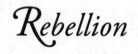

Rebellion

Rebellion

J. A. SOUDERS

TOR·
TEEN

A TOM DOHERTY ASSOCIATES BOOK

NEW YORK

REBELLION

Copyright © 2016 by Jessica Souders

A Tor Teen Book
Published by Tom Doherty Associates, LLC
175 Fifth Avenue
New York, NY 10010

www.tor-forge.com

Tor® is a registered trademark of Tom Doherty Associates, LLC.

The Library of Congress Cataloging-in-Publication Data
is available upon request.

ISBN 978-0-7653-3247-9 (hardcover)
ISBN 978-1-4668-0097-7 (e-book)

Our books may be purchased in bulk for promotional, educational, or business use. Please contact your local bookseller or the Macmillan Corporate and Premium Sales Department at 1-800-221-7945, extension 5442, or by e-mail at MacmillanSpecialMarkets@macmillan.com.

First Edition: July 2016

Printed in the United States of America

0 9 8 7 6 5 4 3 2 1

Dedicated to the loving memory of my grandfather,

Robert Heiland,

*who proved that love is stronger than diamond,
more precious than gold, and as infinite as a ring.
He taught me that love can't be bought, and it
can't be hidden away, but most importantly
that a true love story never ends.*

Rebellion

Chapter One

Sacrifices must be made for the greater good.

—Citizen's Social Code, Volume VI

Evie

My life is just about perfect.

These are the words Mother has permanently etched into my memory, as if it's nothing more than another of the stone plaques placed around the city bearing her Motherisms.

There are times I actually believe it.

But it's not true.

At least not yet.

I've been beaten down. Chased away. Used as a pawn in Mother's sadistic games. My own people see me as a monster and have turned against me. Even my memories have been stolen from me and tampered with or just plain damaged beyond repair.

However, although I'm metaphorically crippled, I've not been broken.

For the past month I've been watching. Waiting. Planning.

Today's the day it's all going to come together. The day we remove Mother from office and put her where she belongs. The Surface.

Luckily, even as messed up as my memories are, the one thing Mother never fiddled with was my knowledge of the city. It's a simple matter to walk through Sector Two from the Residential Sector. I stride right past the Guard at the tunnel to the Palace Wing. My heart skips a beat when he looks up. But like everyone else, he quickly returns his attention to the podium, and I breathe a bit easier.

One step down, and so far everything is going according to plan. That's probably a problem.

From what Father told me and my own warped memories, I know Mother will be holding court during what I'd called Request Day once upon a time. The Enforcer currently in the room will be rotated out in a few minutes, and thanks to Father's interference there will be no one to take her place.

No one but me, that is.

When Father first brought me an Enforcer's uniform, I'd been convinced I wouldn't be able to pull it off. Even with my memories back, it's been so long—I was only ten when I was relieved of duty. The next six years were devoted to being groomed to become the next leader of Elysium. The Daughter of the People. And I'd spent those years being as afraid of the Enforcers as every other Citizen.

But the minute I pulled the cloak around me, everything about me changed. My mind easily adapted. It terrifies me how my brain works now. Gauging everyone and everything and its threat level.

But now, face-to-face with the doors to the Enforcer entrance to the request room, a few doubts slip in. Will Mother see who I really am? Surely she will. Who knows me better than the woman who watched my training personally and then raised me as her own when I "failed" in my Enforcer directive? Even if my mind has changed, my appearance has not.

But that doesn't mean she pays attention to the girls she orders to kill for her. Hopefully, she won't even glance at me.

I push the uncertainty away. I have to make this work. There's no room for failure. I close my eyes and take a deep breath, then blow it out, slow and measured. When I open my eyes again, I've forced all my emotions down. I'm not playing an Enforcer now. I am one.

I push open the doors and step into the large room. A line has already formed inside and extends out the main door. The Citizens step away from me as I pass, avoiding my grazing glance. But then I turn my attention toward the reason I'm here.

I freeze when I see her.

Mother.

A dose of terror makes it impossible to move for a second, and I'm bombarded with a barrage of memories. None of them are nice. I have to clamp down on the emotions they cause.

Mother glances up, and for a second that stretches into eternity I'm sure my cover's blown. But then she turns away again, dismissing me to resume her talks with the couple in front of her.

I force myself to move, slowly making my way around the perimeter of the room, as an Enforcer would. Using the shadows as my cover until I'm standing in the corner—still in the shadows—practically behind Mother.

I survey my surroundings. My position is fairly ideal. It's exactly where an Enforcer would be to make sure Mother is safe from any potentially brave but foolhardy Citizens who think they can take Mother down. I also have a view of all the doors and can see anyone who leaves or enters. The corner is to my back, so no one can sneak up behind me, not even a real Enforcer, should Father be wrong and I'm not alone as an Enforcer in the room today. It's not that I don't have faith in Father, but Mother is far from foolish. She's never trusted anyone but herself, and I can't imagine she'd put enough confidence in Father to tell him the complete truth about anything.

Exactly as I'm thinking that, I look into the corner opposite of where I'm standing and meet the eyes of an Enforcer. A real one. My heart stops as we stare at each other. I'm not sure what to do. She isn't supposed to be here, but she is. And obviously she knows who I am.

One corner of her mouth slides up into a half-smile that chills the blood in my veins. I don't know what that expression means. Enforcers don't show emotion. It's the biggest thing drilled/brainwashed into us. But then something catches my eye and I glance down at the only skin an Enforcer can show—the half circle right under her collarbones. She's wearing a necklace. I reach for my own and worry the pendant between my thumb and first finger. Father told me we had an insider. He wouldn't tell me who it was, just that I'd recognize her when I saw her. He couldn't have meant an Enforcer, could he? If he had an Enforcer on his side, why would he need me?

I meet her eyes again, my mind shouting questions at her from where I stand. She glances at my hand and her smile grows a fraction before she nods and backs into the dark, where I can't see her or where she goes. *If* she goes anywhere.

Warning? Or greeting?

I don't start breathing again until I hear the side door open and then close. That *must* have been our insider. But . . . why? And if she wasn't, what . . . ?

I don't even know where to start with the questions. But I haven't seen anyone else that it could be, and I need my team to know I'm in place.

For the next hour, I stand behind Mother, a pistol held tightly in my hand and hidden in the special pockets of my skirt, waiting impatiently while everything sets up. Or, more accurately, while I hope everything is being set up. This next part has to go flawlessly. One tiny mistake could mean failure.

I stand straighter as the last Citizen vacates the room. It's showtime, as Asher would say.

As if on cue, Asher walks in, dragging a struggling Gavin. Even though I knew this was going to happen, my heart lurches. I want to run to him and drag him out of here, but I can't. So I bide my time, as Father follows directly behind him.

Gavin shouts curses at Asher, who keeps a tight hand on his bound arms. He tosses Gavin to the ground at Mother's feet. I can't tell from my angle what her expression is, but she does lean forward.

"What have we here?" The unmistakable sound of glee in her voice makes me want to hit her, but I stay quiet and slip closer like any good Enforcer would do.

"The Surface Dweller." Asher's voice is deep and sans accent. I have to admit I'm impressed he was able to pull it off. We've worked on it for two weeks, but he never really lost the slight twang. "We caught him skulking around the Medical Sector."

Mother steps down off her throne—I don't really know what else to call it; it's too lavish to be simply a chair. She bends down and then grasps Gavin's chin in her hand. He tries to shake loose, but she holds tight.

"I never thought I'd see you again . . . Gavin, isn't it?"

Gavin only glares at her.

Mother claps her hands twice; my cue that she needs me. I should have already moved closer. A real Enforcer would have, but I'd frozen at the sight of Gavin. I brush off the emotions as best I can and step completely out of the shadows now, my head held high as I slowly walk to her and Gavin.

Making sure my arm doesn't shake, I pull the pistol from

my skirt and aim it level at Gavin's head, as if I'm awaiting orders to shoot him. It gives me the uncomfortable reminder of the time in Sector Three when I did the same thing—when my Conditioned programming took over, and I had every intention of actually killing him. When he glances at me out of the corner of his eye and visibly swallows before turning a glare at Mother again, I wonder if he had the same thought.

"What brings you back here, Surface Dweller? Have you brought my traitorous daughter with you?" There's a slight sound of a laugh in her voice, as if this is just some great joke to her. It sends my instincts humming.

Gavin spits at her.

She jumps back and wrinkles her nose. "Well, I see she hasn't been able to teach you any manners. Pity." She turns to Asher. "How were you able to capture him? Why did you not alert an Enforcer?"

Asher averts his gaze. "He seemed quite desperate. He was muttering something about someone named Evie and infections. It took me only a moment to realize he was the Surface Dweller who kidnapped the Daughter. Forgive me, Mother, but I thought time was of the essence and I did not want him to get away again. I had hoped to find an Enforcer along the way."

Mother jerks her gaze back to Gavin. "Is this true, Surface Dweller?" He doesn't answer, but she nods. "I think it is. Why else would you risk another trip here, knowing what fate awaited you? Did you bring Evelyn with you?" He still doesn't speak and she pushes his head away in disgust. "Just the same as before. But this time, there is no one weak enough to help you escape. You've sealed your own death sentence." She looks to Asher. The way she studies him has me wishing I'd insisted he cut his hair—and the blue streak completely out—instead of just dyeing it. I'm certain she sees a shadow of the blue tint. But then she waves him away. "You may go." She turns to Father. "Escort him from the Palace Wing and then make sure he's fairly compensated for his . . . bravery."

My blood freezes at her tone. She's going to order me to kill Gavin. It's what we've been expecting. It's also the moment I've been dreading. The true test to see if the other side of myself—the Conditioned Enforcer part of me—is wiped out, or at least destroyed enough that I can refuse a direct order.

Father's convinced that this won't even be an issue for me. I've been able to resist her orders before. And the hard reset caused by leaving Elysium in the first place should have erased enough of the old programming.

She glances over at me and I fight the urge to look down. An Enforcer wouldn't. I keep my eyes focused on Gavin.

She stares at me so long, I start to worry she knows who I am. If anyone here knew who I was, it would be her. It's why I've kept my distance and made sure the hood, and its shadow, covered my face. But she's my adoptive mom, and a mother always knows her child.

This was a mistake. I should have listened to Asher and Gavin, not Father. I should have taken more time to hatch a better plan. One that wasn't so bold and risky.

But then she surprises me by saying, "Take him to the

Detainment Center. This time I'm going to get answers from him, whether or not he wants to give them to me." She waves me toward him.

Trying not to show my relief that the plan is working, I pocket the gun, then reach down and yank Gavin to his feet. He fights me as I drag him from the room. I'm slightly worried that I'm hurting him as he struggles against me. But I can't do anything less or Mother will suspect something. We're lucky she hasn't already. But, as expected and hoped for, Mother follows as I drag him across the marble floors of the Palace Wing and then over to the concrete of Sector Two and the Detainment Center.

So far everything has gone as planned, and that worries me. Nothing ever goes as planned. There's always bound to be mistakes. But this is going so smoothly I *know* something's wrong.

It doesn't take long to figure it out. My stomach flips when we step into the Detainment Center.

There's no one here. There's supposed to be members of the Underground waiting to help us subdue Mother and remove her from Elysium. There's supposed to be backup.

For a moment I think something must have changed in the plans, but Gavin stiffens when he sees the empty room. Even from my less than ideal vantage point as I drag him to the cell door, I can see his eyes darting all over the room as if he's expecting the people that are supposed to be here to jump out of some hidden crevice.

I don't know exactly what to do, so I keep walking, then

turn at the glass door of the cell, as if waiting for someone to open it. That's when I notice that Mother has stopped at the door to the Detainment Center. She's smiling at me.

Not Gavin.

Me!

My stomach doesn't just sink; it drops.

She knew the entire time and we fell into her trap like rats.

At least I can be grateful that Asher and Father got away. With only Gavin to protect from Mother, I can do this. I might have to kill her to do it, but if it's a choice between her and Gavin, I don't even have to think about it.

She starts clapping. "Well done, Evelyn. I was beginning to worry that you weren't going to pass."

"What the hell are you talking about?" Gavin demands. His entire posture has changed from the defiant one he'd had before, to angry and protective as he steps a little in front of me. But when his hand takes mine, it trembles a little and I know he's just as afraid as I am.

Mother scoffs. "You didn't think I'd let my daughter just walk out of Elysium, did you?"

"I'm *not* your daughter."

"Of course you are." She sighs. "I raised you. Loved you."

"What you did wasn't love."

"You'll see it my way soon." She purses her lips. "But now we have a problem. You brought *two* Surface Dwellers back with you. That wasn't part of the plan. We only need one."

Mother steps to the side and out of the doorway, revealing

a group of people standing behind her. Two Enforcers rush into the room. One levels a pistol at Gavin, but before I can protect him, my body erupts with a million tiny fires. My screams echo throughout the tiny room as I collapse into a mass of writhing muscles on the hard concrete floor.

I know exactly what's happening; I've felt it before. Every time Dr. Friar brainwashed me with some new memory. Or when Mother wanted to punish me for some wrongdoing—intentional or not. But it had always followed an injection of the nanite serum. I don't understand how it's happening now. My ears ring from my screams and even though my vision tunnels, I can see Gavin struggling to get to me, until an Enforcer hits him over the head with the butt of her gun and he joins me on the floor.

Then, just as my vision almost completely fades, the pain stops as suddenly as it began.

Every single muscle in my body is pulled taut. To even think about moving is a fresh agony, and I'm still whimpering from the memory of the pain, but at least the raging inferno in my body has been doused. Gavin lies on the floor next to me, a trickle of blood seeping from the cut the Enforcer gave him. He seems to be out cold. I try to push myself up to at least crawl to him, but my arms can't even handle that little amount of pressure and I collapse onto the ground again.

The sound of more tussling comes from the doorway and I glance over in horror to see Asher struggling with another Enforcer. The one who saw me in the Palace Wing.

That's why she smiled. Why she let me know she was there. She'd known the whole time. And apparently so did Mother.

Mother crouches down next to me. "I wish you wouldn't have done that, Evelyn. You were doing so well. I hoped not to have to use your nanos like that again, but it's for your own good." She pats my cheek. I have the quick thought that if I could move, I'd rip her arm from her body. She turns to the Enforcer looking down at Gavin. "Pick him up." Once the Enforcer does, Mother smiles at me. "It's too bad he hasn't learned how to control his emotions better. I believe he would have made an acceptable match for you."

I don't really pay attention to what she's saying. I'm starting to get the feeling back in my muscles, but I don't move. I don't want to waste the energy I have. I need it to get to my pistol. I have to get Asher and Gavin out of here.

She turns to Asher. "This one, though." She smiles at him. "He reminds me of Timothy." She looks down at me. "Do you remember him, dear?"

I glare at her. There are no words to describe the amount of hate I feel for her in this instant. "I remember you had him killed so you could Couple me with that *Guard*."

"Ah, yes. A mistake on my part. I should have just let you Couple with Timothy. The Guard was an unfortunate failure and had to be put down after he attacked one of my Enforcers."

"Put down? Like a dog?" Asher asks. The incredulous tone to his voice makes me want to laugh. Of course she killed him, then dismissed him like he was some sick animal she was putting out of its misery.

All of her experiments with the Guards were a failure then. How can someone be so callous? "How can you be like this? How can people be nothing more than toys to you that you just throw away when you break them?" My voice cracks just thinking about how many lives she's destroyed.

"They were broken to begin with. I'm trying to fix them." She shrugs. "You should be grateful."

The feeling is almost completely back in my legs. If I can just move them without her seeing me, I could knock out the Enforcer next to me and then grab Mother. If I held her hostage, she'd *have* to let Asher go. Other people may be disposable, but *she* isn't.

"Bitch," Asher spits at her.

She immediately stands and walks toward Asher, giving me the opportunity to make my move. I jump up and shove the Enforcer leaning over Gavin aside, wincing when she hits the wall and crumples to the floor.

Oops, I think, but wrench the gun from her hand and swing around to grab Mother. She'd make a better hostage anyway. Even though I hold the gun against her temple, Mother laughs.

"You can't do it." Her voice sounds almost like she's singing it. "You can't kill me. I'm Mother."

I merely lift an eyebrow at the other Enforcer and cock the gun. "Wanna try me?" Mother stops laughing. "Let Asher go."

The Enforcer glances at Mother, then at me. Just before she releases him, something crosses her eyes. The look she gives me next is almost an apology as she shoves Asher at me. He

Chapter Two

At least in this place—a place I'd equate more to hell than the heaven the name suggests; A place where god himself has abandoned us—it seems that Mother Nature has blessed us with one last gift. A place to hide and gather in that not even mother knows.

—Eli's diary

Gavin

There's nothing like waking up from a concussion. I've had enough of them in my lifetime that waking up is the easy part. After that? Yeah, I'd rather have stayed knocked out.

Bright red-and-black lights flash in front of my closed eyes when I move my head. That's only a small part of the agony ripping through me, but I force myself to open my eyes. I'm immediately confused.

Where the hell am I?

The ceiling is red rock. As is the wall immediately to my left. Moving at all is a fresh torment in my poor head, but I shove myself to a sitting position. My head spins and I have to press my forehead to my knees.

"Easy," a voice I don't recognize says.

"What the fuck happened? Where am I?"

The voice has an accent I can't quite place. But it does remind me of one of the villains in a pre-war movie I saw once. The one with the spy and his fancy cars.

"You're in the Caverns. We rescued you after Mother tried to have you killed."

It all comes back then in almost as painful an explosion as being hit. "Evie! Where's Evie?" I jerk my whole body around and slide off whatever I'm lying on to stumble around like a zombie.

We're not safe here. Mother knows everything. She's probably already here. I have to find Evie.

"Sit down before you hurt yourself," the woman commands. It doesn't take much for her to push me back down on what I see now is a cot. My head spins so much I feel nauseated. Even though the room itself is fairly dark, it's still too bright as lights flash behind my eyes. I lean forward, placing my head between my knees to rest my forehead on my palms.

We're not safe here. We need to leave.

"You took a hard hit, Gavin Hunter. Luckily your head seems to be harder than the walls around here."

I peek through my fingers at the person talking. I'd have said she was from Elysium, but her eyes are hazel and her skin is olive-toned. Her clothes are ratty—even more so than the villagers' from my Surface town—and covered in dirt. She's pretty and petite, even despite the wrinkles and silver hair.

Like Evie, though, there's a hardness to her that says despite her small stature, she could easily defend herself.

"Do you work for Mother?"

She laughs. "No."

"Then why are you here?"

I take another sweep of her body to see if I can see any telltale signs of a weapon. I see none. Not even so much as a bulge that shouldn't be there, which, considering how sickly thin she is, should be obvious. I give the room another once-over, but the only thing I see is a black medical bag in the corner. I'd get to it before she does, so I'm not worried at the moment. Careful? Yes. But not worried.

"I am Nadia. I live here. I'm part of the Underground. What there is of it." She gives me a wry smile. "I'm a doctor here. Well, the closest thing they have to it in the Caverns. Father is never here and he's busy with . . . someone else, right now. So, you're stuck with me. And I need to make sure your head is still as hard as it was when you started your foolhardy mission this morning."

I relax a little at her being a part of the Underground, but I'm still wary. Just because she said it, doesn't mean it's true. And even if she doesn't work for Mother, Mother knows everything. She knows where we are. She's going to come for us. She's going to finish what she started.

"I need Evie." Why won't she tell me what happened to Evie?

"You'll see the girl in just a minute. Right now you need to rest."

She reaches for my shoulder, but I grab her wrist. It surprises me how fragile the bones feel. It's that underlying strength throwing me off again. "Please. Just tell me. Is she all right?"

"Stubborn as a mule," she mutters, just loud enough for me to hear it. She sighs, then says, louder, "I'll take you to her, but you *must* let me examine you after that." She helps me to stand and then walks away, leaving me to limp out the door of the room after her.

I realize the minute we step outside the room that I'm really not in Elysium anymore. Where I am is impossible to tell. A quick glance to my left shows the shell of what could possibly be the beginnings of another area like Sector Two. There's half-constructed buildings, none of which have glass in the windows or roofs—it reminds me of the propaganda videos they showed us in school of what a city looked like after an atomic blast. The pathway down the middle of the buildings looks like some sort of railway track.

"Where am I? How did I get here?"

"We call it the Caverns."

I give her a look. While a name is nice, it is absolutely the least helpful information I've gotten yet.

"And . . . that is . . . what?"

She doesn't even bother turning around to face me as we continue at a fast pace away from the half-buildings. "You're aware this was a resort before Mother turned it into what it is now, yes?"

"Yes. Her dad was some sort of hotel tycoon and he used Elysium as a refuge from the war."

For the first time, she twists her neck to smile at me. "Yes."

She turns back around. "Before that he'd started construction on a new wing to be built into the other trench wall." She shoots me a quick look. "Where we are now." She continues forward. "Before his resources and workers were needed for the war effort, they'd managed to dig out a sizeable hole, pump out the seawater, and construct the entrance and airlock. They'd even installed a rudimentary life support system. A smaller one to be used in the interim before the main one would be plumbed into the buildings as they were finished, but enough to keep the hundred or so workers comfortable while they were here."

I finish with the obvious, "But they never got to finish those buildings."

She bobs her head once. "Correct."

I glance around at the walls surrounding us and see little doorways like the one I came from clustered together in two rows of ten. One row is stacked on top of the other and accessible only from decrepit-looking ladders leading to each doorway. "And the room I was just in?"

"We built those ourselves." Even from behind her I can see her pull herself straighter. It's obvious she's happy with what they managed to do. "They're primitive, but sufficient for our needs."

"How many of you are there?"

"Only forty."

My brain tries to wrap itself around the math and logistics and I want to ask more, but she suddenly stops and I almost crash into her.

"We can explain the rest later. Here is your lady now." My eyes follow her gesture and land on Evie, who's sitting outside yet another hole cut into the wall. She's got her legs drawn up to her chest and her arms wrapped around her legs.

"Evie!" All my other thoughts rush from my brain when she jerks her head up at the sound of my voice. Her eyes are red and there are tracks in the dirt on her cheeks.

She jumps from the ground and rushes to me, her deceptively thin arms wrapping around me in a vise grip. Her scent—the mix of roses and lilies she seems to carry with her always—fills my nose.

"Gavin." Her voice is like a sigh. Relief pours from her and the way she leans her body into me makes me fold her in my own arms and want to apologize for everything she's worried about since she last saw me.

"You're safe." I feel the words against my chest, more than I hear them, and in answer I pull her closer to me. "Thank goodness. I'm so sorry I wasn't there when you woke up, but . . ." She trails off when her voice breaks.

I press my lips against her forehead. "Shh," I say against her skin. "It's fine. I'm just glad you're okay."

She glances up, then touches a hand to the goose egg on my temple. "Are you all right?"

"I've been told I've got a hard head."

A laugh slips out of her lips and she goes back to resting her head against my chest. She just stays like that. As if the key that was giving her her energy for the past however long has suddenly stopped turning and she just can't anymore.

"Mr. Hunter, it appears you are well enough that you don't need me. I will leave you two to yourselves. If you require anything from me, you need only to ask anyone you happen across." She turns to Evie. "We really must speak soon, Miss Evelyn."

Evie's whole body stiffens at her words as the woman turns and leaves.

"What's going on?"

"Asher . . ." Her muffled voice trails off.

"What happened to Asher?" When she doesn't answer me, warning bells clang in my head. "What happened to Asher?"

"He . . . I . . ." She sucks in a shaky breath. "I—I made a mistake." Her whole body trembles.

My blood turns cold and I want to demand she tell me what that means, but she doesn't need that from me right now, and panic has never solved anything. "We'll figure it out. Just tell me what happened."

"I didn't know what to do. Mother was right there and you were on the floor. Asher was being held by another Enforcer. I thought if I could just get to Mother and hold her hostage, she'd make the Enforcer let go of Asher." It comes out in a spurt of words I barely understand, but then she just stops with a sob and presses a fist against her lips. She looks up at me. "They shot him, Gavin. Just shot him." The words are barely a whisper, but it might as well have been a shout.

My entire body goes numb, except my head, which feels like my brain is trying to push its way out through my eyes. "Is he all right?"

She gulps in air and another sob escapes. "When I woke, he was still breathing, but it sounded bad." Her hands pinch mine as she grasps them, causing my fingertips to go numb. "Like he was drowning, Gavin. And there was nothing I could do about it, because they were pushing and poking at me."

"Who?"

"Father and the woman that brought you here. I don't even know *how* we got here. They won't tell me anything."

I remember then that Nadia easily ignored my earlier question, too, but I'll worry about that later. "Why were they poking at you?"

"The bullet went through Asher and into me. My nanos were healing me and they had to get the bullet out because it didn't go all the way through. Right here." She places my hand on her stomach, holding it with her own against her bare skin. For the first time since I saw her sitting all curled in on herself, I notice there's blood all over her. Her shirt's torn just below where she's pressing and there's a fresh bandage peeking out from the scraps of her shirt.

"Are *you* okay?!" I can't breathe, and my voice comes out all screechy and scratchy, like someone is choking me.

What the hell happened after I got knocked out?

"I'm fine. My nanos protected me. But Asher . . ."

My head is spinning. I'm worried about Evie, but she says she's fine. But she's crying and Asher's gone. And he's been hurt. Where is he?

"What happened to Asher?"

She turns away from me as if she can't bear to see me when

the next words tumble from her lips. "I let them give him nanos," she whispers.

Dread pools in my stomach and my mind tosses information at me like one of Asher's data screens.

Nanos. Tiny robots everyone in Elysium has. Originally designed to keep people healthy, and heal them should they get hurt. But like most things Mother has a hand in, they had a second, darker function: they were also used as a safety protocol should people escape. They're the reason why Evie forgot everything but her name when we escaped from here the first time. And the reason she can't escape now until Eli finds a way through the EM field surrounding the city, so they don't reset again.

I force myself not to shudder and focus back in on what she's saying. "I didn't know what else to do. He was dying and Father said it was the only thing they could do to make sure he didn't. I just did it. I didn't even think what that would mean. Or what would happen later. I just wanted him to live."

"Did he?" I ask cautiously.

Her eyes meet mine and she nods. "But how much of a life will that be, when he's stuck *here*? Mother has to know this place is here. It's just a matter of time before she finds us. I screwed up, Gavin, and now he's stuck here. Forever."

A feeling of insane relief washes over me. I pull her to me again, hugging her tightly, before I push her away slightly and hold her by the shoulders. "But he'll live, Evie."

She shakes her head like she does when she's going to argue, so I place my finger gently over her lips. "Eli said that he was going to try and find a way around the EM field so you could leave. When that happens, Asher will get to leave too. It was the right call. Maybe the only one. You saved his life. That's all that matters."

I agree that Mother must know, but Eli had said he'd help. We fulfilled our bargain. We tried to take Mother down. It almost killed us. That's got to be enough for him. He'll have to help us.

Just then Eli steps from Asher's room and Evie immediately turns to him. "Is he all right?"

Eli looks exhausted and much older than he had this morning. The creases in his face seem to have deepened, as have the shadows under his eyes. Even his eyes exude weariness.

"The nanos are doing their job," is his only response.

"Can we see him?" Evie asks, twisting her fingers together in front of her.

He nods and runs a hand through his hair. "Don't stay long. I have to get more electrolytes. We've already gone through three bags, but the nanos are still trying to eat him alive while they heal him."

He moves as if to leave and I grab his arm. "What do you mean?"

"The nanites are healing him, and not just from the gunshot wounds, but every injury his body has ever had, including the damage due to the normal processes of aging. They work at an extremely accelerated pace. His body is physically unable to keep up with the metabolic demands. The only way to help is to provide him intravenous hydration with an electrolyte-infused solution."

Since my brain just exploded from all that information, I let him go and follow Evie, who's already in the room. A room that, despite the fact that it's only slightly larger than the one I woke up in, is filled with surprisingly sophisticated equipment from the looks of it. I couldn't even begin to say what it all is, but everything else I've seen in these caverns so far looks so primitive, I have to wonder how they managed to get their hands on this.

Evie's eyes are wide when she looks at me. They're almost black with how dilated her pupils are. "This room looks just like ones in the Surface hospital. Not Doc's, but the ones in Rushlake."

I wouldn't know, but I'll take her word for it. It smells like Dr. Gillian's house did from time to time. It's a scent I've long associated with people and animals that are extremely close to dying. It's an easy smell to recognize and one not easily forgotten.

I brush off the thought, shuddering, and focus on Asher instead.

He's so pale, he's gray. His breaths sound wet and I get now what Evie meant when she said he sounded like he was drowning. There's almost a gurgle coming from him—like soap bubbles running down a drain—despite the plastic mask resting over his nose and mouth. A large white bandage splotched with red covers the skin just under his rib cage. Wires spiderweb across his bare chest, leading from white pads on his pale skin to the beeping machines set up just a few feet away. More wires are attached to a cuff wrapped around his right bicep and something wrapped around his left index finger.

For the past six years, I've hated him for what he did to my family. My father. But seeing him splayed out like this terrifies me. He was my best friend once upon a time. And less than two hours ago, he was fine. Now he's at death's door and there's nothing I can do but wait.

He'll be fine. I know he will. Or at least I have to trust he will. Eli's the one that cured the people here of all the diseases that ran rampant on the Surface after the war. Because of his nanos, no one here got so much as a sniffle. He fixed Evie; he'll be able to help Asher.

Evie sits on the floor close to Asher, but out of the way of the staff helping Eli, and I sit next to her. She leans into me and I wind my arm around her waist, taking comfort in our closeness. For the next several hours we sit side by side. Sometimes, I'll feel antsy—Mother is coming, she has to be—and I have to walk around, but Evie stays just as she is. Her legs crossed in front of her. Her hands in her lap. Her eyes stay fixed on Asher or move to watch Eli whenever he changes out the bags of fluids on the metal pole and hook by Asher's head. The only sense of agitation she ever shows is when she twists her hands together as if she's putting lotion on. Whenever she starts doing that, I sit back next to her and pull her into me, and she stops and rests her hands in her lap again.

Finally, color begins to creep back into Asher's face and the awful gurgling sound fades from his breathing. Eli visibly relaxes and for the first time since I woke up, he sits in the only chair in the room.

"Is it over?" Evie whispers.

"I think so." His voice has the hollowness of bone-deep weariness. The kind you only get from complete exhaustion.

A knock on the wood of the makeshift door pulls my attention from Eli. The woman from earlier steps in. She glances at Asher, nods once, then focuses her attention on Evie. "I'm sorry, ma'am, but we must talk now."

Evie stands, stumbling a little when she takes her first step forward, but catches herself before she can fall. She starts to follow the woman out, but I say, "Wait! Where are you taking her? *Why* are you taking her?"

The rumble of the woman's accent is thick when she says, "To a place we can talk privately. Not everyone here agrees with what we're doing. But you may come, if you wish."

I glance toward Evie, who nods once and holds her hand out to me. I jump up and cross the room to take it, then we both follow the woman into the main Cavern. A familiar noise vibrates in my ear, but I can't quite place it. It's kind of like a rumbling, or maybe a crashing, but mixed with something like static.

"What is that noise?" I ask.

"This section of the ocean floor has lava tubes and vents—"

"You're living in a volcano!" My words are pinched as I try to push them out through the lump in my throat.

Evie squeezes my hand. "Dormant. It's a dormant volcano and has been for a very long time. We use its geothermic energy for everything from heating to electricity. It's nothing to worry about."

I'm not so sure, but considering it's been stable for years and Mother is anything but, I decide to focus my energy on Mother.

Nadia continues as if I didn't interrupt her. "There are also places with underground waterways. That 'noise' is from a waterway we uncovered in the trench wall."

"So . . . there's water *under* the water?" Jesus, it only gets worse with everything I hear. Maybe I should just stop asking.

"Yes." She smiles. "I'll explain more later, but please, we must hurry. We don't have much time."

She continues straight to the unfinished buildings. It's so strange. I was right about there not being windows and ceilings, but in this particular building a lot of the walls themselves aren't there either. Most of them are just skeletal innards, studs and crossbeams. We pass through doorless doorways and walk down wall-less hallways.

Then, in the center of the building, is a room that's actually a room. With thick, heavy doors. Walls covered with strange drawings and a projection screen on the far side. In the middle is an old saggy table that takes up most of the space in the room. Papers of every size and color cover the top. Dilapidated rolling chairs circle it. Surprisingly, the room is completely quiet. It reminds me of the Detainment Center. My ears ring from the sudden silence.

"Sit." Nadia gestures for us to take one of the chairs and I do so very gingerly. I'm not sure the chair is strong enough to support my weight.

She waits until Evie takes her seat, then says, "I must ask a favor of you, Evelyn Winters, former Daughter of the People. I know you have questions." She twitches her gaze toward me. "Both of you. I promise I'll explain everything, but we don't have much time." She focuses on Evie again. "There's a doctor whose work is important to us. Dr. Moreau. He worked with Dr. Friar on the 'special projects' that turned out to be the disaster in Sector Three." It takes me a minute to figure out Nadia is talking about the monsters that tried to kill us in the abandoned sector back when we first escaped Elysium. "Since the experiments failed, leaving Mother with almost no Guards and a dwindling number of Enforcers, Mother's decided to fire him."

"Okay, so what do you need us for?" I ask.

Nadia gives me an apologetic look. "Not you." She gestures to Evie. "Miss Evelyn."

"But she can't do anything! She's still hurt."

"Her nanites are effectively healing her. She is well enough to perform this mission."

"What mission?" I demand, flabbergasted. Why would they need Evie to help a doctor who's going to be fired?

"Mother doesn't *fire* people. She kills them," Evie says from next to me. Her voice is quiet, almost emotionless, but there's some tiny hint of something I can't quite place when she says, "They want me to stop it and bring him here."

CHAPTER THREE

Mother's word is law. Everyone must follow the law. If you do not, then you are a traitor and will be treated as such.
—CITIZEN'S SOCIAL CODE, VOLUME III

Evie

I don't know what I'm doing. Two hours ago I was determined not to leave the Caverns. Not until I was sure Asher was fine—I'm the only family he has, and I put him there, after all. But then Father and Nadia told us about what was supposed to happen to the doctor and I couldn't just let that happen. Not if there was something I could do to stop it—and a former Enforcer is better than no one. So now I find myself waiting in a dark room in the Medical Sector.

I have my memories. And my emotions. Two things Enforcers don't have. Mistakes happen when emotions get in the way. And emotions get in the way when your mind reminds you why you should feel them. That's why Mother made sure Enforcers didn't have them. I don't know how anyone expects me to actually pull this off, but I can't let another person die if I can do something to stop it.

So I wait crouched in the darkest corner of the doctor's office, behind a large potted plant. I'm not even entirely sure how I got here. I just know Nadia dragged me through a bunch of tunnels. By the time we got out of them, I was completely confused. I have no idea how I'm going to get back, since she wouldn't come into the lights of Sector Two.

My left leg is starting to cramp and I'm fairly certain my right one has fallen asleep. I adjust my position and bite down on my lip to stop from crying out when my leg suddenly bursts into flames as sensation pours back in.

I've been here an hour. The assassination was supposed to happen thirty minutes ago. Either it was a hoax or someone forgot to check their clocks.

Restless and not sure how long I should wait before I consider it a bust, I decide to do a little snooping on my own. If this was the doctor that helped Dr. Friar and Mother with trying to turn the Guards into Enforcers, maybe there's some evidence—paperwork or something—to use against her.

I root through the drawers of the metal desk, but there's nothing of importance as far as I can tell. So I move on to the file cabinet. Again, nothing important in the first two drawers. But in the third, there's a little box hidden all the way in the back, just under the files. A person glancing through for a file even with all the lights on wouldn't have seen it. I *just* barely catch a glimpse of it as I move papers around.

The box is locked, so I shove it in my bag to force open back in the Caverns. Just as I slide the drawer shut again, a door whispers open at the other end of the hallway. Lights flicker to life and footsteps draw closer to me, echoing off the walls and scattering their sound around the empty hall. Only from the heavy thudding sound they make can I tell it's probably a man. I dive back into my hiding spot behind the plant.

The footsteps stop outside the door, and I'm blinded when the lights blare to life. The footsteps become muffled as he crosses the carpeted floor toward the filing cabinet. I blink a few times to get my eyes to adjust to the light as I peek over one of the plant's long leaves. I don't recognize the man, but then again, I probably wouldn't. Mother only entrusted me to the care of Dr. Friar.

This man is considerably younger. Closer to my age than either Dr. Friar *or* Mother. He's not all that tall, probably just a few inches taller than myself, and he's extremely lanky in a way that suggests he's probably quite clumsy. Or extremely graceful. There's no in-between on this one.

He pulls open the bottom drawer and yanks the files toward him. He stops, frowns, and yanks each file toward the back of the cabinet, before reversing it again. He slams the drawer shut before I hear him curse. Now I'm glad I grabbed the box. It's obvious it's what he's looking for. And if he's looking for it, it's definitely worth something. He stands and frantically pats at the pockets of his pants and lab coat, muttering to himself, his back still to the door.

That's when a sound from the hallway catches my attention. The Enforcer!

It has to be her. I adjust my position and posture so I can take her out the minute I can confirm it's her. I have just a moment to think about warning the scientist she's coming, but she's there before it's more than an entire thought. With no more than a rustle of her clothes, she slips into the room. I have to admire her for that at least. She's as graceful as the gazelles on the Surface I've read about. She's probably one of Mother's greatest achievements.

It's the same Enforcer from earlier, which worries me. I've already dealt with her once and failed. I'm not sure I can actually win against her. Then again, this time neither Asher nor Gavin are here. My only concern is the doctor and the box in my bag. And *I* have the element of surprise.

I plan on taking full advantage of it.

The minute she's fully in the room, I move like lightning and pounce on her before she can even turn in my direction. She slams into the wall. She didn't even have a chance to react. But I don't take the time to gloat. I have to stop her. My body works on instinct and I pull my fist back and punch her in the chin, slamming her head back into the wall.

"What in the name of Mother?" Dr. Moreau pushes himself against the wall as if trying to crawl through it.

While I'm distracted by the doctor, the Enforcer is able to get her legs between us. She kicks hard against my chest, sending me flying across the room. I'm able to soften my landing, but I still come back with rug burns on my palms and legs.

In the time it takes me to get up, she's pulled something silver from her cape. The doctor's eyes widen when he sees it and his entire face pales, making his eyes seem even larger and darker. I've never seen anything like it before, but it reminds me of some kind of remote control. Her thumb presses one of the buttons and almost instantly the doctor's blood curdling screams threaten to break my eardrums.

I cross the distance between us in a leap and try to sweep her legs out from underneath her, but she jumps neatly out of the way and brings her arm down on the back of my neck, which causes my entire spine to protest. My body goes limp long enough for me to hit the ground face-first. It knocks the breath out of me, but I sweep my leg out again the minute I hit. I'm not going to let her get the best of me. This time I'm able to catch her by surprise and she falls backward. She drops the silver remote, but either doesn't care or doesn't notice.

With a growl, she pounces on me and punches me repeatedly in the stomach, right where she shot me earlier. While completely healed, it's still tender to the touch, and after the fall I just took, this new assault makes my eyes water. I shove her away, and reach toward the silver device. I'm sure it's what's causing the doctor's screams. A thought flutters through my brain that this must have been what sent my nanites into chaos before without the normal injection first.

My fingertips barely touch the cold metal before she jumps on my back and yanks my hair. My vision wavers. I jam my elbow backward as hard as I can, managing to connect with something that makes her howl. I'm pretty sure I hear a crack.

She jumps off me, and I whirl onto my back and shove to my feet. But she's nowhere in the room. I run into the hall just as she pushes through a door at the end of the hallway. She stops a moment. Her eyes meet mine. Then she's gone and the door slams behind her.

When I turn to get back to the doctor, something crinkles under my foot. I glance down. I've stepped on a sheet of plastic. It's absolutely clear, but is a similar shape and size to a sheet of paper. It's curled in on itself right now, but I know exactly what it is. When it's flat, it'll operate like a Slate—the clear glass hand held computer every Citizen is issued after they come of age. But this one is different. It's just for Enforcers. That means it has only one function: to give the Enforcers their orders.

It's Mother's way to ensure orders can be given to any Enforcer, at any time, without delay or confusion. No matter where they are in the facility. As soon as the Enforcer reads them, Mother and the Lead Enforcer get a notification on their Slates. When the order is finished, the Enforcer checks it off and again Mother and the Lead Enforcer are notified it's done.

There's also a fail-safe. It reads DNA. Should a regular Citizen pick it up, the entire sheet erases itself. No need to worry the Citizens with messages of death and murder.

Not holding out much hope that I'll actually be able to read it, I pick it up and unroll it. The e-ink flashes to life and I'm surprised to see this Enforcer's orders are still on it. Complete with date and time the order was sent. Date and time it was expected to be carried out. And exactly what was to be done.

I shudder as I read through it. This assassination was not

going to be pretty. And the device is the reason for it. It's something called a nanite telemanipulator—in other words, a remote control for nanobots.

I wonder briefly why I was able to read the orders. Considering I haven't been an Enforcer for a long time, not to mention I'm public enemy number one. I should've been erased from the mainframe. But I'll worry about that later. I don't have time now, especially with the doctor still screaming. I slip the sheet into one of my many pockets.

The silver device is still on the floor where I left it, so I rush to it and press a button, then run over to the doctor. He's holding his arm and howling as though it's been ripped off. I can't say I blame him. Whatever this thing does, it's horrible.

I help him sit up. "It's all right. I've got you." The scent of blood assaults my nose almost instantly and a warm, sticky fluid pours over my fingers.

A quick glance shows my hand covered in blood. The floor around us is rapidly turning redder.

"What in the . . ." I break off when I see what's caused all the blood.

I'm not holding his arm. I'm holding the stump of what's left.

Chapter Four

I'm tired of hiding. I've hidden behind a mask that Mother made for me my entire life. First as an Enforcer, then as Daughter of the People. I refuse to hide any longer.

—Evie's journal

Evie

I stumble my way back into the Caverns, following behind Nadia—who'd met me in the Maintenance tunnels—with the unconscious doctor slung across my shoulders. By the time I lug Dr. Moreau all the way to the room Asher had been in—the Caverns' medical area, apparently—my legs feel like rubber.

Even though I'd tied a makeshift tourniquet around the stump of his arm, he'd still lost a lot of blood between now and then. I place him on the cot Asher had been occupying—I hope that Asher's absence means he's recovered enough to be moved elsewhere and push any other thoughts from my head.

Luckily Father is still there and takes charge of the situation immediately. I try talking to him about what had happened, but he either grunts out terse answers or refuses to answer altogether. Eventually I take that to mean I'm in the way, so I leave Dr. Moreau and go to find Gavin.

I find him pacing in front of a little dugout in the Cavern wall. When we see each other, relief flashes into his eyes for that half a second before he takes in everything about me, including the blood staining my clothes. Before he can say anything, I bolt into his open arms. He holds me so tightly it almost hurts, but I need it. After everything that's happened, I feel like a statue littered with cracks and he's the glue keeping me from falling apart.

We don't say anything to each other. There's no need. He holds me for several minutes, while I rest my cheek on his chest and let his heartbeat soothe me . . . until a noise behind him draws my attention over his shoulder. I break into a grin.

"Asher."

He stands just inside the dugout, leaning against the limestone. He's a little pale and he looks like he hasn't slept in a week. But at least he's not death gray anymore. Coming back and seeing him, if not well, at least alive and awake, seems like a pretty great reward for being mostly successful in my attempt to save Dr. Moreau.

Gavin lets me go so I can carefully hug Asher before helping him back to the cot in the cutout. He grumbles but doesn't protest, which tells me he's still not feeling a hundred percent, but the small grumble gives me hope it won't be much longer.

I sit in a rickety chair by the cot Asher rests in, my hand clasped in Gavin's when he takes the equally shaky chair next to me. I quickly fill the two of them in on what happened with the rescue.

"What do you mean his arm was *missing*?" Gavin demands, leaning forward so his elbows rest on his thighs.

"I searched that place from top to bottom, it's just . . . gone." I spread my hands out to symbolize an explosion. "Poof! What was left looked like something had been eating it from the inside out."

Gavin winces. "Ouch."

"If what I felt earlier today was anything close to what *he* went through, I think ouch is an understatement." I shudder again and let Gavin retake my hand. "That's not what worries me, though."

"A guy's hand disappears and you're not worried about it?" Asher's voice is incredulous, even if it's weak and raspy.

I furrow my brow. "Something felt very wrong about all this. The Enforcer was the one from this morning. Not counting the fact she had that apparatus and the advantage, she took me out easier than I'd like to admit earlier. She should have been able to do it again. She gave up way too soon."

"Maybe you're just better than you think," Gavin suggests. "You've gotten your memories back, but your Enforcer Conditioning was the deepest buried and had the strongest ties to who you were. You could have easily tapped back into that. I've seen you do it before."

I glance over at him. "There were several times she could have killed me. She didn't take a single one. Plus she dropped both the device *and* her orders. I'm not buying it."

"Think it was a trap?"

"I don't know. Maybe." I pause, then shake my head. "I don't think so. If it was just a trap, why didn't she take me out, or at the very least to Mother? Why did she leave all that stuff, including her target, behind? It doesn't make sense."

"What did Eli say?" Asher asks.

"Not much. But he was busy." I frown, rethinking our non-exchange when I dropped off Dr. Moreau. "I think she used that device on me when they tried to incapacitate me earlier. It felt like a worse version of when Father introduced the working nanites into me." I shoot a meaningful look to Asher. "It's definitely something they're using to control nanos. I don't know for sure, but I think it did something to cause his nanos to turn on his own body."

"Jesus!" Gavin hisses. "If that's true, we're in trouble. Everyone but me has them now." He winces and gives Asher a sheepish look. "Sorry, dude."

Asher shrugs. "Are you kidding me? This is the best thing to have happened to me. Did you see how quickly Evie healed? Now I might actually be able to kick your ass if I need to. I'm a fucking superhero!"

Gavin simply leans over and presses a finger to Asher's shoulder to push him back to the bed. "Lay down before you hurt yourself."

Asher frowns. "Guess not."

Gavin and I burst out laughing. "At least not yet." I pat his leg gently. "Soon, though."

Father steps into the room at that moment. "Well, this is a welcome sight. Finally the three of you getting along."

I jump to my feet. "What's going on with Dr. Moreau?"

"Well, he definitely lost his arm, but everything else is fine."

"Did he say anything about the gadget? He seemed to know what it was."

Father runs his hands through his hair. "When he came to, he was delirious from pain. We've got him sedated now."

I toss my hands in the air with frustration and turn around to stomp back to my seat. With him sedated, he's useless. Gavin gives me a sympathetic look, while Father looks like he's arguing with himself about something. Finally he sighs. "Just as the sedation started to kick in, he was able to tell me something." I spin around and Father gestures for me to settle. "It's not much, but he said he hadn't created the monsters in Three—that was all Dr. Friar's doing. But he says he found a way to stop them."

It doesn't take a genius to do the math. "The device," Gavin and I say together.

"He made a bunch of them and gave them to Mother." Father pushes his hand through his hair. "But he found out Mother wasn't just going to use them on her abominations, she was giving them to all the Enforcers, so they could be more . . . efficient."

I exchange a horrified look with Gavin. "We're going to be in trouble if the Enforcers are all equipped with these things. No one will be able to stand against Mother."

"Is there a way around it?" Gavin asks.

"I don't think so. I asked him and he just kept saying Dr. Friar was the only one who could."

"What about the box?" I demand.

"Empty. There's some spots for data cubes, but they're all empty. My guess is he took them out and never got to replace them before you took it."

"Did he have the cubes on him?"

"If he did, they're gone. There was nothing in his pockets."

"Damn," I mutter and tug on the ends of my hair. "There was nothing else in that room. Maybe the Enforcer made off with them."

"That could explain why she dropped her orders. She was too busy trying to make sure she had the cubes," Asher says.

"Maybe." Could be, but I doubt it. I turn back to Father. "What are we going to do about this new device? We can't just let Mother use it on the Citizens."

"Dr. Moreau is the only one with the answers right now. Getting answers from him is futile until he heals. That's if he even will help." He looks as frustrated as I feel.

"This changes the game," Gavin mutters to me. He's leaning forward onto his knees again.

I only nod. It changes *everything*.

"What about my grandmother?" Asher blurts out. "She originally designed the nanos, right? Couldn't she help you come up with a way to counteract whatever that device does?"

Father purses his lips, but something flashes across his eyes. Hope? Longing? I'm not sure.

"She might be able to. Probably. Her help would be invaluable." But then he loses all emotion. "But we'd have to send someone to get her. There's no one here we could send. Not without them forgetting the reason they went up there when they pass to the other side of the EM field."

I glance to Gavin. He's the only one left who could go, but that's not an option. We almost lost him once in the Outlands. I'm not losing him again to the same thing. I'd never even know what happened to him. Selfish or no, I'd rather wait to see if Dr. Moreau can help us before sending Gavin to the Surface for a person who may or may not be able to help.

Father's hands drop to his side. "I need to get back to the Palace. Mother's probably wondering where I am. After the failed attack this afternoon and now this, she's going to be angry."

"What about us?" Gavin demands. "You can't just leave us here!"

Father stares at him. "Where else would you prefer? The Residential Sector where Mother knows you've been staying? Or maybe since you're intimately familiar with the Detainment Center, you'd like to be there. Perhaps you prefer more palatial surroundings and would like to stay in the Palace Wing itself. It would make it easier for Mother to find you."

"Mother can find us here! How do we know that these people"—Gavin makes a wide gesture—"aren't working with Mother?"

"We are not," Nadia says from the doorway. She spears Gavin with her eyes.

I clear my throat. "Gavin brings up an interesting question. How can we be sure that Mother won't find us here? She knows everything. She has eyes and ears everywhere."

"We've lived here in peace for almost fifty years. Mother may know almost everything, but she does not know about this place. I assure you."

"And we're supposed to just take your word for it?"

"You do not have a choice," Nadia says. "You have nowhere else to go."

Gavin opens his mouth, but I interrupt. "Maybe it would help us if you could tell us a little about this place. Like why it's here, who you are, and why you want us here."

She nods. "I'll start from the beginning."

"I really must go or Mother will start wondering where I am." Father leaves the rest unsaid, but I get it. If she starts to wonder where he is, then she really *will* know where to find us.

I nod my understanding and gesture for him to go ahead. I'm not exactly comfortable staying here in a place I don't know, with an entire group of people who I don't know, but at this moment *here* is safer than where I was.

He takes a step, then hesitates. "Do you want me to send for your mo . . . get Evangeline? She's been Linking me all day wanting to hear from you."

I glance away from him. "No. She's better where she is."

"Evie . . ." Father starts.

"Don't. Don't push this on me. I'm not ready yet."

"You're going to have to deal with her eventually."

"I'm not ready," I say again in answer. I'm not ready for *any* of this. Especially not her.

No one in the room says anything. If this were the Surface, you'd hear crickets. Finally Father nods. He leaves without looking at me.

Nadia clears her throat. "Are we ready for the story now?" I nod so she continues, "I am Nadia. I was the staff nurse when this was the Elysium Resort. Now I'm the head of the Caverns." I open my mouth to ask a question, but she holds up a finger and continues. "As you know, when Mother took over, she killed her own father, then everyone else she didn't want as a member of her own family. I made it through the first round of her culling."

"How?" I demand. "She only kept those that look most like her."

"Most like her mother actually. But that part didn't come until later. Her first culling consisted of those she disliked. I'd always been kind to her. And at first, that's all that was needed. No one is truly sure how she killed so many people, but I suspect poisoning. Their deaths were hideously slow. And to most of us, it appeared that someone had contracted one of the Surface diseases and it was spreading. Mother used our fear of another outbreak to inject everyone with nanites. She even convinced mothers to allow her to shove them in babies. Before anyone really had time to think about it and the consequences, everyone in Elysium had them.

"Then came the second culling. It started with anyone who Mother connected with the war. Basically anyone who wasn't

American. Since the original hotel employed people from across the world, there were a lot to choose from. Most of the Citizens didn't agree with it, but they all had nanites themselves and Mother could kill them with a snap of her fingers. And did. Eventually Mother decided anyone who didn't resemble her 'saint' of a mother was a liability. The Citizens stopped their objections, ducked their heads, and went about their lives, pretending everything was perfect until they believed it themselves."

Gavin frowns. "So how did you make it out of *that*? Doesn't sound like she cared very much that you were nice to her anymore."

"My husband. He was a close friend of Mother's father and Eli. He remembered this place and that, although it had been boarded up and never finished because of the war, it was finished enough for a small group of people to live. He gathered us in groups of five. He'd successfully gathered four groups here and was bringing a fifth when they got caught. She killed them all. Including Aleksandr—my husband."

"I'm so sorry." I lean over and touch the top of her hand.

She gives me a sad smile. "He managed to save twenty-one people."

"Twenty-one?" Asher asks.

Her smile grows a little wider. "I was pregnant. Alek never got to see his son, but his son knows what he did."

There's an awkward silence and I decide to fill it by asking something that's been nagging at me. "What does Father have to do with all this?" I ask.

"He started his own rebellion right after Mother showed her true colors, after an imagined slight from him. But Dr. Friar had betrayed him and Mother killed everyone who had any part in the rebellion. Except Eli. She kept him around for whatever twisted reasons she had. After that, he didn't trust anyone. For years he kept to himself and just did what Mother wanted.

"But then Evelyn changed things. Unlike the other Enforcers, Evelyn kept fighting her programming. She always broke through her mental constraints. When she completely shoved away her Enforcer protocols to save her stepfather, Eli changed. He had a renewed sense that he couldn't let Mother do what she was doing. That's when he came to us for help."

"You said that you had forty people here, but not that all of those are willing to help. Why are you helping, if most of your people don't want to?" Gavin asks.

She purses her lips. "Most feel it's safe here. That Mother *doesn't* know we're here. And we should leave it be. Not poking at the proverbial hornets' nest." She sighs. "However, there's enough of us that don't agree. And you're right to be worried about Mother finding us. It's only a matter of time before she does. Hopefully, Miss Evelyn will be what Father says she is." Nadia meets my eyes. "Because I'm risking everything my husband gave his life for over it."

She leaves without another word.

The room stays silent. The pressure on my chest is even stronger now than it was. I thought I was just going to remove Mother from power, and Father would fix my nanos and I'd move back up to the Surface with Gavin and live happily ever after. I didn't think about what other people expected of me. I didn't think about what other people were betting on me. What they'd lose, if I did.

"What do you think was on the cubes?" Gavin finally says.

"Proof," I say without hesitation. I slowly lower myself into a chair, kick off my shoes, and focus on the distraction Gavin gave me. He places my feet in his lap and immediately starts pressing his thumbs into the balls of my feet. I want to sigh at the feeling, but only smile my thanks. "He was running. Whoever told us about the assassination, warned him, too. That's why he was late." His frantic search runs through my mind again. "He didn't hide them," I blurt out. "Why else would he be looking for them? Someone else had to have done it."

"Or maybe he just wanted the box," Asher says, his voice almost a shrug.

"He wouldn't have risked it. Not with his life on the line. He was looking for the cubes."

"Where would he have been running to then? He wouldn't have been able to get to the Surface, right? Not without forgetting everything he was supposed to do or even why he was there in the first place."

"Maybe he was looking for us," Asher says. "Or at least you, Evie. It's not too much of a stretch to think that if you escaped, he could, too. And that, Gavin, you'd do whatever it took to get Evie's memories back. With the connection between Eli and my grandmother, he was probably hoping that somehow Evie would know to go to my grandmother."

I shake my head. "There's too many ways that can go wrong. Too many long shots to rely on. I can't imagine he'd take that risk."

"He obviously knew if he was going to stay, he'd die. Better to take a chance, than have no hope at all."

"Even if he did find them and get out," Gavin says, holding up a hand. "Nobody would have been able to read what's on the cubes. We don't have anything up there like the computers here."

"Here then. Maybe," Asher replies. He lays his head back against the wall behind his bed and rests his eyes. "If he was important enough to save, he was probably important enough to be trusted with this location."

I raise an eyebrow. Now *that's* a possibility. "Nadia *did* say his work was important to them."

"You think Dr. Moreau was telling the truth about Dr. Friar being the only one who could get around the device?"

"Probably. He's the only one Mother trusts. And there's no way Mother would permit a device that could kill her without there being a way around it."

"Unless she doesn't have nanos," Asher says.

There's that heavy silence again.

"So . . . we're screwed?" Gavin finally asks.

"No," Asher replies. He glances at me and I shake my head quickly.

"Don't." I know what he's going to say, and if he does, Gavin won't let it go. I won't be able to stop him from going to get help, because there's no way he'd just sit by and do nothing when I'm in danger.

"What?" Gavin demands.

"My grandmother would be willing *and* probably able to not only make that thing useless, but neutralize the nanos completely. What if instead of removing Mother, we could remove her *Citizens*? Leave *her* here. All by herself where she can't hurt anyone."

"There are other options . . ." I say quickly, but I can already see Gavin thinking it over.

He squeezes my toes. "What are they?"

My mind's a blank slate. "We'll figure something out."

"Evie . . ."

"I'm not losing you again, Gavin. Don't do this . . . please."

"It's the only way. You've said you don't want to kill Mother, and she's not going to leave willingly. But your people might. If we can convince them. But none of that even matters if the nanites aren't taken care of." He gently sets my feet to the floor and leans over to take my hands. "I can do this. There's not much I can do here. Hell, I can't even protect you with the Enforcers and that damned death machine—not that I had any hope before either—but I *can* get Lenore and bring her here to help you." His hand cups my cheek and his fingers slide into my hair. "You know I don't want to leave you here. Especially now. But if I can get you out of here . . . safely . . . I will do whatever needs to be done."

This was never going to be a fight I could win. Today was proof of that. I can't deny the Citizens a chance for peace and freedom. But damn it, why does it have to be Gavin who has to go? Selfish or not, I know if there was *any*one else who could go up, I would personally carry them to the submarines and toss them in.

But there isn't. It has to be Gavin.

My heart cracks a little just thinking about him leaving, but who knows, it might actually be safer for him up there without Mother constantly nipping at his heels. And without me slowing him down, the Outlands will probably be nothing but a mere inconvenience.

"I guess we don't have a choice." I run a hand over my face and move onto the next step because I don't want to think about him leaving. That doesn't stop me from gripping his hand just a little bit tighter. "Any ideas on how to get the Citizens to trust me while you're away playing on the Surface? Right now, all they'll see when they look at me is a traitor and murderer, running around with two Surface Dwellers. There's still the mentality of the people here. The rules. The fear. There's nothing I can do to turn that around fast enough. They'll never agree with me that they should leave."

Asher struggles to get more comfortable and I'm surprised when Gavin's the first to help him. Asher nods his thanks. "You're going to have to do it slowly. Methodically. Make them trust you. Show them you're *not* a murderer or a traitor. Show them what Mother's done. She depends on the power of fear to rule her people. All you need to do is show *them* the truth."

I narrow my eyes. "We don't have time for slow. People are

dying. She's already tried killing us. And Dr. Moreau. She won't hesitate to try again."

"We've already seen what happens when you go straight up to her, without the support of the *people*," Asher says softly. "You're just reenforcing everything she's saying: that Surface Dwellers are evil, manipulative, and turn everyone who has dealings with them into traitorous killers."

I'm about to remind him that I'm not planning on killing her, but Gavin clears his throat and both Asher and I turn to him when he says, "Asher's right. We're going to have to be smart about it. We can't take her head-on. But we can take away her support."

"How?"

"The people don't like Mother. They obey her because they're afraid. But they *could* like you. They *could* follow you. They've been so afraid to do anything because every time someone stands up to Mother, they're killed. But not you. You stood up to her by escaping. And now you're back to help *them.*"

"That doesn't even make sense," I mutter. "Why on earth would they trust me?"

"We just need to give them something—someone—to root for. Someone that's a part *of* them. You could run raids on Mother and Dr. Friar. Pull out all their dirty secrets and air them to everyone. There's only so much people can deny before they have to face the truth. Get enough people to follow you and they'll do the rest."

"How?" I demand. "Even if by some miracle I do get the

people to trust me over Mother, they're still terrified of her. How do I convince them to help, if they can't do anything without Mother knowing exactly who they are and *them* becoming the next target?"

"You'd be surprised by what people are willing to do for even the *possibility* of freedom. Even if that means dying for it."

I purse my lips and consider it. "What of their families? The innocent children. Mother *will* retaliate against them."

Asher is frowning, but nodding as well. "Mother doesn't know where you are right now. That's a *huge* advantage in our favor. We can't lose that." He turns to Gavin. "But you're right. People will give their lives for the chance to be free. So how do we keep Mother from finding Evie and allow the Citizens who want to fight the chance to do so without being recognized and targeted?"

"The Enforcer saw me. She went straight back to Mother and told her everything the first chance she got."

"Are you sure about that? How close of a look did she get of you?"

"Pretty damned close."

"But it was dark, right? It's hard enough to tell people apart here. And with you all covered in dirt and blood from earlier, with the lights off, you could have been anyone."

"Who else would have done it?" Frustration leaks into my voice and coats my words.

"Anyone in the Underground."

"Okay, but if I'm hiding, how will the people trust me? If I'm not even brave enough to show myself to Mother, why should they?" I press my fingertips against my temples. This whole conversation is going around in circles and is making my head spin. "Mother is far from stupid. No one but another Enforcer can take an Enforcer down."

The room goes quiet again, before Gavin blurts out, "A mask!"

"That doesn't make any sense. I'll stick out like a sore thumb if I wear a mask. And so will anyone who wears it. That completely defeats the point."

"No. It *is* the point," Gavin says, a huge grin lighting his entire face. He turns to Asher. "When we were kids, you were the best at hiding the button in Find the Button. Why?"

"Because I never hid it," he says slowly. His face looks as confused as I feel.

"Exactly! Because the best place to hide something is right in plain sight. We can't hide Evie unless we keep her hidden away here. She's too prominent. And no one will trust her if she won't get her hands dirty. Mother doesn't want Evie dead. At least not yet. So we use that. Instead of hiding her away, what if we turned everyone into her?" He turns to me, a flush of excitement burning his cheeks. "With a mask, the people will be able to hide who they really are and Mother will never know for sure which one is you, or even if one is you at all."

Chapter Five

Mother always said, "Sacrifices must be made for the greater good." But I've learned that the reward for those sacrifices is minuscule compared to the price we pay.

—Evie's journal

Evie

The room Nadia had taken us to before to tell me about Dr. Moreau is as quiet as a tomb and feels just as somber. Despite that, I like the room. In a way, it's a time capsule from an ancient civilization.

The papers scattered across the sagging table are aged, dusty, and yellowed. The ink is fading and anything handwritten is pretty much illegible. Yet it's obvious this was the room the builders had used as a sort of on-site headquarters.

Drawings of what the facility would look like once finished are the centerpiece, held down by chunks of limestone. A coffee ring stains the left corner of the top page. The only color in a sea of white and black.

I rifle through the pages. I'm not sure what I'm seeing—engineering was never my forte—but I understand enough to recognize this area was going to be the crown jewel of the resort.

The rooms are bigger. More opulent. Less of them in general. More suites as opposed to rooms. There are separate pages for places called Spa, Casino, and Kid Zone. And plans for different restaurants and theaters. There's even something called a marine habitat. I'm not sure what it is, but it's extremely large and juts off into the ocean with a bunch of different things called moon pools. Each of them are labeled with a different species of marine life. Orca. Dolphin. Stingray.

Fascinated, I move along the table, glancing through folders marked Timetables, Budget, Maps, and Geological Studies. Electronic devices that appear to be an ancestor, or at least kin, to our Slates sit on the table in front of each chair. I wonder, if we were able to make them work again, what they'd tell us.

Oddly, mixed in with the papers and electronic devices are different artifacts. Photographs of people or places. Drawings. Magazines. Paper books. Thin plastic discs with words like *HUNGER GAMES, CALL OF DUTY,* and *LINKIN PARK* printed across one side. I find shattered sunglasses and ancient earbuds like what Gavin's brother, Tristan, used to have. A small black box labeled *CARDS AGAINST HUMANITY.*

Obviously these are things Nadia and her people found and placed in here, and I can't quite help the shiver of excitement as I go through them. Even before I met Gavin, I'd loved Surface objects. An old suitor had helped me fill my little pond in my gardens with contraband items he'd presumably found.

Melancholy at the thought of Timothy pushes delight away. Was this where he got his items? Did someone here know of him? Help him? Did they know what happened to him because of me?

I lurch from the table, dropping the black box and scattering its contents across the floor. I quickly drop to my knees and scoop up the pieces of black-and-white cardboard and shove them haphazardly into the box.

I try to force the thought of him away. But he clings to me like so many of my ghosts. Macie. Nick. The nameless people I killed under Mother's orders as an Enforcer. Shame and guilt war in me and I'm paralyzed with emotion. The room really does feel like a tomb now. Mine.

I no longer like the room; it serves only as a reminder of every single one of my failures. The air is stale and ominous. Expectation and my own inadequacy loom like the dark clouds heavy with rain before a storm. Its weight biding its time before it crushes me.

I go back to the table and grab a coin. The one that most closely resembles the very last gift Timothy gave me. It still surprises me, even after a month, just how strange it feels to remember everything from my life, but not feel like it's mine. The memories I have of the time before I met Gavin are convoluted and blended.

And while I remember Timothy, and that I loved him and

miss him, the feelings I have for him are somehow muted. They're nothing compared to what I feel for Gavin. A side effect of Mother's Conditioning? Or did I never really love him in the first place? And that makes me ponder if it was worth it to him. To die for me. To die *because* of me.

It all seems so needless to me. Even now. Supposedly Mother killed him because we touched while UnCoupled. However, with my memories mostly intact, I know it was because she had decided he was unsuitable and had chosen the young Guard for me. Mother's plan to make me the genesis of the new Enforcer breed.

I know I'd rather die than let that happen. But I worry how many people will go down with me. I'm sure she'll come for me. I'm certain she knows just where I am—she's known everything else—and it's just a matter of time before she decides she's waited long enough. I'm surprised it hasn't happened already.

The coin is cold as ice in my hand, and that coldness seeps into me as I wonder how much of a coward it would make me if I just said, "Enough. This fight is not *my* fight." If I just followed Gavin to the submarines and left with him. If I just let the nanos once again take my memories and all the unwanted emotions from me, so there's nothing left of who I was and what I've done.

The air changes around me and I know, even before I hear his footsteps, that Gavin's found me. As if just thinking of him has somehow summoned him to me.

"We don't have to do this," I tell him without turning or

looking up from the coin when he steps into the room. "We could run again. Leave for the Surface together."

"You'd forget everything." He continues toward me, stopping just centimeters from my back. He's so close I can feel the heat from his body.

"I lived with it before." I shrug. "I could write a note to myself with all the things I want to remember. And a list of reasons why it's better I forgot."

"Is that what you want to do?" His voice is devoid of emotion, as if he's asking me nothing more than what the weather is like.

I look at the coin, then at a paper on the table. It's yellowed with age like all the rest, but it's a picture of some kind, with a hand-printed note in a child's hand that says, "Maggie, 4 years." Surrounding it are old newspapers with horrific pictures and headlines that read: "Air Battle Rages over Los Angeles." "One Hundred Dead, Hundreds Missing after Bombing in Chicago." "New Technology Brings War to U.S. Doorway."

"I *don't* want this," I say, gesturing to the papers.

"No one ever does."

"I used to wonder why the Surface went to war. I never understood the things Mother told us in our studies. That it was over greed, pride, envy, or any number of other things. I never wanted to believe that something so silly as money could cause an entire world to destroy itself. I didn't understand how anyone could feel so strongly about any of those things that they'd die and kill for them."

"But you do now?"

I furrow my brow and slowly shake my head. "No. But I understand *you*. I get why you would rather worry day in and day out about where your food comes from in the Outlands, than live comfortably in Rushlake. I understand why people fought back when other people started war for those reasons."

"Why?"

"Freedom." I clutch the coin tightly in my hand. "And I want that. I want that for me and you and Asher and the people who live here who've never known it."

"Then you know you can't come with me."

I step nearer to him and touch a hand to the stubble on his cheek. "Doesn't mean I don't want to."

He presses my hand closer to his cheek. "I know."

We stand there, just like that. Me staring into his gray eyes. The stubble on his cheek tickling my palm. Our bodies are close enough to touch, but still a hairbreadth apart. Then his lips come down on mine, achingly soft. Sweet. Tender.

Our bodies are pressed so tightly together I can feel his racing heart against my own. But it's not enough. For either of us apparently, because he has the same idea as I do. He pulls me up even as I jump, wrapping my legs around his waist.

His rough hands move up my bare thighs and I give a delicate shiver when they stop at my hips under the skirt, pulling me even closer to him. I have a passing thought that I should feel wrong about this, but I don't. I don't care about anything at all except for what his skin feels like against mine.

His tongue slips between my lips and he tastes sweet like a fruit. I'll miss his taste. His smell. *Him.* My heart pounds so hard all I can hear is the whoosh of blood in my ears and the gasping of our breaths colliding.

But, still, I want more. I yank his shirt out from his pants and arch my back so I can slide my hands under it.

His mouth moves from mine to the delicate area of my throat below my ear, and then down my collarbone to the dip in the center. I tilt my head back and he trails his lips up my throat. The prickly skin of his chin tickles me when he kisses just under my jaw.

I dig my hands into his hair, loving the thick texture between my fingers, and pull him closer to me when he nuzzles the curve between my neck and shoulder.

Eventually we pull apart, our hearts still pounding, and he sets me carefully back down on my feet.

"I love you," we say together and smile, then he leans his forehead against mine. His hands trail up and down my arms as if he can't bear to stop touching me.

"I'm worried," he murmurs against my head.

"Don't," I say, backing away.

"We have to talk about this. I'm leaving. Hopefully I'll be back—"

I touch my finger to his lips. "You will be. It'll be like you're just leaving the room. I probably won't notice you're gone."

He gives me a look. "Evie."

"We should probably plan your trip though. Find the fastest and safest way there and back."

"Evie!" His voice is filled with frustration, but I hear his footsteps following me and that's all I need. For now.

"Hurry. We'll need to make sure you're all packed and have a solid plan." I frown as I step into the main Caverns. Where would I find a map of the Outlands down here?

Gavin grabs my arm and pulls, stopping me in my tracks. "Evie! Stop."

I turn. "I'm not saying it."

"You're being ridiculous."

"Maybe, but I'm not going to say it."

"For God's sake, Evie! I'm leaving for the Surface. Just fucking say good-bye!"

The whole time he's talking, panic creeps into me. The fear I've been trying so hard to push down, so I can let him go and do this, pushes on me from all sides, making it almost impossible to breathe. I shake him off and continue walking toward the cutout.

"So you're not even going to say good-bye?"

"I told you, it's not good-bye. It's as simple as you walking into the next room. I wouldn't say good-bye if you were going to the next room." I almost choke on the words, as tears catch in my throat and I shove them down where he can't see them.

"I don't *believe* this," he mutters.

I press my lips together and continue straight into the cutout where Asher is sitting up in bed, shirtless and pressing on the spot he was injured.

"Hey! Look!" he says. "They're not even sore. It's like nothing—" He stops when he sees me. "What's wrong?"

"We need a map of the Outlands. We're going to need to plan out Gavin's trip to Rushlake," I say.

Asher lifts an eyebrow. "O-okay. But we left it at Evangeline's . . ."

Of course we did. Why would I think he'd have that here? We've been at Evangeline's the last month. Tears immediately burn my eyes. "Well, we're going to have to get it. I'll find Nadia." I start out the doorway, but Gavin stands in my way. "Please move."

"I don't need a map. I know how to get there."

I swallow. My body starts to tremble, but I clench my fists and try to hold it together. "Then we'll just need to come up with a plan to get you in."

"He doesn't need to get in. He just needs the guards at the gate to get my grandma. He'll probably have to bribe them, but that's easily taken care of." Asher slips the watch off his wrist and holds it out to Gavin. "This should do it."

I can feel him staring at me as Gavin takes it without taking his eyes off me. "Thanks."

"You'll need food," I say quietly.

"I'll stop by my house. The less I take with me from here, the easier it will be to leave."

"We need to get Father."

"He's back," Asher pipes up. "He's with Dr. Moreau."

"Actually, I'm right here," Father says from the doorway behind Gavin.

"Well, that's just great then. I guess you're all ready to go." My voice catches and I almost lose control of myself as I think of all the things he's going to have to do.

I think I'm going to be sick.

"Damn it, Evie. Just say it! I'm leaving! Through Sector Three, which has twice proven it wants to kill us. If I make it through that without Mother finding me, it'll be a miracle. Then I have to get through the Outlands and bribe the guards to get Asher's grandmother and convince her to come with me. Then make it *back* through the Outlands, back through Sector Three with her. And if I manage to make it through all that, there's no guarantee you'll still be here and still be you."

"Don't you think I know all that? I know the dangers. I know that Mother probably knows we're in here and that the next corner I take could have Enforcers around it. I know that Mother probably won't kill me when she finds me, and that she'll either make me kill all these people or watch as she has someone else do it, then scramble my brains so I don't even know who I am anymore. I *know* that," I say in a pinched voice.

"Then what are you doing? Why are you acting like this?"

"Because I *have* to. If I even *think* about what *could* happen, then I won't be able to let you go."

He's quiet for a moment, then he jumps forward and gently takes my head in his hands, pulling my lips to his. I return it, putting everything I have into the kiss, because there's a whole lot that can go wrong and we'll need a miracle to make it all work. This could very well be the last time I'll ever get to do this.

The thought causes the dam to break and tears finally run down my cheeks.

I pull away immediately, but he keeps his hands on my face, his thumbs rubbing the tears away.

"I can't do this," I whisper, my voice clogged with tears. "I can't watch you leave." But I kiss him again. Harder this time, pouring everything I have into it, before breaking away. "I love you," I say. The closest I'll let myself get to saying good-bye. Then I bolt out the door, past Father and a stunned Nadia, so I don't have to see the person I love more than anything walk away from me, possibly never to return.

CHAPTER SIX

Stephen: The council is disappointed to learn of your failure to discover the whereabouts of your son and, most importantly, that of the girl from under the sea. As you well know, she is thought to be an invaluable asset to us. If you do not find her, alive, by month's end, we will be forced to take action on our own. Might we suggest you start with the boy who found her.

—LETTER FROM AN UNNAMED INDIVIDUAL IN RUSHLAKE CITY TO MAYOR ST. JAMES

Gavin

I can't believe Evie wouldn't say good-bye! I mean, I know how she feels. I saw the fear in her eyes and her tears and felt it in her trembling body. Hell, I'm terrified. Not of the Outlands, but of returning here to find her either dead, or worse, with no memory of me as anything other than a Surface Dweller who must die. But damn it! She could have at least said good-bye.

Of course, the way her blue eyes bored into me and pleaded with me not to go before she ran away was almost my undoing. I think if she would have asked me to stay, I would have. Which I know is why she couldn't. Still, I don't know how many times I want to turn back around and demand a good-bye. I almost do it when Father leads me to a rock wall blocking our path. We climb carefully up a ladder they've carved into the wall next to it and through a tiny hole I'm not entirely sure how we fit through. We then let ourselves drop to the concrete floor. What looks like a Tube track is blocked off by an airlock like the one at Sector Three.

"What is this?"

"The original way into the Caverns. There was going to be a train like there is from Two to Three, but that of course never happened. Shortly after work stopped, there was a minor tremor and it caused the cave-in we just crawled through." He pushes on the airlock door and it slides up just enough to let us belly crawl through it.

"And Mother has no idea that it's here?"

He pushes the airlock back down. "She's sent Enforcers from time to time to check it out, but even though they managed to get through the airlock, they couldn't get past the rocks. It was a terrifying time for the Caverns, so I'm told, but the Enforcers never came back. As far as I know, Mother has no idea what's on the other side of those rocks."

"How do you know that?"

"Because they wouldn't be there if she did." He says it bluntly and without a hint of emotion. "She wasn't even born yet when her father stopped building that. And it was never talked about when she was alive, as far as I know. None of the plans for the hotel have anything other than that tunnel and a note about possible future expansion. I assure you, she doesn't know."

"You'll have to forgive me if I don't trust you."

He only shrugs in answer and continues through the Tube. When we get to the airlock on the other side, he does the same thing as he did with the one by the Caverns, but before I can slide under he says, "You have to be careful here. The cameras in this Sector are still working and I'm not there to monitor them."

My nerves ramp up so they're at an all-time high, but I nod my understanding. I knew this wasn't going to be easy. I'll just have to trust Eli knows how to get around the cameras.

When we enter Sector Three, Eli doesn't even appear nervous. He barely glances at the green people-shaped globs I remember from the last time I was here. I, on the other hand, steer as far from them as I can without straying too far from Eli. One tried to eat Asher when he accidentally stepped in it, and another attacked us when we were briefly trapped with it.

However, I do notice that they have moved from their original location. At least the ones on the main floor that were from where all the people from this Sector were massacred. They're closer to the windows, and there's a small track in the cement. As if it had melted away.

I shudder at the thought of any of it touching me.

Eli clears his throat and I jerk and look over at him. He's already at the elevators, holding the door open for me. He looks pointedly at the green stuff. "It's all over this building. We've permanently closed it and have built a temporary connection to the Agricultural Sector, because it appears that whatever it's made of is eating at the structure of this building."

"Any idea yet what it is?"

He doesn't say anything for a few seconds, but then he sighs. "*My* mistake. After . . . everything last time. Mother just left all her failed experiments here to kill each other until no one was left. When she was sure it was 'safe,'" he makes air quotes with his fingers, "she sent someone to clean up all the bodies. I went with the crew, because I wanted to try and gather the nanites and see if they were still operable. But when we got here, we saw the oldest of the bodies had been liquefied."

I glance at the green stuff and feel my stomach twist. "Liquefied?"

He barely glances at me. "I haven't quite figured out how that part happened yet, but I believe it has something to do with the nanites trying to clean up the dead tissue like they're programmed to."

I swallow and nod.

"Naturally I was upset. All those nanites. Lost."

"Naturally," I say, and want to roll my eyes. Of course he'd be more concerned about the nanites than actual human life.

"I was eager to study what was left of the bodies to find out what had happened, and found out the nanos were still working. Still trying to perform their primary function: Keep the body running. And some were succeeding. Not all the parts had liquefied in some of the bodies and the nanites were trying their damnedest to get them working again. Then it hit me. I thought, if Mother could take men and make them monsters, maybe I could take monsters and make them men. Reanimate the bodies. Use them against Mother, like she uses the Enforcers." He closes his eyes. "But it failed. Miserably."

"What happened?"

His eyes open and he stares into mine. "Can't you see? I reanimated the bodies, but not like I expected to. And now they're this . . . substance. Worse than anything Mother programmed. It destroys almost everything it touches or comes near. And turning off and destroying the nanos has done nothing. The stuff is reanimated and operating somehow on its own. So now I spend my free time trying to figure out how to get rid of it, but I'm worried it's too late. Mother has her own ideas of how to handle it." He gives me a look. "If you plan on returning, I'd make this a fast trip. I'm not sure there will be anything to dock to if you take too long."

I look back at the Tube, then nod and step into the elevator. "I'll make it fast."

For the rest of the trip to the submarine bay, we don't speak. I don't know what to say to him and he isn't exactly sending off the vibe he wants to talk to me.

When we get to the submarine bay, the one we'd used before, he places his hand on the hand plate. The door opens and he gestures toward it, handing me my bag. "Your ride awaits. I trust you remember how to operate it?"

I'll do as well as I did the first time, I guess. At least I'm not being attacked by a bunch of crazed Enforcers this time. I just nod, then glance toward the door again. Once more stopped by the desire to go back to Evie.

"There's a button on the console that will bring you back here."

I take that step into the submarine, but it's almost impossible. My heart and my head fight against each other the entire way. I can't believe how hard it is to leave. It's not like I'm not going to return.

I turn around just as he's about to press his hand to the plate again to shut the doors from his side. "Wait!" I say.

He lifts his eyebrows.

"What happens if there's no place to dock when I come back?"

"Just hurry and we won't have to worry, will we?" Then he shuts the doors before I can say anything else.

I take that to mean I'm screwed if this building is gone when I get back. It really will have to be fast.

I take the controls. I don't really know how to drive this thing, but I just press the same buttons I pressed the last time as best I can remember. The sub bursts away from the facility and, for some reason, this trip feels a hell of a lot faster than the last time I took it. Probably because I don't have someone dying next to me. I sigh. No. Not just someone. Evie.

When I get to the Surface, I almost steer directly onto the beach near my house like I did before. But I know if I do, Asher's father will just take the sub away again.

So I moor it to the island across from the village, making sure it's anchored securely and won't float away before I can get back to it.

This is the island that fuels my nightmares. Not because of its eerie fog or that there's absolutely no game on it, despite its deep forests. It's the island I came to with my hunting partner, Con. The one that had me careening down a cliff and forced to wait in a cave. The one where I stupidly made the decision to venture into the tunnels that eventually led to Elysium. The one that led to Con's death.

The place where I anchored is right near the cave and I can't stop myself from peeking into it. The ghosts of those that came before me beckon like the Sirens from long ago to lead me back to the tunnels. Con's voice is the loudest, and for one second I can almost believe he's been at the end of the maze of tunnels the entire time and needs my help.

But when I get about a hundred feet into the tunnel, water splashes against my ankles, soaking my shoes. I remember seeing water puddled along the sand floor last time I was here and thinking the tunnels must fill during the rainy season. I guess I was right. The whispers I hear are just the slap of the water against the cave walls.

Guilt pulling at me, I force myself to turn around and step back out through the cave's wide mouth onto the rocky ground at the bottom of the ledge of rocks. Carefully, I pull myself up hand over hand to the top of the cliff and wind my way through the foggy forest, to the beach where Connor and I left what could roughly be called a raft.

There's not much left, but I have to hope it's enough to get me across before it falls apart altogether.

After dragging it into the water, I use a stick to push toward the cove. Luck seems to be a little on my side this time, at least. The tide is coming in and I'm able to use that as a propellant to get me across the cove toward my beach as quickly as I can. I take a few minutes to hide the raft in the underbrush again.

I rush toward my house, more eager than I expected to see Mom and Tristan.

I stop on the threshold of the door, suddenly anxious. What the hell do I possibly say to them?

Sorry for taking off for over a month without telling you where I was going or what I was doing and probably dredging up old feelings from when Dad died. Or maybe: *Hey! I know I just got here, but I have to go right back out and find Asher's grandma because I'm in the middle of a mutiny and it turns out she's the key to everything after all.*

For a moment I even debate just getting Lenore without seeing them at all. I'll be back after everything is all over and they'll never even have to know the dangerous parts. But then it hits me that even if everything turns out for the best and we do get Evie's people up here, there's the distinct possibility I won't be returning. That it isn't just a simple mutiny, it's a full-out revolution, and every revolution throughout history has had casualties. I have to accept I may be one of them.

I can't just leave them like that.

Not again.

Not like Dad.

After taking two deep breaths that really don't do anything to relax me, I push open the door and walk straight to the kitchen, where I know they're either eating, or Mom will be cooking.

I'm right. She's at the stove, stirring something in a pot. It smells so good my mouth waters. I've had to endure Elysium's food for entirely too long. I smile when I see her. I can't believe how much I've missed her.

"Mom," I say.

She spins around so fast, the pot she was stirring catches on her apron strings and flies off the stove to drop at her feet.

"Holy shit!" I run to her, dropping all my stuff as I go. "Are you burned? I'm so sorry. Are you okay?"

She doesn't answer; she just wraps her arms around me. Her whole body is shaking and I realize instantly that she seems so much thinner than she was. I can almost feel every bone in her back as I hug her.

Was she always like this? Did I just never notice how thin she was?

I push her back a little and really study her. Her face is drawn and thin, her eyes all red from crying. And there's a bruise on her right cheek.

Guilt tears through me. "What happened?" I touch her cheek.

Something like fear fills her eyes, and she glances to the door. "Did anyone see you come? Did you talk to anyone? Did you come straight here?"

"No. No. And yes," I say with a frown. "What's going on? What's the matter?"

She shakes her head. "It doesn't matter," she chokes out, pulling me to her again. "It doesn't matter. You're home now and it doesn't matter." She's still surprisingly strong for as thin as she is. "They said you'd died. That you'd been lost on the trip to Rushlake. But I knew that wasn't true. It couldn't be."

I close my eyes and clench my fists. I know *exactly* who told her I'd died. Asher's dad. The mayor.

"I didn't die. I'm sorry, Mom." I hug her tightly and tell her the whole story, starting from the time we left here, being attacked by the vulture hawks, then getting lost and almost killed by coyotes in the Outlands. Getting to Rushlake City only to find out that Asher had left with Evie to take her back to Elysium, and then following her to Elysium and everything that's happened there.

She looks around me. "Is she with you?"

"Evie? No. She had to stay there. In fact, she may not be able to come back here. Ever. Her . . . sickness is keeping her there."

Mom frowns at me. "And you came back?"

"I had to check on you. And Tristan." I want to tell her the real reason I'm here, but I can't force my lips to say the words. Besides, it'll only worry her and she obviously doesn't need any more of that right now. I can tell her when I get back with Lenore.

"But you're going to go back, right?"

Something about her tone throws me off, but I say, "Yes.

Evie's going through a hard time right now and I have to be there for her. I love her, Mom. I have to be where she is. No matter where that is."

"I know." She smiles, even though her lips quiver a little. She touches a cold hand to my cheek. "But you have to promise to come back and visit."

"Is that a 'here's your coat, what's your hurry' thing?" I laugh. "I'm not leaving yet. I have to handle a few things first. And one of those things is to make sure you guys are taken care of."

She shakes her head quickly. "You need to go back to Evie. She needs you. We're fine. We'll be fine."

This time warning bells go off. Why is she in such a hurry to get rid of me? It's obvious they need me back. I touch the bruise again. "Are you going to tell me what happened here?"

She looks down and I know she's not going to tell me, but a voice behind me says, "Mayor St. James hit her."

I whirl around to stare at my brother, Tristan, then turn back to my mom. "He *hit* you?" I demand at the same time she hisses, "Tristan!"

She doesn't answer me; she looks to the ground, though, and I have my answer. "Why did he hit you?" When she doesn't answer, I twist back around to Tristan. He looks just as gaunt as she does. "Why?" I repeat.

"She couldn't tell them where Evie and Asher went." His voice has changed, too. He's lost a little of the innocence he had before. And his mannerisms. I can see Dad in them, in him, so clearly it makes my eyes sting.

"She didn't know."

"She told him that. He didn't believe her."

"Well, beating it out of her isn't going to give him the answers he wants." I clench my teeth. "It's him that deserves a beating."

"Don't worry," Tristan says. "I took care of that already."

My eyes widen. "What?"

"When he hit her, I saw it. I made sure he didn't do it again." He looks to the pot lying on the ground. "We're not allowed in the village anymore."

"Wait. What?" My head feels like it's going to explode. I'd expected them to be in a bit of trouble, not a full-blown epic mess.

"We're not allowed in the village. Mom or me. Because I attacked the mayor and that's our punishment. We can't trade Mom's sewing or dresses or embroidery for money or anything. We can't go to the general store or even the doctor. And it's my fault." He looks back up at me and tears are welling in his eyes. "I shouldn't have hit him. But I couldn't let him hurt Mom like that. And it wouldn't have been so bad, but I can't hunt like you did and the other hunters aren't allowed to teach me. So we just have what we can grow and what I do manage to catch. Mostly fish." He makes a face. "I'm beginning to hate fish."

I hold my arms out to him and at first he just stands there. Then he rushes into them, and his tears start soaking my shirt, because ultimately, he's only ten, and he's had to carry the weight of a man. I close my eyes. This is my fault. How many times did he beg me to teach him to hunt, but I said no, because I wanted the quiet, the false peace?

I pat and rub his back. "Shh. It's okay. You did the right thing. It's not your fault." It's mine. But I don't say it. I just let it fester. "I'm back now. And I'm going to fix everything."

There's no way I'm going to let Mayor St. James get away with hurting my mom, not after what he's already done to my family. He's going to pay for what he's done and I don't care what I have to do to make sure of it.

CHAPTER SEVEN

Building hope through sinking dreams! Join us for a 5- or 7-day vacation and get 1 night free!

— ELYSIUM TOWERS RESORT FLYER

Evie

I may not have been able to say good-bye to Gavin, but that doesn't mean I didn't watch him go. Was it silly and stupid not to say it? Yes, but I felt like if I said it, it would be forever and if I didn't, he'd have to come back. To argue with me at least for *not* saying it.

I know it was logical for him to go. That in order to give the Citizens even a chance at the freedom I've known because of him, he had to go. But that doesn't mean I have to like it. Or sit around and twist my hands together and wait. With Asher still confined to bed, I decide to start the other part of our plan by myself.

Getting the people to trust in me and turn from Mother. And I know exactly what to start with.

Dr. Moreau.

Father checked on him earlier, but I didn't get a chance to talk to him myself. Seems the perfect time to do so. Hopefully he's able, not to mention willing, to see me.

I peek into the nook that's his room. It's not far from Asher's. He's lying on his back, but he's awake. He's just staring at the ceiling.

I clear my throat and step in when he twists to look at me. "How are you doing?"

"I hear I have you to thank for saving me from my own device."

I bite my lip. His tone is so accusatory I don't know what to say, so I smooth my skirt and then take the seat next to him. "Should I apologize?" I ask.

A smile finally creeps over his face. "No." He shakes his head. "In fact, I probably should for being rude to you."

"Don't worry about it," I say. "You have every right to be as angry and rude as you want to be." I gesture to his missing arm. "Does it hurt?"

"No. Surprisingly. Father's got me on a pretty good dose of painkillers while the nanos finish repairing it. But it's strange to want to reach for something, only to remember I can't."

"I'm sorry."

He doesn't say anything. He just stares at where his arm is supposed to be and I don't know what else to say. It's not like the nanos will be able to help his arm regrow. That would have been a nice feature, but I'm fairly certain it wasn't one of

Mother's priorities when she was having Lenore and Father design them.

Lost for words, I press my lips together and swing my legs between the chair legs. "I . . . I guess I should let you rest."

I start to turn away, but he grabs my wrist with his one hand. "You have to tell people what Dr. Friar did. All those people. Dead."

"What are you talking about?"

"You have to find his documents. It's all there on the data cube. The people he kidnapped. The experiments. What happened. Who died. How." He pulls me closer. "They all had families. Every single one. They need to know what happened to them."

I nod. "Where do I go?"

He lets go of my arm and leans back against his pillow with his eyes closed. "If I knew that I wouldn't be missing an arm."

I press my lips together and move my gaze to the floor. I have to remind myself that his tone has nothing to do with me, and more the situation.

For a few minutes, we sit in silence, with only the beeping of his machines to mark the time. Finally acknowledging that my visit here was a lesson in futility, I push my chair back with a squeal of its legs against the rock. "I'm sorry for bothering you." I nod once and twist my body to start walking toward the door.

"He knew I took them," Dr. Moreau says, stopping me in mid-step. I turn to face him when he continues. "I thought I was being slick, by taking them a few days ago and not planning on doing anything with them until later, but Father says you found the box in my drawer, which means that Dr. Friar knew. He has the cubes."

"Do you know where he might keep them?"

"He thinks I'm dead and his little hidey hole is safe. He's going to be smug. And that means he put them back exactly where they were before I took them. In his office. In the same cabinet as he does the Conditioning serum." He's staring at me, meeting my gaze full on. "You have to stop him from doing *this*," he gestures to his missing arm, "to anyone else."

"I will," I promise, but I have no idea *how* I'm going to do it. I don't even know if I *can*. Just the thought of having to enter Dr. Friar's office again sets off every horrible memory I've ever had there. My whole body shudders as I stand and leave the room. And that's if he's right and the cubes are even there. If they aren't, I've no idea where to start looking.

I'm not sure what to do now. It's still too early to even think about going to Dr. Friar's and I *don't* want to think about Gavin and everything that could be going wrong right now.

So I wander around until I find my way back to the room with all the artifacts. I don't know how long I spend sitting at the decrepit table looking at everything and taking it all in. All of the items are so captivating, it's easy to lose track and just let my mind wander *and* wonder over the pieces. I have to admit, I'm most fascinated by the electronics, but no matter how many of the buttons I press and no matter the order, nothing happens.

"Whoa!" Asher says from behind me. I'd heard him coming. In this quiet tomb, it would have been impossible not to.

He stares around the room, wide-eyed. "What is all this?" He walks over to another of the electronics, one similar to the one in my hand, and picks it up, frowning at it. "My grandmother used to have something like this."

"What is it? I can't get it to work."

"She called it a tablet, I think." He turns it around and around, looking at it from every angle before pausing at the hole in the bottom. "Oh yeah."

He looks around the desk, then picks up a white cord that's plugged in to the outlet in the center. He slides it into the hole. Nothing happens, so I shake my head and put mine down. He continues to play with the machine. Jiggling the cable. Pressing the buttons. Turning the whole thing facedown. The screen remains blank. I decide to glance through the drawings of Elysium Towers again.

When I'm flipping through the drawings for the umpteenth time and spinning the coin from earlier on the table, his machine suddenly makes a strange dinging sound and a little rectangular red picture with a lightning bolt inside it lights up.

"What did it do?" I ask, giving it the side eye.

He laughs. "It's working. That's what. I can't believe something this old is still working."

I get up to stand next to him. "What does it do?"

"You'll see."

It takes another few moments before a white symbol—the same one from the back of it—pops onto the screen. A few seconds after that another symbol—the one that's on the bottom of all the blueprints—replaces the first one. The screen asks us to unlock it and Asher slides his finger across the bottom of the screen.

The entire screen fills up with a dozen or so symbols. But these are all different colors. There's one that looks like a music note inside a circle. Another that looks like an old analog clock. One with an *A* made of pencils.

"It's pretty," I hedge, not exactly sure what I'm supposed to be seeing.

Asher's lips quirk into a grin and he touches a finger to a symbol that has the caption, PHOTOS. Dozens of tiny little pictures pop onto the screen with dates above them. They're all from about ten years before the war ended.

He taps the screen and the original symbols are back. He clicks on one called VIDEOS. There's only one. More curious than I'd like to admit, I touch it. The whole screen blips and then the video starts playing.

The "camera" pans over a surprisingly horrible animated picture of Elysium with even more horrible animated pictures of dolphins and whales and rays swimming by, before panning in to reveal happy smiling people looking at the creatures from the other side of the glass in Sector Two.

"Has the war got you down?" a male voice blasts from the ancient Slate. "Dive into the exquisite beauty of Elysium Towers. A place where the fun never ends. A world filled with wonder and amazement. Where you can stay and play with your favorite creatures and fall asleep to the songs of whales.

Where the memories you make will last lifetimes. Book now and receive rates as low as two hundred dollars per person per night. Plus a six hundred dollar airfare credit. Kids under twelve eat free at any of our sixteen famous restaurants. Make time for fun. Make time for Elysium Towers."

"What was *that*?" I ask, laughing so hard I have tears pouring down my face.

Asher's laughing too hard to respond, but he taps it again and the video replays, panning over different aspects of Elysium as it was before Mother made it a city. It shows people lounging, people reading, people having fun. People, people, people. All of them smiling and happy.

Nadia pokes her head into the doorway. A strange expression crosses her face when she sees the images on the screen.

"I remember that," she says quietly. It's almost sad how she says it, and immediately both Asher and I bite our lips to stop our laughter. She shakes her head. "I *hated* that commercial." She gives us an amused look. "Strange, the things you miss after a while." She shakes her head and goes back to her normal irritated state, staring daggers at Asher. "You, young man, were supposed to stay in your room. You may feel better, but it will take a while for your body to get used to the nanos. Get back to your cot."

His eyes plead with me to let him stay and play with the neat new gadget, but I just give him my "not a chance" look and shrug. He pouts, but stands and walks from the room.

Nadia turns to leave as well, but I shove up from the table. "Nadia. I need a way to show this order to everyone in Elysium."

I unroll the Enforcer's order I picked up in Dr. Moreau's office and hold it out to her. "I figure we can make copies of it and hand them out to people in Sector Two."

She narrows her eyes when she sees the order. "How do you want me to copy this? And if you go out there, they will know you're still alive. There will be no doubts. I didn't save you to have you killed twenty-four hours later."

"I know. That's the problem. We'll need some sort of distraction." I glance down at the pre-Slate in my hand and a smile raises the corners of my lips. "I don't suppose Mother would be too happy to have her Citizens realize that their 'city' was just a really expensive hotel."

She gives me a considering look. "That is a good idea, but might I suggest something a little less . . ." I think she's going to say *stupid,* but she only says, ". . . obvious than you outing yourself? How about we give this to Father. He'll know how to get it off that and onto everyone's Slates without Mother knowing where it came from."

"He's not going to risk that." A sense of déjà vu hits me and I frown, but shake it off.

"I'm sure the distraction will help with that."

I weigh the benefits of that against the drawbacks. I somewhat begrudgingly have to admit her idea is better. "Okay. Sure. Thank you."

A lump forms in my throat at the thought of entering Dr. Friar's office again after all this time. But I don't have a choice. Exposing the assassination orders is a good first step to showing who Mother really is, but it's also easily dismissed. However, if I can prove what happened to people's lost family members, it's not something they're likely to forget.

Luckily Father agreed it was a good plan and knew just who to give the commercial to, along with the orders. According to him, Mother wants to address yesterday's incident with the Citizens. He said she's going to hold an assembly tonight to quash the rumors that we were there and that will be the perfect time to disseminate the information. I have to admit, I'm a little worried about him playing double-agent, but he's the only one in Mother's inner circle that both Nadia and I trust.

Nadia helps me retrace my steps from last night. Following her through some tunnels that lead to Sector Two, I watch our path carefully this time. Even though it's dark, my eyes adjust quickly. I pull from my Enforcer training to create a map in my head of what we're doing.

Thick cables lay across one side of the tunnel, leaving just a small walk space on the other. "What is this place?" I whisper. My nerves are humming, but I'm pretty sure it's just stress and panic from the thought of going into a room that holds so many bad memories.

"They're the old conduits that run from Three to here. They would have powered the life support systems for the entire complex, but since it was never finished, it only powers the supplemental one now."

Well, that answers my question about electricity, but only feeds my concern that Mother can easily get to us. "And

Mother? She has to know this exists. Especially if you're pilfering her electricity to run your systems."

"Mother knows nothing of how her 'city' is run. And as long as she has what she wants, she doesn't question anything when it comes to power. Besides, there's no way for her to know the usage. It's not like there's a bill she has to pay." She laughs at her own joke, but I don't know what a bill is so I don't join her.

"I'm sure she knows there's a tunnel here though."

"We've taken precautions to make sure the entranceway into this particular tunnel is hidden, but yes, it is a concern of ours that it could be found." Nadia shrugs. "We have measures in place should someone other than our own stumble across it."

"And they are . . ."

"We are nearing the connector to Sector Two. It is best if we make as little noise as possible."

I don't like that she didn't answer my question, but her advice is prudent at the moment. She peers through the small peephole, then presses a code into an apparatus hidden on the side of a junction box.

"I shall wait here for you as before. Same signal."

I fight the urge to roll my eyes. Like it won't be obvious I'm standing in the middle of a maintenance way, knocking on a wall. But I don't have a better idea and I know she won't leave the presumed safety of her tunnel again.

I'm at least a little relieved that the shafts are quiet since it's after curfew, but I still feel the tingly sensation in my spine that tells me I'm being watched. I don't know how many times I turn around to see who it is, only to find no one, but by the time I get to the exit into Sector Two my skin feels like it's just going to crawl right off my bones.

It's late, but not too late. Just after Mother's imposed curfew though, so Sector Two is as eerily quiet as Sector Three. I slide along the outside walls as close as I can, so I can stay in the deeper part of the shadows and hopefully avoid being caught in the crossbeam of the sensors of the turrets and cams.

Finally, I slip into the Tube of the Medical Sector. This is it, I think. This is the moment Mother's Enforcers ambush me. I'm trapped. There are only two ways out of the tunnel—back the way I came, or straight forward. But nothing happens. No one stops me from accessing the Medical Sector. Enforcers don't block the exit. The airlock doors on either side of it don't even close.

It's just like last time. Quiet. Almost peaceful. Dark. So I make my way to the hallway I've traveled hundreds of times to get to Dr. Friar's office. At his door, my panic returns. My chest pinches so I can't breathe. My heart attacks my ribs as it pounds away, announcing my fear for anyone to hear. I force my emotions down and take a deep calming breath before I push open Dr. Friar's office door. It's empty, but that looming doom feeling is back, so I make quick work of crossing the room and opening the cabinet.

As Dr. Moreau said, Friar's data cubes are in plain sight.

Smug doesn't even begin to explain Dr. Friar. But, since his arrogance ensured I got what I wanted, I'm not going to complain.

With a quick glance to make sure, yet again, that I'm alone, I sweep the cubes from the shelf and into my satchel.

It feels entirely too easy, and I'm still not convinced that Mother doesn't know what I'm doing, but I'll take it and whatever comes next and hope it goes just as smoothly on the way back.

I'm heading back to the main waiting room to start the slow arduous path back to the Caverns when there's a flicker of light in the corner. My heart leaps into my throat when I see Mother standing there, but I stand my ground. Hiding isn't going to prevent the worst from happening, and I'll be damned if I go down easy.

My mind immediately starts to process escape routes and different scenarios of how this is going to go down. But then I see the telltale flicker of a holo-projection and realize that Father is next to her on one side and an Enforcer on the other. And she isn't looking directly at me. She's focused on the camera.

It hits me then. This must be the assembly she wanted to have. The one that Father was going to have someone interrupt with our commercial. I debate whether or not to leave, but curiosity gets the best of me and I decide to stay and see how she handles the intrusion.

"Citizens of Elysium! I apologize for the inconvenience and untimeliness of my announcement. However, I know many of you are concerned with the incident that happened yesterday during the hours of Request. The 'Surface Dweller' seen in my chambers was nothing more than a Citizen, hand chosen by myself, to test the effectiveness of the new protocols put in place to prevent another such incident from happening. I'm pleased to announce that the new measures have worked perfectly and—"

Her image cuts out and is replaced by the opening image from the commercial. "Has the war got you down? Dive into the exquisite beauty of Elysium Towers . . ."

At that moment, the Slate on the nurse's desk beeps and flashes, lighting up the area around it.

That's it! I think, and rush to check it out. Sure enough, it's the Enforcer's orders, plain as day and not a thing missing, including who sent the order. Mother herself.

A huge grin spreads across my face. I can't wait to see Mother's reaction.

The entirety of the commercial plays out and then, without warning, the image cuts back to Mother, whose entire face is red as she yells at someone off screen.

"We're back," Father mutters and Mother jerks back around to face the screen.

A laugh fights its way through my barrier as she visibly struggles to pull herself together, before finally wrapping composure around herself like a cloak.

"I apologize for the technical error. I'm not sure what that was." She laughs as if it's just some funny glitch. She clears her throat. "As I was saying . . ."

I take advantage of the uproar I assume is happening and make my painstakingly slow journey back to the door where Nadia should be waiting. I knock the signal and wait for her to make sure it's me and I'm alone.

The door yawns open and I slide into the darkness to follow her back. Even though I know what we did is a good idea, that déjà vu feeling hits again and I can't help but feel like I've made a very big mistake.

Chapter Eight

The boy has returned. However, he has not brought my son or the girl. He also refuses to divulge their location. However, necessity does make the strangest bedfellows. I will have an answer on their location by the end of the week!

—LETTER FROM MAYOR ST. JAMES TO AN UNNAMED
INDIVIDUAL IN RUSHLAKE CITY

Gavin

It's late when I finally get to bed. I spend most of the rest of the night tossing and turning and missing Evie, but I wake as soon as the rooster crows. I have business in town and it's not going to wait.

I quickly check the traps I set last night and find two rabbits and a coypu. I clean them and put them where my mom will find them, then shower, dress, and search my weapons cache. I take my shotgun. I have no plans to use it, but I'm also not stupid enough to walk into a lion's den without backup.

I take my normal route from the house to the village. I'm

not all that surprised to see two guards standing at the pass-through from the lighthouse. They look half asleep as they lean against the ruins of the old stone wall, but when they see me they immediately jump to attention.

I don't recognize them, but from their clothing I can tell immediately they're from the city. Flippin' fantastic. I don't know exactly what Tristan did to the mayor, but I'm strangely proud. If the mayor brought in guards from Rushlake, he must be at least nervous.

They block the pathway when I walk up to them. "Sorry, sir. No one can pass from this side. Mayor's orders."

I nod like it's no big deal. "I understand that." I twist like I'm about to leave, but instead pull my shotgun over my shoulder and point it at them before they even move. "What I don't understand is how the *mayor* can decide that two of the people in *his* township—the very people he's supposed to protect and serve—should be denied the basics that they need to survive."

They swallow and stare at the gun, but don't say anything.

"So *I'm* going to clear up this little misunderstanding, and *you're* not going to stop me." I rack the slide of the shotgun, getting a little personal satisfaction from the sound and the whitening of their faces. "Are you?"

They both lift their hands in the air and step to the side. As I pass I see one of them reach for something and I spin around, the gun still at my shoulder. He's holding a walkie. I grin and aim my gun at his groin. "If you value that part of your anatomy and don't feel like bleeding out all over the sand here, I would highly suggest *not* letting anyone know I'm coming." I signal with my gun to have him toss it toward me.

The man's Adam's apple bobs. He tosses the walkie to the ground close to my feet. His partner's eyes are so wide I'm almost surprised they don't pop out of his head. I grab the walkie, shoving it into my pocket before taking their rifles and slinging the straps over my shoulder.

Can't be too careful.

But I'm not done yet. "If I find out that either of you tell anyone that I'm coming, I promise you'll be making a permanent blood donation to the sand. Understand?"

They both bob their heads.

"Have a great day."

I give them my sunniest smile. It feels oddly awesome to not be afraid for once. I sling the gun back over my shoulder, still racked, just in case, but I'm sure I won't have any further problems.

As I walk through town, I'm surprised at how quiet it is. Normally people are walking around, greeting each other, passing gossip from one person to another. But now there's no one. It almost reminds me of the way Elysium looked when we first returned. A ghost town.

It gives me the chills.

What is the mayor doing?

Time to find out.

When I walk into the mayor's office, I instantly stop in my tracks as my body rebels against being here. It's the ingrained fear and hate of him I've had over the years. But I force myself to keep walking straight to the secretary's desk. To Asher's mom. She isn't bad most of the time. A little quiet and obviously scared of her own husband, but she's always been nice to me. Even when I stopped being friends with Asher.

She's typing away at something I'm sure the mayor thinks is important, but glances up as I walk to her desk. The look of surprise on her face when she sees me is almost comical. As is the sound her computer makes, since she's pressing down on all the keys at once. She jerks her hands off the keyboard immediately.

"Gavin," she says, her voice almost a whisper. Then the shock gives way to hope—I can see it fill her eyes—and she peers around me. She frowns, then glances over her shoulder and gestures me closer.

"Asher?" Her voice is so quiet I practically have to read her lips to understand her.

At first I open my mouth to lie, but the look she's giving me reminds me so much of my mother's from last night, I can't do it. I lean closer. So close I smell the scent coming off her skin. It reminds me of Rushlake City, and all the women there that smell like flowers, without the flowers actually being there. Evie kind of smells like that. Except her scent came from actual flowers. Even when she was here, away from her gardens, it remained. Like the flowers had permanently soaked into her skin. I mentally shake myself when I remember Asher's mom is still waiting for me to reply. "He's not with me, but he's safe."

She lets out a breath and leans back in her chair. "Thank

you," she mouths and I have to give her credit when I see real tears in her eyes, even if she doesn't let them fall—or maybe it's *because* she doesn't. It surprises me that she doesn't ask where he is. Considering what her husband did to my mom to get that information, it seems weird.

I nod in recognition of the thanks and lean back so I'm standing normally in front of her desk, and wait for her to gather her emotions. Finally she says, louder than before, "Mr. Hunter! What a lovely surprise to see you again. We'd feared the worst. How can I be of assistance to you?"

I harden my tone. "I'm here to see the mayor. I'm sure he knows why."

She pushes up from the chair, but before she can go any farther than two steps from her desk, Mayor St. James himself opens his office door. As his wife did, he stares for a few seconds, before nodding. "Mr. Hunter. Rumor had it you died in the Outlands."

"Well, you know what they say about rumors, Mayor. They're carried by haters, spread by fools, and believed by idiots."

"Indeed." His eyes narrow. "Why don't you join me? We have much to discuss."

"Without question."

I follow him into his office and he takes the seat at his desk. "Shut the door. There's no need for more rumors to be spread. Is there?" He says it like a man accustomed to giving orders and having them instantly obeyed. I guess he'll just have to be disappointed.

"Fact is different from rumor, Mayor. I own my words and I don't care who hears them." Still, I shut the door, then drop the rifles and walkie on his desk—to show just how easy it was for me to get in here. And, hopefully, to show him I'm not afraid to do what needs to be done. I take the seat across from him before being offered it. I'm done taking orders from this man.

That doesn't mean being here doesn't make my skin crawl. I'm just not going to let him get away with what he's done. If there's one thing I learned from Evie, it's that this man is nothing more than flesh and blood. No more important than any one person and a lot less important than he thinks he is.

Evie stood up to him when she didn't even know who he was. Who *she* was. And she'd won. Because she had—has—something I lost somewhere in all this. Confidence. To stand up for the things she believes in, even if that means getting hurt, or worse, in the process.

The memories of everything the mayor's done to my family make me falter a little when I speak, but if Evie can do it, I can. I'll just have to channel her when I stumble. And I know I'm going to have to channel a lot of her to get what I want.

He leans forward over his desk. "I'm not going to beat around the bush, Mr. Hunter. We both know why you're here and we both know how it can be resolved. Let's get to the point, shall we?"

"Yes. Let's." I lean back in my seat, forcing my muscles to relax and be a direct contrast to the tension coming off him.

"I want my son back, Mr. Hunter. You want your family safe. I think we can both get our way, *if* you tell me what I want to know."

"Where Asher is?" I smile. "I don't know where he is. And if I did, I wouldn't tell a snake like you."

"Watch your tongue! You're here, sitting in front of me, only because I allow it. Keep that in mind."

I slowly stand and lean closer to him, lowering my voice. "I'm here because *I* choose to be here." I eye the weapons on his desk to punctuate my meaning. "And nothing you or your goons can do can keep me from being here. What *you* should keep in mind is that you're not laid out on the floor for what you did to my mom because I choose not to be like you."

He tilts his head and leans back in his chair. "I see your time in the Outlands has not done you any favors. And with age has not come wisdom. You're turning more and more into your father every day, aren't you?"

For a moment I see nothing but a red blur across my vision. I bang both of my fists against his desk, startling him into pushing his chair farther from me. "Do *not* speak of my father. You have no right to even *think* about him. I know what really happened to him and so do you. And yes, there is one thing my time in the Outlands has taught me." I slide my shotgun around and point it at him. "Survival is all about who has the best weapons. Where's yours, *Mayor?*"

He licks his lips. "Now, now. I understand you're angry, but there's no reason to resort to violence."

"Tell that to my mom."

"I admit I was hasty, and regret losing my temper in such a violent way. But you must understand how it feels to lose someone you love. I'm just looking for my son. That's all."

"So you beat an innocent woman and child?"

"It was wrong of me."

"And then take away their only means of survival?"

"It was a hasty decision made in the heat of the moment." He spreads his hands in front of him. "I'm sure you can understand that."

"No, actually. No, I can't."

"Mr. Hunter . . . Gavin. Please. Put your weapon away and let's talk. Gentleman to gentleman. I just want to know where my son is."

"If you're a gentleman, I'd rather not be one. Thanks." But I put my gun down and sit. "I told you. I don't know where he is."

He narrows his eyes. "I think you're lying."

"And I think you're an asshole."

"Name calling is so passé." Pink flares in his cheeks, but his words are smooth and without a hint of emotion. "Until and unless you tell me where they are, the restrictions remain."

"They?"

"H-him." His voice cracks before he clears his throat. "Asher. My son."

I blink as I realize something I should have known from the beginning. "You're not looking for Asher at all, are you? You want Evie." I shake my head. "You're such a bastard. You don't even care about your own son. He's just a means to an end like everyone else here."

For the first time in a long time, I feel bad for Asher. While I've had to deal without my dad, at least I had one once. Asher's had to deal with having one that doesn't give a shit about anyone but himself.

I lean forward. "What do you want with Evie? You've wanted to 'help' her since you met her. Why? And why are you willing to have your reputation damaged by beating a woman to get to her?"

"As much as it pains me to work with someone like you, here's my deal. You tell me where my son and that girl of yours is, and I'll release the restrictions on your family and give them full protection. I can even move them into Rushlake as citizens with full access and more money than they could ever dream of. They'll never run out of food. Never worry about whether their house will survive the next rain shower. Never worry about electricity or water. They'll be welcomed into Rushlake with open arms, and fortunes will be tossed at their feet. They will be like royalty." He pauses and it's obvious he's letting all that sink into my head. "If you don't tell me . . . well . . . there's no telling what will happen to them, is there?"

It's tempting. For a second. To never have to worry about my family. To never have to get up at dawn to hunt and spend the day shivering in a tree as I wait for something big enough to wander by, only to never see anything. For my brother to grow up never having to hunt, to regain some of the innocence he lost. For my mom to never have to sew until her fingers bleed to make just a little extra that month. But as tempting as it is, I can't. I won't be responsible for what would happen if I told him where Elysium is.

"I don't know where they are. And I can take care of my family just fine without your help."

"Then our business is concluded." He stands and walks to the door, opening it. "Good-bye, Mr. Hunter."

I laugh and start to walk out the door, but pause just as I reach him. "Actually, there *is* just one more thing I have to do before I leave." I punch him as hard as I can in the exact same location he hit my mom. He flies into the door, then falls to the ground, out cold. "*Now* our business is concluded."

CHAPTER NINE

Our little fish has found a hidey hole to wait us out. It seems we
need to draw her out. The only way to do that is with bait.

—MOTHER'S JOURNAL

Evie

The next morning, my birth mother Evangeline is the one
to wake me.

"What are you doing here?" I mumble into the blanket I'd
balled into a pillow. It took me forever to fall asleep last night
with all the adrenaline and worry pumping through my veins.
I feel like I didn't get any sleep at all.

"Father sent her," Nadia's clipped accent tells me from my
doorway. She lifts a Slate. "And this."

I push myself up and see Evangeline's smiling face and
Nadia's annoyed one blur together when my eyes cross from
exhaustion. I rub my eyes with the backs of my hands until
they're two separate people again.

Father may have sent her, but I have a feeling that since she's filled to bursting with news, there probably wouldn't have been any stopping her regardless.

I slide my legs off the cot and push out of it to walk toward the washbasin and splash the freezing water onto my face. The water does a decent job of waking me up, but what I'd really like is a giant cup of coffee.

I yelp when my hair is yanked back so hard it hurts. I twist around to glare at Evangeline. "What are you *doing*?"

"Just trying to get your hair under control." She smiles and holds up a hairbrush. "You can't lead the rebellion with messy hair!"

"Give me that!" I wrench the brush from her hands. "I'm quite capable of brushing my own hair. And I'm not *leading* a rebellion, I'm *failing* at even starting one."

Evangeline backs away. The smile that had seemed a part of her face when she came in falls from her lips, and she nods. "I'll just wait until you're done getting dressed."

She leaves the room with Nadia sticking to her like glue. I can't say I blame her. I suppose for someone who's lived for so long in constant fear of Mother finding them, Evangeline is a threat. It's a bit worrisome for me, too. Evangeline isn't exactly the stealthiest person I've known in my life. Wouldn't surprise me in the least if Enforcers followed right behind her and she didn't even know it.

When Evangeline does finally tell me her news, there isn't much to tell. It seems the commercial itself created more of a stir than the announcement that flashed across everyone's screens, but people are talking about that, too. Especially since the doctor in question has gone missing. Well, missing for them. Of course, I know exactly where he is.

So far there's no word from the Palace Wing about any of it. I can't help but wonder why. Is it just another ploy? Mother's way of saying, "Nice try, but I'm so not worried about what you're doing that I'm not even going to acknowledge that it happened"?

That would make sense. If I were her I'd just ignore it and wait for everything to die down before doing anything else. Maybe, if I'm thinking like Mother, I might kill the Enforcer who dropped her orders.

No, my mind argues with me. There aren't many Enforcers left. And hardly anyone is qualifying these days to become one. That being the case, I would ignore it and punish the Enforcer for her blunder, but then move on as quickly as possible.

But then that leads to an interesting question for me. Did she see the orders flash onto the Slates? If not, her people had to have. They *had* to have told her. Of course, there's no way to tell without Mother making a move, which she probably won't. Unless she thinks it'll garner her the best benefit. If that's the case, then a swift strike to the people who breached her system and the person who's responsible for the integrity of the computer mainframe would be ideal. Which might be another reason Father told Evangeline how to get here.

Ugh! I press the heels of my hands against my eyes. Thinking like Mother is exhausting! I just want to know what my next move should be. Clearly I need something bigger and better than just the Enforcer orders. It's caused a stir, but I need to cast real doubt. I need to prove that Mother is behind everything that's wrong in this city. Since Dr. Friar is her closest and most trusted friend, it seems most logical to sift through his files as the doctor recommended.

Evangeline seems to want to say something else when I tell her what I'm doing and that I wish to do it alone, but she just nods and slinks away like a chastised dog. Guilt pinches me, but I don't know what to do about it. She may be my birth mom, but I don't feel any kind of connection between us. If I really try to feel something, the only thing I muster is anger. Anger that she gave me up to Mother so easily. That she let Mother do what she did. That the reason I don't feel anything for her is basically her fault altogether and forcing herself on me so we can try to recapture something we lost when *she* gave me up is only making it worse.

I shove the guilt and anger away when I slip into Asher's dugout. He's still asleep, but I'm in just a sour enough mood that I don't care. I plop onto his cot and he grunts.

"Hey! I'm sleeping here." He opens suspiciously clear eyes and grins.

I shove his shoulder. "No, you're not. How long have you been awake?"

He shrugs, then yawns and stretches his body across the cot.

I narrow my eyes at his shirtless chest. A little because he looks like he's gained some muscle mass since the shooting, but mostly because he's completely healed. There's not even a bruise or a scar. "Looking good."

He grins. "Of course I do. Was there ever any doubt?"

I shove him again. "Come on. I need your help going through Dr. Friar's cubes."

He stands and pulls a shirt over his head. "How are we supposed to do that? There's no computers young enough."

"Father sent Evangeline with two data screens. They're off grid."

"Off grid?"

"Not connected to the mainframe, so the hope is Mother can't trace us through them."

"I sense you're not convinced."

"Mother's smart. She knows we're here. She has to. And if she doesn't, she will. It's just a matter of time. I don't plan on taking what she knows or doesn't know for granted."

He takes the second data screen from me. "Then it's time to work."

For the next few hours we focus on pulling information off the data cubes. It's long, tedious work. And while I learn a few things that prove Dr. Friar's responsible for the new additions to the nanos, there's not much I can use.

It's Asher, sipping from a cup of electrolyte water, who finally finds what we need at hour six of reading the files.

A complete list of every person Dr. Friar has ever experimented on, broken down by experiment—or experiments— and dates. Including date of arrival, date of testing, and date of disposal.

And I'd bet money that's also a fairly comprehensive list of people who've gone "missing." Of course, it's not labeled that way, it just says "test subjects." Since these tests more than likely included some form of torture—how else do you test a device that causes a person's nanos to eat them?—I can't imagine anyone willingly submitting themselves to them, but who knows.

This might be just the thing we need to get people to start questioning, if not Mother, then at least Dr. Friar.

Or maybe nothing will come of it.

I drag my hands through my hair and tug on the ends. I *hate* being this indecisive.

"Are you all right?" Asher glances up from his data screen.

"I'm fine. I just don't know what to do." I get up to pace his little dugout. "I want to share the list."

He lays his screen down. "Some of these people's families probably still don't know what happened to them. Remember what it was like not knowing if Gavin was alive or dead? I'd imagine it's the same for these families. At least telling them their family members are gone can give them a type of closure."

"I agree with that. I'd be helping them. But how do I do it?"

"Like you did before."

"I can't just pop a list of people onto their screens with the note, 'Do you know anyone on this list? If so, they're dead. Have a nice life.'"

Asher lets out a strangled laugh. "Well, no, I wouldn't be *that* blunt, but there's no reason why it can't say, 'Is anyone you know on this list?' The list itself will do the rest."

"Don't you think it's a little harsh?"

He shrugs. "Maybe, but do we have any other choice?"

"Do you mind going through the rest of that? I'm going to find Nadia so we can get ahold of Father."

He waves me away. "Take your time."

Finding Nadia proves easy. The area is small and most of the people here ignore my presence. They're not rude about it. Just . . . unsure of where I stand, I guess. And I can't really blame them. If the situation had been reversed . . . Say I'd been the one living in a cave my entire life, always worried that today's the day I die. Then here comes a girl who's never had that worry. Who is the epitome, and essentially the off-spring, of everything I feared. I'd be more than wary. I'd be downright terrified.

But I have the run of the place, more or less. So I find Nadia as she's walking away from Dr. Moreau's dugout and tell her what I want to do.

She scans the list. "It is a sad day for these people. But I agree it's the right thing to do. They must know what happened to their loved ones and the woman responsible for stealing their lives." She takes the cube from me. "I will make sure Father gets this."

She continues on her way as if I hadn't stopped her at all. I turn back around to help Asher sort through more of the files, but stop short of taking my first step when I almost barrel into Evangeline. She's standing with a family. A husband and wife and their daughter.

They're obviously from Elysium and not the Caverns because there's not a smudge of dirt on them, not to mention they're a bit more . . . fleshed out than the people living here. Probably because they get more to eat than the mush that's all the Caverns have to offer. The parents are both tall and Mother's requisite blond with blue eyes. Their daughter is a perfect mix of both of them.

Evangeline gives me another of her hopeful smiles. "Evelyn, this is Kara and Tate." I nod my head at the couple, not exactly sure what's going on, but willing to wait and find out. They are the first new people besides Nadia who've given me even the time of day. "They . . . they've been a part of the Underground for a while and couldn't wait to meet you." Kara and Tate exchange a look, and a buzz of nervous energy tingles up my nerve endings. They shouldn't be here, I think. It's too dangerous to be bringing people here. I'm just about to chastise Evangeline for bringing them, but then the little girl, who's more like a little two-foot bundle of energy, captures my legs in her arms.

"Are you Miss Evelyn?" She stares up at me with big blue eyes.

I kneel down so I'm eye level with her. "Yes, but you can call me Evie. What's your name?"

"I'm Myra!" She grins at me, showing two missing teeth. "Did you really go to the Surface?"

Her pleasure over it reminds me of myself and I grin back. "I did."

"Was it pretty? Mom says it's pretty."

I smile at her and her mother. "Yes. It's the most gorgeous place I've ever seen. Especially at night."

Evangeline, smiling, folds her hands, delight surging from her. "Come. Let's find a more comfortable place to talk."

She starts to take us in the direction of the dugouts, but something makes me stop them. "I think I know just the place. Follow me." I lead them to the artifact room.

The nervousness I'd felt earlier continues to stream through me, but I'm excited to talk to them. Find out why they joined. It had to take a lot for them to both join. I can't imagine what Mother would do to their little one, should she find out they're helping. That thought instantly makes me want to tell them to go back to their apartment on the other side and forget this place ever existed. But I don't think that they would listen.

When I show them the room, they stop and stare, then slowly walk around the room, taking everything in. Myra finds some dirty, dingy stuffed animal in the mess on the table and carefully takes it in her hands to show it to me. "Is this from the Surface?"

I nod. "I believe so. Yes." She grins, then declares it's hers. She looks so smitten with it and hugs it so tightly, I don't have the heart to tell her to leave it. In fact, I start going through the piles on the floor looking for more toys for her to take or at least play with while she's here.

A few minutes into the hunt, Kara kneels down next to me. "Still into the Surface treasures, aren't you?"

I frown at her as my heart falls into my stomach. There's only one person besides Mother who knew that, and he's dead.

She smiles knowingly at me. "Timothy was my brother." It's said so quietly I'm almost sure I'm mistaken.

"What?" I whisper.

"I'm Timothy's sister."

I stand so fast the blood rushes from my head and I sway as a wave of dizziness washes over me. I grab the nearest seat and sit in it before I fall over and pass out. Kara takes the neighboring chair.

"You remember him then."

I nod, because I don't know what else to do. Of course I remember him. I was just thinking about him.

She smiles at Tate as if this is just what she wanted to hear. "My parents were both part of the Underground. They were friends with your mom. My mom and yours were extremely close and I think she was the only one who knew who your real father was. But she's also extremely loyal, so she kept to herself until your mother came to her for help when Father decided to restart the Underground. We've been a part of it since then."

"And Timothy?"

She exchanges a look with Tate, her lip trembling slightly. "He was, too." She smiles at me and places her hand on my leg. "He was so thrilled when Father told him that they needed him to become your Suitor and convince you to Couple with him. He couldn't wait to start."

Ice water flows through my veins as my memories of him take on new meanings. I'm numb, but my heart pinches at the same time. "He was *chosen* to be my Suitor?"

Something in my voice obviously hints at my distress, because Tate touches my shoulder, but I can't even look at him. I turn toward the table and grab the coin I'd been playing with yesterday. Timothy was a lie, too? Everything that happened to us? My heart cracks a little more, allowing more of my icy blood to numb my body.

"It was just a mission for him when he started," Tate says. "He went into it fully expecting for this to be just like any of the others he'd been asked to do, but that changed the first day he saw you." He pauses, but I can't stop staring at the coin. "A few months after that he told me he was compromised."

I look up at him through tear-filled eyes. "What does that mean?"

He gives me a sad smile. "He loved you, Evie. He was compromised. He was no longer an impartial member of the Underground."

I take the coin and hold it tightly. "I loved him, too," I say quietly, trying to wrap my brain around this newest info. "Mother stole the emotions I felt for him, but I still have the memories." I glance at the coin. "It's like those memories are from someone else. Like I'm reading them from a book, but I loved him. I know that. And I know I'm the one who killed him."

Kara glances at Evangeline and something passes through her eyes. Tate grabs my shoulder, his fingers pinching into my skin. "Mother made you do it?"

Tears spill down my cheeks as a crack finally opens the fuzzy door between me and those memories. "She made me watch. Made sure I knew it was my fault he was killed. That if I'd just chosen the Guard over Timothy, that he'd still be alive. I tried to stop her, but she gave the order and the Enforcer didn't even hesitate. He died in my arms and then Mother took even my memories of him away."

Kara lets out a breath and says my name. I glance up at her. Her eyes are red and sparkle with tears. "He knew it was a risk. He knew it was even more of one when he fell for you. But he knew you loved him." She reaches a hand out to me and squeezes mine. "He'd be so happy that you remember him now and that you're going to help take Mother down." Then she smiles at me. "And he'd be happy you found your Surface Dweller."

I don't know whether or not to feel guilty. I should. But when I fell in love with Gavin, I didn't remember Timothy. According to what Mother reprogrammed my brain to think, Timothy had never existed.

Myra pulls on the hem of my dress and I realize she must have heard everything. She lifts her arms to me in the universal sign of "pick me up," so I do and she hugs me so tightly I'm surprised at the strength in her arms. "Are you my aunt?" she asks.

Tate and Kara immediately try to shush her, but for some reason, her simple question makes me feel better and I smile at her and return the hug. "Of course. Nothing would make me happier."

For the next few hours, I talk with Kara and Tate. They fill in gaps I had of Timothy and tell me stories of him when he was young. And I, even though it's embarrassing, tell them of the times we were together. Of how we'd spend hours just talking. Or sometimes of how we'd just sit, doing nothing and enjoying the time we had together. It seems to give Kara peace. At least a little bit.

She tells me of her parents and Tate embarrasses her with his own childhood memories of them. And when Kara asks about Gavin, I tell them everything. Of the Surface and how at points it's scary, but most of the time it's peaceful and amazing and beautiful. And when I talk about Gavin, Kara gives Tate a knowing smile. It should embarrass me I'm so transparent, but it doesn't. It just makes me happy.

And Myra. She's simply an amazing ball of energy that you can't help but fall in love with. Which makes me think I should make them stay in the Caverns. To not only protect them—the only connection I have to Timothy—but for Myra's sake. If they're found out, Mother will not only kill them, she'll make an example of them, like she did of Timothy.

But when I suggest it to them as they get ready to leave, they refuse and assure me that staying where they are is the best thing. They'll be able to give me eyes and ears where I don't have them. Help grow the Underground from that side now that it's sure to grow.

As a more than unhappy Nadia escorts them to the tunnels, I'm, again, hit with that déjà vu, sick-to-my-stomach feeling. But I watch them go, because I know nothing I say will change their minds.

That night, I'm preparing more files for Father to send out the next day, when Father and Nadia find me. They've gotten word there will be another assassination.

"It's a nurse this time," Father says. "She works almost exclusively with Dr. Friar, so she's probably no innocent either, but we can't let her die."

"Why are they going after her?" Asher asks.

I hold up the data screen with our list on it. "Because of this." I let out a long breath. "They're going to kill her because she's probably the only one besides Dr. Friar with access to these records."

Father merely nods and tells me everything he knows about the planned assassination, one he says he helped plan in order to give me more of an advantage when I get there to save her. I can't say I'm pleased he's helping plan these, but I don't see where he has a choice either. If he refuses, Mother will know something's up. At least this way, I have some idea what I'm walking into. I'm not looking forward to another confrontation with an Enforcer, but I can't let this woman die for something I did. Besides, she could have more information the doctor didn't have. Or at least information that can be used to corroborate what we found on Dr. Friar's data cubes. We could use her.

But when I get there, even though I'm early, it's quickly obvious I'm already too late. I hear the screaming the instant I push open the door from the waiting room. I race down the hallway, following the screams to an open door. There I see the nurse on the floor, blood everywhere and the Enforcer waiting to clean up the mess.

It's not the same one as before, but she doesn't even bother to fight with me. She bolts the minute she sees me, bumping and knocking me to the ground in her hurry to get away.

The wheels spin in my head. Why would she do that? Enforcers don't run. They're supposed to stay and fight, no matter what their chances of survival are, but this makes two who ran from me. Someone they could easily take down. It doesn't make sense!

I don't have time to think about it as I pull out the device used on Dr. Moreau. The plans in Dr. Friar's notes say that the device can start and stop the disruptions in the nanos, but not if one particular device works for everyone, so I don't know if this one will work on the nurse, but I have to try. I hit the button and almost immediately the woman stops the bloodcurdling screams and folds in on herself, sobbing.

So I bend to help her up, only to stop short when I realize just how late I am. Both of the woman's arms are gone and half of her left leg. There are missing chunks all over her body, including one that allows me a glance into her stomach. She's bleeding out so fast from everything, I don't think there's anything I can do to stop it.

Chapter Ten

Mr. Hunter is much like his father in that he believes he is above the law of common men. A reminder that he is in fact below common man might serve him well.

—Mayor St. James's journal

Gavin

I walk out of the mayor's office, confident I made my point. Of course, there'll be a consequence to my actions. I either made this worse or I fixed it. Either way, it feels great having done *something*.

Mrs. St. James stops me as I'm leaving, and for a minute I stand frozen in front of her. I did just knock her husband out.

"I'm sorry—"

"Shh!" she hisses, glancing at her husband, who still appears to be out cold on the floor. She grabs my hand and yanks me to the far side of the office. She glances back at the office door again, but only the top part of the opening is visible.

"I'm so sorry for your mother," she whispers. "She's a good woman and doesn't deserve what my husband is doing to her or your family." She glances back at the door. "But right now, you're making a big mistake."

Of course I am. Maybe I was wrong about her. Maybe she *is* just like *them,* even if she grew up here. I give her a look filled every bit with the disgust and anger I feel.

"I know what you're thinking, but hear me out. I've been married to my husband for over twenty years. I know him much better than you do. And I will tell you that he is much worse than you can even fathom. He always gets his way. At whatever the cost. I do mean whatever the cost."

"I've dealt with people like that before. He doesn't concern me," I say, thinking of Mother.

She frowns. "I don't doubt that, but you must listen to me. He never says anything he doesn't mean, so he very much meant that your family will suffer if you don't do as he asks."

"I don't know where—" I start, but she holds her hand up and I stop.

"We both know that's not true, but it doesn't matter, because I agree you shouldn't tell him where they are."

I blink and stare at her. That is totally not what I expected from her. "You . . . don't want to know?"

She gives me a look filled with longing and hurt, but something else, too. Something I saw on Evie's face just before I left. Determination. To do the right thing, no matter what the personal cost is. "Of course I do, he's my son and I love him. But if my husband even thinks I have an idea where Asher is, I'll have no choice but to tell him."

"Why?" But I already know the answer. I've seen the look

in her eyes when I was a kid—it's the same look I saw in Johnson's dog's after Johnson had gotten done beating it. I was only six, but even then I knew what it meant.

She looks away from me and her voice is so quiet I have to strain to hear it. "Do you really think that he'd be any different with me just because I'm his wife?"

"Why do you stay?" I can't stop myself from asking, but I know the answer to that one, too. It's the same reason the dog stayed with the Johnsons and the same reason Evie stayed with Mother: because they didn't know there were other options or were too scared to leave.

She finally looks at me, her eyes brimming with tears, but they don't spill over. Somehow that makes it even worse. "You have your secrets and I have mine. Let's just leave it at that."

I nod, not sure what else to do or say.

"But never mind all that. You're going to need to tell him something and you're going to have to make it sound believable."

I narrow my eyes. "What?"

"That's something you're going to have to come up with on your own, but I suggest something that puts Asher and Evie together. Like they've run away together or something."

"And me?"

"Well, you'd be hurt, right? You'd need time to accept that the girl you loved left you for your best friend. Don't you think?"

"He's not my best friend," I mumble out of habit, but I'm not sure I mean it anymore. I did trust him enough to protect Evie in Elysium while I'm gone. "You really think that'll work?"

"I know my husband, Gavin, but I'm not an oracle. Just think about it. And steer clear of him until you're willing to give him an answer. He's not going to be happy with what you did." She looks back at the door to his office. This time there's a slight groan, and panic crosses over her face. "Go! Now! I'll take care of this mess, but if you wish to help your family you need to go." She practically pulls me to the front door and out of it. "Take some time to think about it. But not too much. He tends to get grouchy when he doesn't get his way." The groaning grows louder and she slams the door in my face.

I do as she asks, but not without a bit of guilt. I wince at the sound of the mayor's angry shouts. I don't want to cause her any more problems and I have a lot to think about.

I leave the village. It's obviously not safe there. Nowhere to hide, even if the villagers were to help me. I don't want them involved in my mess.

I pass the guards and they back completely away from me. I don't even bother looking at them. I'm too busy trying to decide whether I should trust Asher's mom or not.

For hours I walk around the other side of the cove, where I did most of my hunting while Evie was here. There are lots of trees, so small game mostly, but it kept me close to her. There are plenty of spaces to hide, should the mayor decide he wants to come after me.

I still don't know what to do when night finally falls and I realize I haven't eaten anything all day. My mom is probably worried about me. So I make my way through the woods and to the edge of the cove, only to stop short.

There's an orange, flickering light emanating in the distance. A long column of smoke drifts into the sky from where my house is located.

"Shit!" Something's on fire. I just have to hope it's not the house. I'm able to delude myself into thinking maybe Tristan accidentally spilled some of the tallow oil when he was refilling the lighthouse and somehow lit the spill on fire while igniting the wick.

He's too small. Too young for all the duties that I've tossed at him. I want to scream and rage at the winds of fate for making me put him in the same position I was in at his age. Guilt eats away at my insides, though, that I didn't at least prepare him. For God's sake, I never even let him take care of the lighthouse. There's no one to blame for this mess but me, and I have to teach him to take over for me. I *will* be going back for Evie, and he'll have to take my place here.

I race across the sand, slipping in it, scraping my palms and face on it. People think sand is soft, but when you fall it can burn just like a cheap rug.

I reach where the fire is and stop short as I gasp and suck in air. But I'm already too late. The fire's obviously been burning for some time. The pump house is almost completely decimated.

Conflicting emotions clash in me. Relief it's not the house

and pain for having lost the pump house, the one Dad and I built together. But it's just the pump house. Not the house. Not my family.

They're standing, watching it burn. I go to my mom and brother. Mom's crying a bit, and poor Tristan is standing there with a bucket of seawater, looking lost and slightly afraid. I don't even think they've noticed I'm here. I try to take it from him, but he turns to me, terror flying over his features before he yells, "No! Don't!"

"What . . ." I trail off when I see the two guards from the gate and Mayor St. James come from around the side of the house.

"Pretty sight, that, wasn't it? Fire always is. It purifies. Cleans unworthy things." He smiles at me. The light from the fire dances off his face, making him appear more evil than even Mother. "This is your last warning, Gavin. Tell me where they are or your house will be next."

I clench my hands into fists, and start to move in his direction, but Mom stops me by hugging me and pulling me back. "Don't, Gavin. Just leave him be."

"Want a go at me again, boy?" He touches a hand to his cheek where I hit him. "I wouldn't suggest it." The guards move forward to the well, and start destroying it and its components with sledgehammers.

I rush forward to stop them, but a man pops up behind me, grabbing my arms. He yanks them behind my back so hard the muscles in my shoulders would scream in pain if they could. Another guard slams his fist into my jaw, and I have just a moment to think how lucky I was I didn't bite off my tongue before he punches me in the stomach. Stars fly into my vision and I try to double over, but I can't because the other guy is holding me up. The second man hits me again in the same spot and this time when the stars burst into my eyes, the first guy lets me go and I fall onto the ground in a ball of agony.

Mom rushes to help me, but I spit out the blood that's accumulated in my mouth and push myself up to a standing position, even if I do stagger a bit. I won't give that bastard the satisfaction of seeing me down.

I glance over at the men smashing bits of the well off. I've fixed the damn thing enough over the years to know that even though the pump itself probably works, and water isn't spraying everywhere, the whole damned thing is toast. Anger fades to anguish as I realize what this means for my family. It's completely decimated, and we have no access to the parts we need.

The mayor grins at me in the still glowing embers from the pump house's remaining wood. "It's going to be tough living out here without fresh water, don't you think?" He wanders away, murmuring,

". . . *Day after day, day after day,*
We stuck, nor breath nor motion;
As idle as a painted ship
Upon a painted ocean.
Water, water, everywhere,
And all the boards did shrink;
Water, water, everywhere, Nor any drop to drink . . ."

I wait until the sound of his footsteps die off and then kick at the sand. "God damn it!" I yell and spin around and kick the sand again. I pace, and even though my face, stomach, and head are pounding, I still pull at my hair.

Mom puts her hand on my arm. "It's all right, Gavin. We'll find a way to make this work. We always do." I spin around on her, ripping my arm from her hand, choking on the hot ball of rage, pain, and anguish in my throat. She doesn't even wince, just lets her hand drop as I swallow several times, trying to get my breathing and emotions under control again.

We *do* always make it work. The pump has broken several times over the years and every time, Dad or I fixed it. But that was when we could go to the blacksmith for parts. Now we can't even do that. It seems I wasn't proactive enough. I ended up having to react. Again. Exactly what Mayor St. James wanted.

Dealing with him is like playing poker—a game my dad taught me to keep me busy on long hunting trips. No matter what hand you're dealt, there's always a way to win. Even if it's bad, you can still walk away with everything if you can bluff right. And if there's one thing I know about, it's how to keep a poker face.

In any deal, if you play your cards right, there's always a way to win. Even if you have to cheat a little to get it.

CHAPTER ELEVEN

Today is to be a holiday in the memory of my daughter and her heroic sacrifice. Halt your duties, dress in your finest clothes, and join me in the Square to celebrate our safety, peace, and freedom! Long live Elysium!

—MOTHER'S SPEECH ANNOUNCING THE INAUGURAL DAUGHTER OF THE PEOPLE DAY

The nurse never stood a chance. She was lost before I even tried to save her, but I had to try. I grabbed gauze and dressing and tourniquets from the closet cabinets. Wrapped and covered and tied everything that even appeared to be injured. But still the pool of blood just keeps growing. My legs are coated in its sticky heat. My hands are stained red to my wrists as if I'm simply wearing gloves. I watch helplessly as my fight—and my pleas—to keep her alive go unheeded. The light in her eyes fades as her life flows out of her into the puddle I kneel in.

Suddenly, a door at the end of the hall clicks open and footsteps quieter than anyone's should be make their way to me.

I scramble to my feet, slipping in the ichor on the floor, but managing to keep my balance to dart to the doorway and peer into the hallway. My heart slams into my rib cage when I see it's the first Enforcer.

What is *she* doing here? Did Mother send her after the first returned? Is it even possible the first made it back there already?

But none of that matters, because I'm trapped and dripping the nurse's blood and I can't get the smell of it out of my nose. A glance around the room tells me there really is no place to hide, but if I don't I will end up like the nurse.

The door! My mind screams at me as the footfalls draw closer. It's a horrible place to hide, but it's the only choice I have. So I dive behind the door and press myself as close as I can to the wall.

The Enforcer steps into the room and stops in her tracks. Confusion is as plain as day on her face. I can see it in the crack left by the hinges. If she turns her head just a fraction of a centimeter, she'll see me, too. I force my racing breaths to slow so she can't hear them, but my heart hammers so loud, I'm fairly certain my breathing is the least of my problems.

She mumbles something under her breath, but between my heart and my breathing, I can't make it out. She strides forward now, almost leaping across the distance between her and the nurse. She crouches, the hem of her dress swirling in the gore. Her hands travel the body starting at the neck, apparently looking for a pulse. When she finds none, her fingers trail over my bandages and everything else I used to try and stop the nurse from dying.

She stops then and tilts her head, before she turns it slowly, her eyes narrowing at the drips on the carpet leading to my hiding spot. She remains hunkered down next to the nurse, but stares at the spot where I'm hiding so long I have to wonder if she sees me. But she turns back around to study the body.

"Should've came earlier," she says, startling me to the point I almost gasp. But then she laughs. The half-crazed laugh gives me goose bumps down my back and I squeeze myself closer to the wall. "Mother always knows what goes on behind every door. In every passageway. She's always at least a step ahead." She stands then and I wonder again if she knows I'm here. If she's talking to me. But she continues staring at the nurse. "You shouldn't have sent that transmission."

When she turns, there isn't even a hesitation as she saunters straight out the door past me and down the hall. The door at the end swings open and then shuts with a whoosh a few seconds later.

I don't move—I barely breathe—as I stand trembling by the wall.

That's when what the Enforcer says clicks in my brain. Mother knows. She knows we're hiding in the Caverns. That's what the Enforcer meant. She thought the nurse was working with those in the Caverns. Mother caught the message between us and Father.

The revelation finally makes my frozen legs move as I barrel around the corner and back the way I came until I reach the door to the other tunnels. I didn't even worry about the cams this time. Mother already knows. It may already be too late.

I knock the signal and when nothing happens, my heart feels like it's going to take off out of my chest. I knock again. Louder. I'm about to knock a third time, when I hear the tell-tale clank of the lock opening. I don't even wait for the door to open all the way before I push it open, and slam it shut.

"Where is the nurse?" Nadia asks.

I grab her by her shoulders. "Has she come?"

"Who?" Nadia asks.

"Mother! Has she come?"

"No. I told you, she doesn't know we're here."

I let her go and jog down the tunnel. "We have to find another place to hide. Now. Mother knows. She knows everything."

Nadia stumbles next to me as she obviously struggles to keep up. "Are you sure? How do you know?"

"The Enforcer said it to the nurse. Said that Mother knows what's behind every door and in every passageway. Then she said the nurse shouldn't have sent the transmission. She must have intercepted the message we sent to Father." I burst into the Caverns and stop to get my bearings.

"Miss Evelyn, what you're saying isn't possible."

"Anything is possible," I mumble, moving directly toward where I hope Asher is.

"But there wasn't a message to intercept. Nothing to trace back to us."

I finally stop and frown down at her. "Of course there was. That's how Father got the message on everyone's Links."

"That's precisely why we don't use the electronics to send messages," she says.

"Then how do you send each other information?"

"We leave a paper with a coded message in a predetermined location," Father says from behind me.

I spin around to see him with his brows knit together as he takes in my appearance.

"What's going on?" Asher says from beside him.

Confused, my body still filled with so much adrenaline it doesn't know what to do, I pace in a circle around them and tell them everything.

"There were *two* Enforcers?" Father asks when I finish.

"Yes. One was already there and the second came after the nurse was dead."

"This is troubling information, but not for you. It's possible Mother doesn't trust me as much as I'd thought."

"Or she didn't trust the second Enforcer to get it right. She'd already screwed up with Dr. Moreau. She didn't want any more mistakes."

Father gives Asher a look before rubbing his hands over his face. "For my sake, I hope you're right. Either way, Mother is preparing for some assembly. Mandatory attendance by all Citizens."

"Are you crazy? You just said you thought she didn't trust you. This could be a setup!" Asher says.

"But if he doesn't go, he's proving it. He doesn't have a choice." My stomach twists as I watch him.

"Then he stays here."

"She'll look for me." His voice is so defeated already it makes my heart ache.

"You said she couldn't find this place." Asher's face is all squished up as he tries to figure everything out.

"I *won't* take that chance." He focuses on me. "There are too many things here that I'm not willing to risk."

I swallow the sudden lump in my throat. "Go. You should be there."

"Evie—"

Asher stops talking when I stare at him. "Mother always has a backup plan. It's as simple as that." I meet Father's eyes. "Just . . . watch your back."

He gives me a grim smile. "Distrust is what keeps you alive." He walks away looking as miserable as I feel.

Nadia pats my arm. "He will be fine. He's made it this long." She marches away in her normal fashion, but even she's missing something in her step.

I turn my attention to Asher. "I need a way to watch the festivities."

"You've got to be kidding." Asher groans. "You can't go back there *now*! Even with everyone milling around, you'll be spotted in seconds."

"I'm not planning on actually *being* there. I'm not a fool. I just need to see what's happening."

"And how do you plan on doing that?"

"I'm not sure," I say, but then what the Enforcer said to me, about Mother always knowing, gives me an idea. "The same way Mother knows what's going on everywhere. Her cameras."

He knits his brow together. "Gavin said something about them being activated by DNA."

"The cameras are always watching. Always. They only trigger a signal when something out of the ordinary trips them off. Such as the wrong DNA. But the cameras are always watching, and Mother will definitely have them on and trained on the Square."

"So we just need to use the cameras to watch? How do we do that?"

"There is a central monitoring area. In the Palace Wing. All the cameras are hardwired to it through the maintenance tunnels. I'm going to cut into the feed and watch what's going on in the Square from the tunnels."

". . . twenty-five . . . twenty-six . . . twenty-seven . . ." I almost laugh when I find S2-A8-J28. "This is it."

Asher doesn't even ask if I'm sure, he just nods and hands me the tools I stole from a maintenance worker's bag left unattended. Sloppy of him, but good news for me. It has everything I need. Including the mini holo-projector they use to test the feeds to make sure they're working right.

"Let's get to it then."

I pull out the Slate I also stole and pull up the circuitry map, then I open the juncture box. It's frustrating work, and while I vaguely remember how to read a wiring diagram, it isn't enough. Even with Asher's help, we're taking entirely too long. Sweat trickles from my forehead and down over my face into my eyes, blinding me.

"This is insane." Asher blinks at the Slate. "We have as much chance of figuring this mess out as we do the meaning of life."

A message beeps through onto the Slate. I press the ignore button, but it immediately rings again, and without me even touching anything, the Slate automatically answers for me. A scowling face pops onto the screen. He looks familiar. I know I've seen him before, but the memory that goes along with him is just out of reach.

But he smiles when he sees me. "Miss Evelyn. It's a pleasure to see you again."

With a frown, I glance over to Asher, then back to the Slate. "How—?"

"How do I know you?" he asks, then answers without waiting for my question. "I'm Joseph. I'm the one who's been helping you send your messages to everyone's Slates and slipped that amusing video into Mother's speech." He smiles at me, but it has this sadness to it that makes my heart hurt. "You don't remember me, because of what Mother did to you, but I was one of your Suitors. Along with Timothy. Father tells me you remember him, which makes sense, since it was obvious to all the rest of us that he was going to be the one you chose."

"I-I'm sorry." I wish I could remember him, but all I can come up with is a fleeting sense of familiarity.

He waves it off. "Don't be. I've been paired with a wonderful girl."

I nod. "That's good. I'm very happy for you. Thank you for helping me."

"You were always kind to me, Miss Evelyn. It's my pleasure to return the favor." He grins. "Having trouble hooking into the cameras?"

It makes me nervous that he knows exactly what I'm doing, but I guess that's his job. "Right the first time."

He laughs. "It's simple really. I'll walk you through." He glances at something over his shoulder and a shadow of panic crosses his face before he blurts out, "Just match the colors. Gotta go."

"Thank you!" I try to say, but the connection cuts off before I've finished the first word.

I close my eyes and take several calming breaths. It's easier than I'm making it. The answer is right there in front of me. Just match the colors.

I know this. I know this.

When I open my eyes, I'm surprised to see the diagram looks completely different to me. It's the same, of course, but I understand it. I can read it like I would any book or my Slate. And I know exactly how to do what we've been trying to do for almost an hour. I dig into the box without so much as a second thought.

Asher sits beside me, handing me the tools I request, and I only have to show him how to read the map once before he's digging in right next to me, speeding up the process.

Finally, I'm connecting the final wires and hoping I actually did understand what I was doing and wasn't just making things up.

When everything is in place I turn on the mini holo. Immediately a picture of a section of the Square lights up. I almost shout in happiness at our success.

"One down. Three to go," Asher says, interrupting my thoughts. We dig back in, setting the rest up in a matter of minutes.

Finally I have four views of the Square. After a few minute tweaks, we have a perfect view I can shift by moving my finger around the mini holo of the view I want. I can also "pinch" the "screen" to zoom out and drag my fingers apart to zoom in. There are a few icons on the side that I don't recognize the symbols for, but for the most part it's really an intuitive design.

For a little while we watch the Citizens chat, but then something starts happening. They all start lining up and facing in one direction.

"There's something happening on the stage," Asher says, pointing to one of the hologram displays. "Can you get a closer view?"

I touch the display of that camera, making it the main view, then zoom in. People are walking across the stage adjusting lights, pulling wires, aligning the podiums and a bunch of other things. It's obvious it's going to be used. After several minutes, Mother walks onto the stage. I freeze when I see her.

But I shake it off and zoom in closer, leaning in as if that's going to help me hear her. I can see her lips moving, but not hear her.

"Are the cameras equipped for sound?" Asher asks.

Memories run through my head of watching people through these cameras, listening through headphones to conversations I had no business listening to.

I nod and press the speaker button. Within just a few seconds the sounds from the camera blare loudly—very loudly—and clearly. Asher and I wince in unison. After a few more adjustments I get the volume to a more manageable level. One that will allow us to hear Mother's speech and to listen for anyone coming at the same time. I drop my hands from my ears, even though they still ring from the loudness of the echoes.

Asher shakes his head as if that will help the ringing, but I just try to listen past it to whatever Mother is saying.

". . . I know these past few months have been difficult since my daughter was stolen from us, but all of you have shown an exemplary model of what being a Citizen of Elysium really means.

"We—the Enforcers, Guards, and certain Citizens—have performed an investigation, and we have found the means by which the Surface Dweller was able to get into and out of the city. How he was able to steal my daughter so easily."

There's a small murmur, but Mother holds up her hand in a stop gesture and the Citizens all quiet. "Now, I know many of you think that Evelyn had no real role in this city. That she was . . . what's the word I heard someone use? Oh yes . . . daft?"

She focuses on someone in the audience, but I don't catch

who, although I do remember that many people here did have a low opinion of me.

"But I'm here to say that is not the case. She didn't just follow that Surface Dweller blindly. He tricked her. And while some of you are thinking that it was an easy task—that she was foolish—I'm here to assure you that it was not. This trickery proves that the Surface Dwellers are much more cunning, ruthless, and dangerous than even I had previously thought."

"What is she doing?" Asher mutters.

"Shh!" I hiss. I'm curious, too, and I don't want to miss a thing.

"My daughter had been, with my permission and encouragement, of course, spending countless hours reading Surface documents and watching historical reports of Surface life pre- to post-war, collecting and cataloging items from the Surface with the help of her betrothed—who is believed to have been killed by the Surface Dweller in his attempts to get to Evelyn." I glare at Mother through the screen. I can't believe I'm even surprised that she'd lie and use Gavin as a scapegoat.

She continues, and it takes everything I have to not slip into Enforcer mode. I can feel it pulling at me, but I get it under control so I can hear what she's saying. ". . . And not only investigated ways Surface cities defended their cities, and their people, from training to weapons to all of their past wars, but taught herself these ways. She used this knowledge to set into place security measures that would prevent the destruction of our wonderful city by the Surface. This knowledge also made way for much of the training the Enforcers and Guards receive to keep our city running smoothly and peacefully. So that what happened there cannot happen down here.

"She was, in fact, in the middle of researching the current Surface Dwellers and their ways, which to my bottomless guilt and dismay, was part of the reason we detained the Surface Dweller instead of eliminating him as soon as we were made aware of his presence . . ."

Asher taps me on the shoulder and I turn. He gives me a questioning look, but I shake my head. "No," I whisper. "I wasn't doing any of that. I've always been interested in the Surface, but . . . I never researched it like she says . . . unless I was doing it without even knowing it. Like it was part of my Conditioning. And Timothy wasn't helping me. He brought me things he thought I'd find interesting and I had a tidy collection built up, but it wasn't to study your ways or anything." I don't know who I'm trying to convince. Me? Or Asher?

". . . So as you can see, if *she*—one of the most well-versed persons of this city—can be fooled and seduced by a Surface Dweller, then the rest of us have no chance against them. Surface Dwellers have changed in the years we've kept ourselves in seclusion. They've become far worse than even I could have imagined and we must be ever vigilant to those that wish to destroy our city. Those who may have been tainted by the Surface Dweller."

She pauses and from the camera angle I have, I can see tears delicately forming in her beautiful blue eyes. She wraps her arms around her stomach as if trying to comfort herself. My stomach twists at the gesture and I tense as I keep my eyes on her.

"I also regret to inform you that during the course of our investigation, I sent out my most trusted Enforcers to get my daughter back from the Surface Dwellers' dirty and blood-covered hands, but before they even left the trench, they found what appeared to be damage to one of the walls. Upon closer inspection, the Enforcers located what was left of a submarine."

"What's she playing at now?" Asher mutters.

There's a loud gasp from the audience and I narrow my eyes. Yes, indeed, what *is* she doing now?

"In the ruins of the submarine, we found the remains of two bodies. After extensive DNA testing, we are positive that the remains are that of the Surface Dweller and my beloved daughter."

Frustration and anger burn just under my skin, but I want to know where Mother is going.

"We believe that Evelyn went willingly with the Surface Dweller due to information she received during her interviews with him. That she believed that he was more dangerous than we previously imagined and that the only way we would be safe is for him to be removed from our facility. We've learned that while we originally thought the murders of her close friend Macie and Macie's betrothed, Nick, were at Evelyn's hand, the Surface Dweller was the one who actually killed these people."

I press a hand to my lips. "Why? Why would you lie? What's the point?"

"To prove Surface Dwellers are evil and manipulative,"

Asher says without a single trace of emotion in his voice. The only hint I get that he's angry is how tense his arms are.

"We believe that the vessel wrecked because Evelyn tried to gain control of it and return home. Because of that, they lost control and crashed into the side of the trench. At this depth, the submarine would have imploded on impact, killing everyone on board."

She sniffs and I can actually see tears running down her face.

"However, due to her sacrifice, we are able to maintain our secrecy and safety. Because she gave her life for all of us, we can live without fear of discovery. My daughter, the Daughter of the People, had nothing but the best interests of her people in mind until her last breath, and for that she deserves our praise and respect. Please, for her sake, let us take a moment in silent reflection of what she did for our city. What *every* Citizen should be willing to do to protect our city."

I sit straight up. "I don't understand. Why is she doing this?"

"She made you a martyr, Evie," Asher finally says.

"Why?"

"We'll find out soon enough." He points back to the hologram.

Mother clears her throat and pats under her eyes with a tissue. "While Evie was sacrificing herself for Elysium's protection, there was another working against us. Against her." She signals someone off stage and I see an Enforcer forcing someone up to the stage. A man with short blond hair, dark slacks, and a white shirt is struggling against the girl, but like any Enforcer worth her salt, she has no trouble shoving him forward until he's standing next to Mother, then forcing him to his knees.

"Joseph," I gasp, when the man looks up, directly into the cameras.

Asher and I share a horrified look. This can't be possible. How did they find him so quickly? How did she *know*?

"Many of you are asking yourselves how did the Surface Dweller get in? How did he know how to get to our Daughter? And I'm here to tell you it was him." She points her hand at Joseph. "This man—no, not a man. A rat. This *rat* is a traitor. It has been proven that he was working *with* the Surface Dweller. That *he* was the reason the Surface Dweller was able to make his way in, and later, escape. With Evelyn. With our Daughter. Without setting off the turrets or the cameras. *He's* the reason. For everything. For the death of our city. For the death of our Daughter. For the disappearance of one of our most talented physicians and the death of his assistant. He's the one that sent the fraudulent orders and the list of missing people to each and every one of you, to wrongly accuse me and cast doubt in the absolute beauty of our city."

She turns to him and more tears—fake ones, obviously—pour down her cheeks in rivulets. I can only stare. That's not right. That's not right at all. Gavin and I escaped on our own. *I* got us out. *I* found the maintenance tunnels. *I* betrayed my city and my people. Not this man. Not the one standing with blood dripping from his mouth, hunched over and holding onto his stomach as if everything inside it might fall out if he lets go. And just like always, there is nothing I can do.

"What do you have to say for yourself?" She kneels down next to him and lifts his chin so he's forced to look at her.

My breath wheezes out of me and Asher places his hand on my shoulder. He just keeps repeating, "Easy," over and over again, but I don't pay any attention to him. I can't. I'm riveted to the screen and Joseph.

He only smiles at her, showing bloodied teeth. "Evie . . . lives." He gasps it out, then spits in her face, coating her white skin in red gloopy streaks.

I gasp along with the crowd, and even though I pray that Mother will ignore the insolence and move on or at least show some mercy, I silently cheer, too. He's not just going to roll over and let her take his life. He must know what's going to happen. Everyone has to. Because mercy isn't something Mother possesses. She lost that long before I ever entered into the picture.

Mother wipes her face with her bare fingers, then flicks them, splattering the bloody spittle to the ground, and glaring at him before standing and turning toward the audience. "Elysium will *not* suffer a traitor to live."

She flicks her hand again, moving away from Joseph. I want to look away. Asher *tells* me to look away. But I can't. I know what's coming, but I can't force my eyes away.

As I expect, one of the Enforcers on stage pulls out her pistol, holds it to Joseph's head, and with only the slightest hesitation, fires, splattering Mother's white dress with Joseph's blood.

CHAPTER TWELVE

Sometimes a deal with the devil is better than no deal at all.
—A BRIEF HISTORY OF THE 21ST CENTURY, POLITICS, FACT
AND FICTION

Gavin

I wake early in the morning and want to scream in agony. My stomach feels even worse than yesterday. The meatheads from the city can really pack a punch. Just pushing myself up to a sitting position hurts like nothing I've ever felt before.

I curse and pant for the entire movement, then I force myself to stand and stumble over to the mirror to stare at my reflection. There's dried blood crusted in the stubble on my face, with a broken line of it running from my mouth down past my chin to my neck, and an ugly bruise on my chin. I touch it gently and hiss.

Damn it!

Of course, that's not the only sore point. I carefully lift the corner of my T-shirt, wincing at the reddish-purpling of my skin that's spread from the two impact zones. It hurts to even stretch my abdomen.

Assholes.

But really I'm more mad at myself. I have to always think things through. Always. Even when my gut is screaming that what I'm doing is right. I should have just listened to Asher's mom. She was right and I knew it. Even then. Asher's father is hell-bent on finding Evie. I don't know why—although, I'm thinking Asher probably does. Which could be the real reason why he was in such a hurry to get Evie out of Rushlake. When I get back to Elysium, I really need to apologize to him.

I do know that Mayor St. James will do anything to get her back. Including making a deal with someone like me. Asher's mom gave me a start on what to do. Now I have to fill in the blanks and make it believable.

Mom pokes her head into my open doorway. Her eyes are sad when she sees me and my bruises. Not exactly what I want to see on my mother's face first thing in the morning.

"It's not ideal, but you can go wash in the ocean. It'll at least get that blood off. The water's freezing, which will probably make those bruises feel better, and the salt will help clean the wounds."

She heaves a sigh, and just before she turns around, I can see the spark of life that she always had, no matter how bad things got for us, is gone. Her shoulders are slumped, and she seems to have aged overnight. There are hollows under her eyes and she looks like she's lost even more weight.

I did that to her.

Because I left her to handle things alone by herself without even teaching Tristan the basics of survival. Because I flew off the handle with the mayor. I stand behind that decision, though. There's never a reason to hit a woman—except Mother; I'd beat the hell out of her if I could—and I've been waiting for years to get my hands on the mayor. I have to admit his hardheadedness isn't just metaphorical. My hand still hurts where I punched him. At least I have some pleasure in knowing that bastard will walk around with a bruise for a while.

Explain *that*, Mr. St. James.

"I'm sorry," I say, before Mom can disappear like a ghost down the hallway.

She turns back around, tipping her head in obvious confusion. "What for?"

"I screwed everything up." My energy leaves me all at once and I sit back onto my bed. Misery makes my whole body ache worse than anything those goons did to me.

She tips her head the other way, her eyebrows furrowed. "How?"

"Leaving you. Not teaching Tristan to hunt—"

"For trying to help the girl you love? For coming back to check on us? For standing up for your family when we needed you?" She pierces me with a glance. "From where I stand, you did nothing wrong. Do I wish you wouldn't have used violence to solve your problem? Yes. But I also know that men like the mayor listen to nothing but brutality." She comes to me and gently takes my face in her hands. "Look what he did to you.

To me. To *Tristan*. This isn't your fault. It's his." She lets go with a smile. That spark of life is back in her eyes. "And I see those wheels turning in that head of yours. You're planning something. Stop questioning yourself. Just do it. Action is the only way to move forward." Then she turns and moves down the hall toward the kitchen. I hear her banging pots and pans around, but I follow her advice and stop planning and start doing.

Without even taking the time to take that dip into the ocean or change my clothes, I grab my gun again and walk straight to the gates.

Every step is a fresh agony in my stomach, but I push the pain aside. I refuse to show the guards how much they hurt me. They'll never let me through if they think I'm a push-over. Which I might literally be if they push in the right spot.

The guards come into view and I recognize them. Not because they're the same as the ones from yesterday, but because I know them. They're brothers. I've taken their family meat from time to time when their father was sick and couldn't hunt.

They stare at me before the one on the right—Nate—says, "Gavin? Is that really you? The mayor said you were dead. That you died in the Outlands."

"Sorry to be a disappointment," I say with a smile, then hold out my fist. I'm surprised the mayor didn't announce my return. You'd think with everything going on, he'd want everyone to know I was back and to avoid me at all costs.

They both bump their fists against mine with a smile, but

then Seth—the oldest—frowns. "We're not supposed to let you through."

I lift an eyebrow. I hate to pull this card, but I'm going to. For my family. "You're not going to let me through, after everything I did to help you when your father got sick?"

"We want to, Gavin. Really we do. But Mayor St. James told us no one is to pass through."

"No one?" I laugh. "What about him?"

They look to each other. "Well, yeah, of course."

"And his son?"

"Well, yeah, I suppose he'd want us to let *him* through."

"What about someone who *knows* something about his son?"

They exchange a look again. "I don't know, Gavin. If we let you through, our family . . ." Nate trails off, but his gaze is directed at my house. Even though you can't see where the fire was, I'm sure word has gotten around that there was one, and who was responsible.

I sigh. "I get it, guys. But if I was here and you were me, I'd let you through and you know it. Besides, what do you think the mayor'll do if he finds out you didn't let me through when I was coming willingly to tell him what I know about his son?"

They glance at each other and I laugh. "Come on, guys, you both know I can take the both of you, at the same time, without even breaking a sweat." I'm not entirely sure about that at the moment, but I'm not about to let them know that. "I did it enough when we were kids. How about you let me through and you can say I forced you if it comes to be a problem?"

They exchange a look, then they both glance at the bruises and blood on my face, before nodding and stepping to the side. "If it's about Asher, I'm sure he'll want to know," Seth finally says.

I step through, nodding my thanks, and they go back to leaning against the wall as if nothing happened.

I follow the same path as yesterday, and again it's just as quiet. No one's out. All the windows are drawn. Even the metalsmith's door is shut, though I can hear him banging around in there.

I step into the offices again and Asher's mom immediately stands. I ignore the look of sympathy she gives me. I know I look like shit. I also know I don't care. The door to the mayor's office is open, so I walk calmly to her desk and place my hands on the top, leaning toward her. I want it to be an intimidating move—in case the mayor's watching somehow—but it's really just to take the pressure off my stomach.

"I'm here to see Mayor St. James about the possible whereabouts of his son and my *former* girlfriend, Evelyn."

She gives me a quick smile and a nod, before turning to the mayor's door. Even though I'm sure he heard me, he doesn't come. He's going to make me come to him.

Fine.

She announces me and he says, "He may come."

Without waiting for her to gesture me over, I step past her, making sure I show no visible pain as I step into his office. Asher's mom closes the door quietly behind me.

The mayor lifts an eyebrow. "I see that you didn't even take the time to clean up after last night."

"There was no need."

"So you're finally going to admit you know where my son is." It isn't a question and I don't even bother to answer it.

"I want you to swear that everything you promised me and my family yesterday will be followed through. I don't care about living in the city. We can have our riches here in the village."

The mayor shrugs. "Of course. I'm a man of my word. You tell me where my son is, I give you everything I promised."

"Your word means shit to me. I want it in writing." This I thought about all night. I have to have *something*. He may be able to revoke it later, even if it's in writing, but that'll take awhile. Long enough for me to figure something else out.

I hope.

The mayor's eyes flash and his cheeks turn red. "How dare you talk to me like that? I can take down that wreck of a house just as fast as I took out your pump house and everything in it."

"Mayor, I have no doubts that you mean what you say, but you can't keep me or my family here. Our house means nothing to any of us. Burn it down and you lose the only thing keeping us here, and any chance of you finding out where Asher may be."

He narrows his eyes, but finally yells, "Caroline!"

She rushes in, her gaze barely grazing me before focusing on her husband. "Yes?"

"Take a note."

She immediately pulls out a pen and notepad.

"I, Stephen St. James, Mayor of Black Star Cove, and due representative of Rushlake City, do from this moment forward provide the Hunter family with full first-class citizenship status and all the benefits, advantages, and boons that that status entails. They will be sponsored personally by myself and under my protection. An account will be opened in their name at the bank in Black Star Cove and another in Rushlake City, where there shall be money deposited to provide for them and their family. This agreement shall be binding upon and inure to the benefit of the aforesaid parties hereto and their respective heirs, successors, and permitted assigns. And shall go into effect immediately." He glances at me. "Does that sound acceptable to you, Mr. Hunter?"

"Quite." What I understood of it, anyway.

"Very well." He turns to his wife. "Make sure to have that drafted on my letterhead and back to me post haste so that I may sign it into effect."

She rushes out and he gestures for me to sit across from him. "I've fulfilled my end of the bargain."

Chapter Thirteen

Subject 121, Evelyn Winters:
Failure to follow a direct order, resulting in the unnecessary deaths of ten Citizens and one Enforcer. Evaluation shows Conditioning has failed yet again. Recommend immediate disposal.
ETA: Mother has taken over control of said subject.

—Dr. Friar, incident report following massacre at festival

Evie

I sit in the maintenance tunnel above the crematorium, looking through a grate at Joseph—a boy I once knew, but remember nothing about. The memories of him are like words written in sand and washed away by the rising tide. And while I feel sorrow, and regret, no tears come.

I want to cry. For him. For his match. For the children they'll never have and the life that wasn't just lost, but tossed away like so much trash, but ultimately I can't. I can only stare through the grates with remorse and the need for revenge flowing through my veins.

When I left Asher back in the Caverns, I had no clue where I was going. I just knew I had to get away. From him. From Nadia. From *everyone* in that Cavern. Because if I didn't leave right then, I would have been exactly what I hated. Mother's puppet. Her murderer. An Enforcer.

The girl pulling that trigger on that stage could have been me. If it hadn't been for a chance encounter, or a moment of clarity, or even possibly what could be considered a wrong choice, that could have been me standing there next to Joseph. The one pulling that trigger with no emotion. It could *still* be me. If I'm not careful. If I don't keep control on those programmed instincts. If I allow myself to forget who I really am.

I tense as I hear the echoes of grunts, and the sliding sounds of someone drawing closer. If it's Enforcers, I'm in trouble. A *lot* of trouble. Because of how I feel now, with the need for vengeance and retribution searing my veins. I know I won't be able to stop myself from giving in to the monster inside me, begging for an opportunity to claw its way out. If it's a Guard, I might have a problem. If it's a Citizen, I don't know what I'll do. I guess it depends on what that Citizen does.

The sounds come closer and I move until I'm in a better position to do something other than sit here and die.

I hold my breath, but the echoes fade and I realize they came from somewhere else in the vast expanse of tunnels. But they remind me that I need to be more careful. More vigilant. I'm not the only one who uses these tunnels.

The door to the crematorium squeals open and two Enforcers enter, dragging what can only be Joseph's body between them. I watch, shaken, as they strip Joseph of his clothes—of his one last dignity—and then toss him, without any sort of care, into the furnace. As if being a traitor is contagious and they might catch it if they touch him for too long. They toss in his clothes and some sort of other linen after them.

I can hear their thoughts as if they were mine, because I've been there. I've done this. Because that's what Enforcers do. We're nothing more than robots made with flesh and blood instead of metal and wire. To them this man is a traitor and deserves no respect or care.

They close the door to the furnace with a slam; the locks thud into place, causing me to flinch. Then they leave. They don't look back. They don't stop or even pause to think about what happened. They simply walk out, the door clanging shut behind them.

I don't move, however. I sit there for a long time—longer than I should—before I glance one last time at the furnace. In several hours, his body will be nothing more than ash and bones. Then his bones will be ground up into dust and used as fertilizer. The thought makes me a little queasy. But another part of me says bone ash is the best fertilizer. The best crops always come from plants fertilized with bone ash.

The idea of that, and the fact that I even thought it, sickens me. I'm disgusted with myself, but a new wave of indignation and loathing sweeps through me. Mother put those thoughts there. Mother made me. Made those girls. Pushed the metaphorical button on Joseph's murder. And Mother needs to be the one who pays.

I push up to a kneeling position and crawl back the way I came until I get to the ladder. I descend it and carefully remove the crawl-through door, peering out into the other set of maintenance tunnels. And then more and more. I'm hyperaware of my surroundings as I make my way around in the labyrinth. I refuse to be the cause of any more deaths. Only when I'm certain that I've shaken anyone who may have followed me and gotten them thoroughly lost do I take the tunnels that lead to the Caverns.

Nadia is waiting when I get back. Her normally agitated face is even more so when I finally see her in the light of the Caverns. "Now is not the time for a tantrum. People here have been worried about you." Her eyes travel from my head to my shoes. "You are still covered in blood from before."

I raise an eyebrow, because I'm pretty sure when she said "people" she meant herself. But I don't call her out on it. I just keep walking to the half-constructed buildings.

"I can wash later; right now I need everyone who's in these Caverns and willing to be an active member of the Underground to meet me in the room with all the Surface artifacts."

She frowns. "Why?"

I stop at the entrance to the building that houses the artifact room. "Because I've grown weary of Mother's games." I step into the building and head directly to the room, taking a seat at the head of the table.

I still have no idea what I'm doing, but I'm going to do something.

It only takes a few minutes for everyone to arrive. That's because there's precisely three people who do. Nadia. Asher. Evangeline.

"Where are the rest of the people?"

Nadia refuses to meet my eyes when she replies, "They do not wish to be involved. Things here are tough enough. They feel you are not what Father promised. They do not wish to bring the wolves to their door without a shepherd. So to speak."

"So there are only four of us?" My voice pinches with a panic.

"Seven," Evangeline says. "Father, Tate, and Kara aren't here."

Seven. I have seven people. Out of at least forty.

Asher leans over. "No one said this was going to be easy."

I stare at him. Anger practically steaming from my ears. "No one said *anything* to me. They just *assumed* I'd come in, take down Mother, and then everything would be wonderful after that."

"I did not think that." Nadia shrugs when everyone looks over at her. "I thought you were too young."

I toss my hands in the air. "Well, you're wrong and so are they. This *isn't* going to be easy. And I was a fool for believing Father that it would be. But Mother isn't as infallible as she thinks she is. She literally killed two people over a list."

"So?" Asher asks. "She kills people all the time."

"Yes!" I say. "But she usually does it quietly. Like she tried with Dr. Moreau and the nurse. Not so publicly. But what we're doing is forcing her hand. We need to keep doing it."

"But," Nadia says, folding her hands on the table in front of her, "as you said, two people died in one day because of that list."

I nod. "We've been too obvious. We need a way to spread the word about Mother and the Underground movement without her being aware. Dr. Friar's files are filled with stuff we can use."

"There's always good old-fashioned paper," Asher suggests, grabbing a sheet from the table and holding it up. "It's slower, but we could pass a few out to the right people and eventually everyone would see it."

"Still could get back to Mother," Nadia says. "As far as I know, Elysium does not use paper anymore."

I shrug. "That could work in our favor. Even if or when she sees what we're passing around, she'll have no way of knowing where it came from."

"How will you pass out the papers?"

Asher purses his lips. "We need more people."

"Who?" I demand. "Everyone's too afraid to do anything. Especially after today, we'll be lucky to add just one more person to our ranks."

"We just need to give them someone to root for," Asher says with a grin. "Like, say, a person Mother convinced them to believe died saving them?"

"Me?"

"She made you into a martyr for her own twisted purposes. Take advantage of it for your own."

"Even if Mother succeeded in making me a martyr, that doesn't mean anyone is going to want to follow me."

Asher looks at his Slate. "Mother said you were the Daughter. What does that mean?"

I roll my eyes. "Nothing. It's just a stupid thing she made up."

"No. Evie. Think about it. What does *Mother* want it to mean?"

I toss my shoulder. "That I was her successor. I was supposed to take over for her when and if she decided to give it to me."

"No." Evangeline pipes up and everyone swings around to stare at her. "Or, more precisely, that's not the only reason. You were supposed to be the approachable one. While she stayed on her pedestal. At least for a time. That's why she had you handle the Request days. Since the Citizens couldn't talk to Mother themselves, she wanted you there to 'carry their voices to Mother.' To be the people's voice."

"The people's voice?" I frown, but a little thought starts niggling at me. I turn toward Asher, who has a small smile on his face like I just solved the problem he knew the answer to all along. "So . . . you're saying I need to be their voice now?"

"Mother's already set it up. You just have to show the people you're here and you want to be *their* voice. Not Mother's."

"How do I do that?"

"What about Gavin's idea for the mask?" Asher suggests.

"Even with a mask you could only be out there a short time

before the Enforcers saw you." Nadia's composure remains the same, but her voice sounds slightly more excited than usual.

"What if more than just Evie did it?" Evangeline suggests. "I'd be willing to help. I'm sure Tate and Kara would, too."

No one argues so I lift a shoulder. "Well, we need a good old-fashioned printer and a few masks then."

For the next hour or two, I scour Dr. Friar's data cubes for just the right passage. I eventually decide on one about the experiments that were in Three, and I now sit by an old paper printer and wait for it to do its job. It's ancient. Nothing like the 3-D printers in Elysium. And it still has the sticker on it that says, Property of Elysium Towers. I'm impressed Nadia and her people were able to keep it running for so long.

When it's finally finished, I gather up all the papers. It's only a small amount considering all the people in Elysium this has to go to, but we'll only have a small window before the Enforcers see us. Hopefully, it'll be enough.

Now to figure out how the masks are coming along. Asher, Nadia, and Evangeline left sometime during my struggle to find just the right file to print. But I eventually find Asher in his dugout, sitting in his bed and staring at something in his hands.

He looks up when I step into his cutout. "There you are. I made you something."

He tosses me the thing he was looking at. I barely catch it before it hits me in the chest. But when I do, I grin. One half is blank, the other a duplication of half my face, obviously taken from a picture. It's slightly crude. The edges aren't perfect and the picture doesn't sit quite flat, but it's close enough that I'm sure it will work.

"Why is half of this blank? Wouldn't it be better to use my full face?"

"I thought it could be symbolic. It'll represent that you are both nothing and something. You are one of them, yet all you."

"How did you make this?"

"Evangeline did. From a 3-D printer. I told her what I wanted and she came up with this."

I blink. "Evangeline? I thought she was only good at standing around and twisting her hands together."

"Evie!"

"Sorry. That wasn't nice. But seriously? She made this?"

"Yep. She was an engineer. Did you know that? She keeps a 3-D printer in her apartment. She went back for it when she went to tell whoever Kara and Tate are about the plan. Brave of her to leave here, considering."

I give him a look. I get the point. He wants me to play nice and get to know her. I'm just not ready to sit down and do it. I don't know that I'll ever be ready.

The mask will look nothing like me when I actually wear it—more like a distorted, possibly even grotesque version of myself—but I can imagine what it would look like with a few minor adjustments and the right material. Asher is right. I am Evie, but I'm also the Daughter of the People. I am no one and someone. I am the people's voice. And I will take Mother's city out from underneath her, remove *her* support system before she even knows there's a problem. Then, when I'm ready, I'll yank the rug out from underneath her and watch her fall.

We meticulously plan the first of what I've now dubbed maskings. It takes more than a few days and squashed ideas to come up with some kind of plan that isn't haphazardly thrown together. While there's still wild room for improvement, it should work.

With Father's help we add biological sensors to the masks to help get rid of the distortion. The next time I put it on, it immediately conforms to the contours of my face. It feels weird as it adjusts, but after a few seconds, it's no more uncomfortable than wearing latex gloves. When I pull it off, however, it feels like when I was sunburned on the Surface.

The others take their turns with their masks, and it's eerie watching half my face stretch and adjust to someone else's features. But I have to admit it's effective. It changes enough so it doesn't look strange and distorted, but not enough to destroy the illusion.

The whole point of the masks is for people to realize I'm back—hopefully Asher's right and they'll see that as a good thing—or that I might be back, anyway, but without giving away my hand too soon. And to start the countdown clock on Mother's reign of terror.

So . . . now it's time to drum up some attention and show Mother there's more than one person behind what we're doing, which, optimistically speaking, should slow down her assassination rate since she'll have no idea who to target. Hopefully it'll also show the Citizens that there *is* a group ready, able, and willing—no matter how small it is—to take Mother on.

Evangeline will start it. Followed by Tate, then me, dressed as an Enforcer, plus Kara, and lastly, Asher. The trick is to move slowly enough through the crowds that with the busyness of the Square no one will notice—except those we wish to show.

We all take our places and I keep my eyes out for as many of them as I can see. Evangeline starts at the dinner club and I watch as she winds through the crowds. When no one's looking, she slips the mask on for a few seconds. Long enough for someone to notice her and for the cameras to get a good view before she disappears into the crowd and removes the mask, hiding it and dropping a handful of the "flyers" I made.

Now should come Tate. I'm not exactly sure where he is, but it's close. I can feel the excitement as the crowd catches a view of the mask again. Suddenly someone bumps me and I look up to see him.

"Pardon me," Tate says with enough of a quaver in his voice to make it appear he's afraid of me, then he bows quickly and drops his sheaf of papers before rushing away in the opposite direction. An Enforcer has popped into view, so I weave my way through the crowd in the opposite direction of her. She pays me no mind, but she's definitely on high alert as the buzz of the crowd gets more frantic and the dropped sheaves of paper are passed around and read. The crowd parts for me like water around a rock.

Finally, I step into the shadows by one of the buildings, slip on the mask, and rip off my cloak, hoping no one can see my "transformation." Then I walk around the side of the building where I know a camera's blind spot is and step back into the crowd to wait for the reaction. Almost instantly someone notices it, and I see them blink a few times, as if they're not sure what they're seeing. When I disappear back into the crowd, I shove the mask under my shirt and keep my head ducked so my hair hides my face, but I hand my entire packet of papers to some random Citizen who's not paying attention to anyone but his Slate. He thanks me as we pass.

I continue along my path, passing Asher, who I nudge with my shoulder. A few seconds that feel like hours later, another jolt of electricity arises a few meters away from where he was. I turn in that direction, as everyone else does, but he's already gone and out of sight. But there's a woman in the middle of the crowd holding yet another sheaf of papers. I continue on my way toward my designated exit, but I make eye contact with an Enforcer before I do.

I feel it the minute she sees me. The confusion. The minute of disbelief. Then the programmed response kicking in as she pushes people away to get to me. My heart kicks in my chest, but I'm gone and in one of the maintenance tunnels before she can catch up to me.

CHAPTER FOURTEEN

One should not be afraid of what they can see, but what they cannot see. For it is what people hide that shows their true intentions.

—LENORE ALLEN'S JOURNAL

Gavin

I don't know where they are." I look Mayor St. James straight in the eyes. "We got separated in the Outlands. As you well know. When I got to Rushlake, they were gone. From what I've been told, they grew fond of each other on their trip there and they . . ." What the hell is that damn word they use in Ann Marie's movies all the time? ". . . 'clicked.' Apparently, *Evelyn,*" I force her name through my teeth like a hiss, as if even saying her name is a fresh brand on my skin, "thought I was dead and Asher did, too. She moved on. They both did. I was told they ran away together somewhere up north."

"And the submarine?" The mayor frowns. It's hard to tell what he's thinking, but I hope he's buying my story, because this is all I've got to sell.

I screw my face up into what I hope looks like confusion. "What about it?"

"It's gone, Mr. Hunter. I'm sure you're aware of it."

I sneer. "Nope. Don't care either. Stopped caring the minute she left me for your son actually." I try to add as much scorn as I can muster into my tone. I really hope this is working.

The mayor laughs. "You really expect me to believe that?"

I shrug and lean back in my chair. "I don't really care what you believe. I can only tell you what I know."

He pauses a minute as if debating whether or not to believe me. I want to go on and plead my case, but I channel Evie. She has the patience of a saint. And she taught me that when dealing with people like the mayor, there really is such a thing as protesting too much.

"Mr. Hunter, that deal we made was that I gave you full citizenship and enough money to take care of you and your family for a very long time, should you give me information about the whereabouts of my son. You are not following through on that deal."

I shrug again. "That's all I know. I can't tell you what I don't know. I heard they snuck out of the hospital she was in, stole a couple of horses, and took off heading north."

"And you were *where* all this time?"

I hiss out an aggravated breath, hoping it's not too overdone. "I told you we got separated." I look to the ground and try to look sheepish. "I came back here right away, but couldn't face my family, so I made a raft and went to the island."

"The *island*?!" Asher's father purses his lips. "You've been at the island the whole time?" Disbelief colors every word, but I think it's more because he doesn't think anyone could actually stay on the island that long. *I* don't even think someone could stay there that long. It's a horrible place to stay for just a few hours, let alone days.

"If you go to the edge of the cove, you'll find the raft I made to get there and back."

"Why should I believe you?"

"Because it's the truth," a voice behind me says.

I whirl my entire upper torso around to see Asher's grandmother standing there, looking just as stern and formidable as she was the last time. I want to gape at her, but I keep my expression as flat as possible. At least that's answered one question and solved a *huge* problem for me.

"Asher and Evelyn left together. When they first arrived she was distraught and completely inconsolable over Gavin's assumed death. But over the weeks, Asher helped her through it, and like Gavin said, something clicked. You had to be blind not to see the two were in love. They ran away together. They left me a note. I don't know where they are now, but I doubt they're anywhere near here."

Asher's father studies the two of us closely, until he finally nods at me. "Show me this raft," he demands.

I don't want to. My gut tells me it's not a good idea. But if I don't show him, he'll know I'm lying.

"Follow me." I stand up, and without waiting for him or anyone else, I head straight toward the shoreline and the buried raft. We pass through the gate, where the two guards stand up straight as the mayor proceeds through.

"Both of you!" he barks. "Come!"

They don't even hesitate; they fall in line behind us. The heat of their stare burns the back of my neck, but I keep my gaze straight ahead and focus on where I'm walking. My nerves are strung as tight as a fully drawn bowstring, but I can't let the mayor see.

Finally, I gesture to the ground. "I buried it around here somewhere."

The mayor signals his guards to start digging and it doesn't take them long to unearth the remains of the raft. It falls apart in their hands. I'm not surprised. I'm amazed it didn't fall apart on my way back here.

The mayor glances at it, then at the water, the island, and finally me, before turning to his guards. "You may go."

They don't hesitate. They run back toward their post before he even finishes the sentence. He doesn't seem to notice. He's just *staring* at me. "You really expect me to believe that you used *that* to get across from the island?"

I fight the urge to swallow the lump of nerves stuck in my throat. I'm sure he has the eyes of a vulture hawk and any show of fear or nerves will give me away.

"Like I said before, I don't really care what you believe. I can only tell you what I know."

He tries staring me down, but years of hunting predators meaner and bigger than me has taught me how to hide my tells, and the one thing I have in spades is patience. I can wait out anything, or anyone, as long as it takes. That doesn't mean I'm not terrified he can sense my fear like a dog sniffs out fresh meat.

Finally, he jerks his head to the side, then pushes past me to trudge back to his office. He doesn't say a single word until we get back. Caroline and Lenore are sitting talking, but whatever it is they're saying is quickly cut off when we walk in. Asher's grandmother stares at me and I don't have to hear her to know her question. Did he see what he needed?

I nod slightly before turning my attention back to the mayor.

"It seems my business with you and your family is concluded." Anger permeates every syllable he utters.

I realize, too late, I shouldn't have said anything until the papers were signed. Not that that would have really changed anything. He could just tear them up. But hopefully Caroline would have made sure to file them in such a way that it would have been too much of a hassle. And with so many witnesses, Lenore, who doesn't take shit from anyone, being one of them, would he have dared?

Caroline hands him some papers. "The letter you requested. In triplicate." He rips it from her hands and for a moment, I'm paralyzed with fear he won't sign it. Then he takes a pen from his drawer, scrawls his signature, and adds his seal to all three pages. He hands—well, more like tosses—two back to Caroline and one to me.

"I do not appreciate being made a fool of, Mr. Hunter."

I straighten my shoulders to argue, but Asher's grandmother

steps in between us before I can. "He did nothing of the sort." She leans into him. I'm surprised to see him actually back away from her. "He told you before he had no information on Asher or Evelyn. Yet you insisted he did. You ostracized his entire family, destroyed their fresh water, then threatened more harm if he didn't give you what you wanted. So he gave you the best answer he could. The only one who made a fool of you is yourself. I suggest, before putting your foot any further into that large yapping hole you call a mouth, that you apologize and do as you promised." She waves one of the pages in the air in front of the mayor's nose.

She reminds me of Evie so much in that moment that I have to swallow the sudden lump that forms in my throat and look away. It's no wonder the two of them, not to mention Asher and Evie, got along so well almost from the minute they met. And the resemblance reminds me there's the possibility that there might actually be a familial connection between them.

The mayor narrows his eyes, but snaps, "I will remove the guards and your family will have their rights returned immediately. As for your water, I'll try to have a crew out there within the hour to fix your pump and replace the pump house." He dismisses all of us with a wave of his hand.

Honestly, I don't believe for a minute that he'll do any of what he says, but as long as he leaves my family alone, I don't really care. Despite what Caroline said yesterday, I'm sure she'll make sure he does.

As we exit, I try not to look at Asher's grandmother. Even

when I hold the door open for her. I'm at a loss as to why she's here. She doesn't fit in our dusty, dirty, falling down village. She fits in perfectly with the beautiful and stylish Rushlake City where she lives. But since it saves me a trip and much needed time, I'm not going to question it too much.

I pause to talk to her when we get into the reception area, but she stops me with a look. "I am parched," she says loudly, startling me. "That was a long ride for such an old lady." She gives me a look full of meaning, before glancing at her daughter, Asher's mom. "Caro, would you accompany me to the bar? I think I could use a drink."

I raise my eyebrows. A drink? This early?

"Not right now, Mom, but we'll do something special for your return this evening after I finish working. Maybe Gavin can escort you. You can teach him all the ways of being a true gentleman."

"That's a grand idea!" She turns to me. "Would you care to escort a lady for a drink?"

I'd have to be an idiot to *not* see what's really going on, so I hold my arm out. "Of course."

She slides her arm through mine and I escort her to the bar, where she leads me to a table right in the middle of the room. She orders a tea for herself and water for me.

I'm not sure why she picked a bar, or why she's being nice to me, but it makes no difference, so I ask, "What are you doing here? How did you know I was here?"

She lifts a brow. "Come now. Surely you can come up with better questions than those."

I stare at her.

She shakes her head. "My daughter and I do talk from time to time, you know. Especially when something as important as your arrival happens."

"What's so important about my arrival? And why did you help me?"

She smiles and leans back in her chair. "Now that, my boy, is a much better question." She taps her foot against the floor in time to the music pouring from some kind of pre-war radio. "Because you've been *there* and made it back *here*. Alive and well and with all your limbs attached." Her eyes run over my bruised face. "Even if you are a bit banged up."

"That's from the mayor." Not sure why, but that's a huge point of pride for me. That it wasn't Elysium that hurt me, it was the Surface.

"I'm sure." The server places our drinks in front of us, before leaving us without so much as a "you're welcome." Asher's grandma takes a sip of the tea, then wrinkles her nose and pushes the cup to the side. "You found him. Didn't you?"

"Who?" I know exactly who she's talking about. Eli. I just don't care to answer. I want answers from her first.

"You know exactly who." She leans forward. "Don't play games with me, boy. I've been playing them longer than you've been alive and I know all the rules."

It doesn't take me long to realize that I'm going to have to play almost the same game with her that I did with Evie when I first got to Elysium. One answer of my own for each answer she gives me. I go first to show her she can trust me. "Yeah. We found him. He's not the same though."

She leans back in her seat. "No doubt." She says it softly, almost sadly. "Any amount of time that close to Mother has to have an impact." She gives me an even look. "I helped you because what my son-in-law did to your mother was as wrong as wrong can get. I've had quite enough of that, thank you. If Caro would listen to reason . . ." She trails off, before refocusing on me. "I was already on my way here when Caroline told me you'd shown back up. That man merits a beating," again she looks me up and down, "and I applaud your restraint in not giving him all that he deserves."

"I still don't understand why we're sitting here having tea."

"Because I know now that you think you've gotten things straightened out you're going to go back to her. I'm here to tell you not to."

I twist my water glass in my hand. Now that Lenore is with me, I should be planning on going back, but the truth is I've been thinking the same thing. That maybe I should wait a bit longer. To make sure the mayor follows through with leaving my family alone.

But . . . "I'm not just going to leave her there."

"That man is going to be watching you closer than a dog watches a bone. You've got to pretend everything is normal, because if he even *thinks* you've lied to him, he won't hesitate to make that contract null and void."

"I'm surprised he hasn't already."

"I knew you were smart." She leans back in her seat and stirs her tea, but doesn't drink it. "Go on, for now, like you would if Evie really had left you." She smiles at me. "Let my son-in-law pretend to make you a king among paupers, then, when his guard is down and he finally believes you, *then* you leave."

"How long will that be?"

"I don't know. A couple of weeks. A couple of months. It just depends."

"And when will I know?"

"I'll tell you." She takes another sip of her tea, makes another face, and places it down again. "God, they really make horrible tea, don't they?" She signals for the server to come over. When he does, she says, "Bring me a whiskey."

"We're not supposed to serve anything before noon."

She glares at the boy. "I don't care what my jackoff of a son-in-law has decreed. I'm Lenore Allen of Rushlake City. I'm head of the board of trustees and I overrule my son-in-law here. I've ordered a whiskey, now bring it." She bangs her cane on the floor and the boy jumps, basically tripping over his own feet. "Bring the whole bottle!" she yells after him.

I snicker as little bits and pieces of the puzzle I've been trying to assemble since she came back start falling into place. The server brings the bottle and Lenore downs two good mouthfuls before I speak.

"Why are you doing this? Really?" I ask. She has some sort of ulterior motive. They always do. "If you're head of the board of trustees and are basically in charge of the mayor, why aren't you turning in Evie yourself? How do I know that you're not the reason they left in the first place? You know exactly where she is and how to get there. You know everything. You sent them there yourself."

"Because I made a mistake a long time ago, and it's high time I fixed it." She takes another swallow of whiskey straight from the bottle. "I know much more about this whole debacle than you can ever imagine. I'm more involved in it than I ever wanted to be. And I need to fix it. The only thing I don't have is a way to get there." She grins at me. "And you can give me that. Now you owe me a favor, and when it's time, I'll come to collect."

There's never such a thing as a favor freely given with people from Rushlake. But I need her to come back with me, so *she's* really doing *me* another favor by coming.

However, there's no need to let *her* know that.

Chapter Fifteen

It is my daughter that hides so boldly behind the mask, of this I have no doubt. And my foolish husband is probably the one that helps her. One must wonder though if she knows her political plays were taught to her by me.

—Mother's journal

Evie

I'm not sure if it's a good thing or a bad thing that Mother's response to the masking was to *not* respond, but since nothing bad happened it's worth doing again. So the next day, I go out, just Asher and I, passing out flyers. This time it's just a note from Mother to her "most trusted scientist" that she needed to make her people better than what they were. Since it corroborates the notes from Dr. Friar that I passed out yesterday, I figure it's a good way to continue my propaganda circulation.

I've made over a hundred flyers this time and split them between Asher and me. Fifty apiece shouldn't be that hard to distribute quickly, especially if you drop the papers and disappear when the people next to you bend over to help you.

I've just dropped the last bit of flyers, when someone grabs my hand. Immediately, my whole body reacts as my brain shifts into that state between Evie the person and Evelyn the monster. But before I can even look up from the hand that clasped mine to the person it belongs to, the hand is gone and so are they. The only thing left behind is a small piece of paper.

"Evie!" Asher hisses so close to my ear I jump.

I glance up and see over his shoulder an Enforcer practically shoving people to get through them to me. I spin around and dash through the crowd to one of the shadowed sections, remove the mask, and yank my Enforcer garb back on to slip back into the crowd.

My heart thrashes in my chest as the Enforcer who was looking for me, steps next to me. "Did you see her?" Her voice is as emotionless and cold as I remember from my training, but I still have to fight not to shudder at it.

My mind races, throwing answers randomly at my mouth before my lips finally spit out, "I thought I did, but when I got here she was gone."

"Mother will be displeased," the girl says, but disappears into the crowd again without saying anything else.

It was a risk answering her. I don't know how many Enforcers are left or how close they are. When I was one we considered each other sisters, but it's been so long since then.

My heart still ramming against my rib cage, I patrol the area I'm in before melting into the shadows to find the nearest maintenance tunnel. The paper burns a hole in my hand.

I'm dying to read it, but I've already almost been caught once today. I don't want to press my luck any further.

The door swishes open the minute I finish the signaling knock, and I'm yanked into the dark tunnel before my brain catches up.

"Are you all right?" Asher demands, his hands holding me in place by my shoulders. "Did she find you?"

"I'm fine," I say. "She did find me, but I already had my cloak on. She just thought I was one of them."

"That was too close. What the hell happened? Why weren't you paying attention?" He yanks me into a hug.

"Trust me. I didn't like it either." I hug him back, before pushing him away. "Someone grabbed me. It startled me so much I almost lost control of myself. By the time I pulled myself back together he was gone, there was a paper in my hand and you were warning me about the Enforcer."

"A paper?" Asher asks. "Is there anything on it?"

"I don't know. I didn't get a chance to look at it."

"It is dangerous to continue this conversation here," Nadia says in her stern voice. "I suggest if you are not injured we continue this conversation in the Caverns."

"Of course."

We make the long trek down the pitch-black tunnels. While I still trail my hand along the wall, I've come and gone so much in the last few days I don't think I actually need to do it anymore.

When we enter the light of the Caverns, I immediately look at the paper. I frown at it. Written in an almost illegible hand are the words "Evie Lives." I flip it over and see, in the same hand, a short note.

"We believe you. We wish to help."

I read it a few times, not sure I'm seeing what it's actually saying.

"What is it?" Asher demands.

"I think someone wants to join us."

"What?" He rips the paper from my hand and I hiss when it slices into the webbing between my finger and thumb. "Sorry," he mumbles, already reading the paper.

"What do we do?" I ask.

"More is better, right?" He doesn't sound very confident in his answer.

Nadia watches the two of us, her face as emotionless as usual, but she's obviously waiting for me to do or say something. "Shall I get Evangeline?"

I nod absently. "Please. We'll be in the artifact room." I walk in that direction, with Asher following a few paces behind.

We sit at the table and stare at each other, both at a loss for words.

"This is what we wanted," Asher finally says.

"Yes." But I personally didn't expect a response so soon. Sure, it was just one, but every journey and all that.

Evangeline walks in then. She's flushed and out of breath. She obviously ran here. Her eyes are excited and she beams at us. "So we got one!"

"Theoretically," I say. Why oh why does her bubbly nature always set my teeth on edge?

"Why theoretically?" She gestures toward the paper. "It's a request to join, right?"

I look at Asher, not sure what I'm trying to say. Thankfully, he knows exactly what I'm feeling. "We don't really know what to do about it." He splays his hands out in front of him. "We didn't expect it to happen this fast."

The room is silent. Then Evangeline asks, "Who was it?"

I shrug. "I don't know. It happened too fast. I just know it was a man."

"How?" Asher demands.

"His hand was definitely male."

"If it's just the one, we could bring him here," Evangeline suggests.

"No," Nadia says instantly. "That is not a good idea. There's no way to tell if he is working for Mother or not. I will not risk my people."

"I agree." I take the paper from Asher and study the handwriting. "It's too high of a risk."

"There's nothing stating he *has* to be here to help out. Kara and Tate aren't. Right now we're just planning on more information drops, right? Just give them the papers like we did with Kara and Tate."

"But we don't know who it was."

"Another pamphlet drop." Evangeline folds her hands on the table and leans forward. "Instead of information about Mother and her atrocities, we give them a place and time to meet."

"And then Mother ambushes us." I scowl at the paper.

"There's no reason for us to be there to give it to them," Asher says. "Just leave the papers for them to grab. If we're suggesting they do it at a certain time and place, then one of us can drop it off and wait to see who shows up. If it's an Enforcer, then we know it's a trap and we continue as we have. If not, then we've just added another member to the roster."

"If we're just handing out pamphlets with a place and time to meet, how do we control how many show up? How do we make sure the people who show up are ones that want to join our side?"

"I do not believe," Nadia pipes up, "that you will get a lot of people to join your cause. Even if you asked straight out, which I highly recommend against doing. I would just leave the bare essentials in a simple format. Such as time in just numerals and maybe a coded location. Those waiting for a response from you will guess to its meaning. Those who are not, will not understand it."

"But how will they know where to look? They won't know our code," I ask.

"What about a symbol? We can put it on the paper and, like Nadia said, no one but those specifically looking for the answers will understand. They'll look for the symbol at the appointed time."

I nod my understanding and agreement. "It shouldn't be either of us who are waiting, though," I say. "It's already risky, us going out there with all the cameras to do the drops in the first place."

"Kara and Tate," Evangeline says. "I'd consider it a safe bet that she doesn't know about Kara or Tate."

"Maybe," I say, but I don't see where we have a choice. There is nothing unusual about them wandering around Sector Two, but every time I leave here, I put forty people at risk. It's a chance, but less of one than if I go.

"Well, then," I decide, crumbling up the paper. "I guess we better get to work. We've only got until tomorrow."

We spend the next few hours hashing out the details. We decide to have the meeting during the dinner hour, when Sector Two is busiest. The papers—ten of them—will be hidden slightly behind the sign for the theater near the Residential Sector. There are plenty of hiding spots there for Kara and Tate to watch and see who shows up. We're not going to leave masks. They're too hard to hide and I don't want to give Mother anything easily. Once we determine this person is really on our side, then it'll be easy enough to make sure he or she gets one. Asher draws up a simple lotus flower to use as our symbol. He says it means freedom and rebirth in a few ancient cultures, which is good. Elysium will have both by the time I'm finished.

The next day we do our drop. Again only Asher and I. Kara and Tate will have enough to do later. No reason to double their risk. I slip from our secret door first, dressed once again as an Enforcer, and make my way through the maintenance tunnels to an exit close to the Palace Wing, where the Enforcers are kept. However, the minute I step foot into the Sector,

I want to turn right back around. Apparently yesterday's near miss has made Mother up the ante. I spot four Enforcers and ten Guards off the bat.

A sense of déjà vu settles over me again. I feel like I've done this exact thing before, and I almost turn around. My body tells me to, but the last few times I listened to what my body said to do, people died. This time, I keep going and the sense of foreboding flits away, like a bumblebee from a flower.

I straighten my shoulders and make sure the hood is pulled all the way up to cover my face as much as possible. I push forward and try to keep my breathing even and my pulse steady. Not an easy feat when every few meters there's a Guard or an Enforcer. I don't know how we're going to pull this one off, but we're going to have to.

Ten minutes pass before mumblings begin to make their way to my ears of the latest pamphlet. The excitement is even more than it has been and it has all the Enforcers near me migrating toward where Asher should have started and finished his drop. I follow just long enough to make sure he's gone and not raise suspicion. From what I can tell, Asher left and his papers are nowhere to be seen. I hope that's a good thing.

This time, I don't even bother removing the Enforcer garb before I slip the mask on. It's too much of a risk with so many Enforcers around. Plus, who knows, it could be another blow to Mother to think one of her precious Enforcers could be helping the Underground. That gives me an idea, but I shelve it for later.

My heart lodged in my throat, I start handing papers to the nearest people. I want them in actual hands this time. Not just on the floor for anyone, including an Enforcer, to grab. I've just handed out my last one when someone grabs my shoulder and spins me around. I have just enough time to rip the mask from my face, but not enough time to hide it in my pocket. I just keep it crumpled in my fist.

"Was that a paper in your hand?" a Guard asks me.

I shake his hand from my shoulders and glare at him. "It was." I try to project the same amount of coldness as I was Conditioned to do. "I took it from a Citizen. It was the same from yesterday."

"You gave it back?"

"Mother already has the lies. She will not wish to see it again."

"Are you sure?" the Guard asks.

I narrow my eyes into slits. "Are you questioning me?"

It's at that point something appears to click in the Guard. He backs up. "No, ma'am. Not at all."

"Do not grab me again."

"Yes, ma'am. Of course. I'm so sorry." He stumbles over the words as much as he does his own feet in his hurry to get away.

A real Enforcer probably wouldn't have let him go. That part of me urges me to follow him, but I resist and turn away.

The buzz is still there from my drops, but no one looks at me as I pass them. I wander around another few minutes before I once again disappear into the shadows of the buildings and make my way back to the Caverns.

Asher is waiting as before and he seems to sense immediately the waves of energy I'm producing. "Are you all right?"

"I'm fine," comes my clipped response.

He doesn't push for an answer and for that I'm grateful.

For the next several hours we wait—silently—for the word to come, and when it does, I still don't know how to feel.

Several people had come to the spot marked by the lotus according to the missive. Each one had come separately or, at the most, in a pair. None seemed the least surprised to find only a tiny stack of papers. They'd only paused long enough to grab one, pretend to read the sign they were hidden behind, and go on their way.

Six people came in total. Not many, but it's a start. And I'll take what I can get.

Kara also stated that the Enforcers this evening were nowhere near what they had been at the earlier drop, which tells me Mother has been watching patterns and we need to change them up.

For the next few days, with the help of our newest members, we continue to chip away at Mother's pedestal. We change around the times we pass out the information on what this city really was, what Dr. Friar has done, and what Mother really is. Twice we run out of what Evangeline is calling membership packets because of the people wanting to join. Especially since Enforcers have stepped up their patrols. Mother has made the curfew even earlier, and twice now a Guard has attacked an innocent person for no reason other than they were in a place longer than they should have been.

It's also becoming extremely clear that Mother's defectors are expecting an experienced leader out of me. And, at first I was sure I could do it, but I find myself second-guessing every decision I make and every request I ask of them. I'm so un-confident in my leadership skills that I've started going to Asher first so he can help me make the right choice. I remember from the Surface how well he knows his way around a political power play, having lived in one his entire life.

The one thing I'm sure of, even though Asher and Father don't agree with me, is that I can't stop getting my hands dirty just because we're gaining members. I can't just sit around and do nothing.

So I go out into the crowds of Citizens with my mask on to extend some kindness to whomever I can. People are still disappearing. Still dying. The Enforcers are still out in full force. I can't tell if Mother is bringing more into the fold or if it just appears that way. But either way, I can't let her scare tactics work. So, despite the risk, I go out of my way to show the Citizens that the Underground is there to help anyone who needs it. And that while Mother is something to fear, I'm not, and I'm not afraid of her.

Even though my efforts are small—bandaging and kissing the knees of a little girl, pressing credits into hands of people I know need it, distracting Enforcers so the Citizens can breathe a little easier when they're out and about—the mixed looks of shock, relief, joy, and gratitude on their faces when they realize it's really me, is giving me faith that I'm offering them hope that things can be different. If they want them to be.

Chapter Sixteen

Anyone who even dares to wear the mask is considered a traitor of Elysium and is therefore a threat to our fair city. If you find someone, no matter who they are, shoot them on sight.

—Mother's instructions to Guards

Evie

It's not surprising that it doesn't take long for Mother to call another assembly. Despite her increased security measures, the earlier curfews, and her ever-present Enforcers, nothing has stopped the trickle of people who've decided to join. I'm positive it hasn't been lost on Mother that the reason her Enforcers can't catch the mask wearers is because the Citizens are protecting us.

Enforcers and Guards have stepped up their patrol, but there are simply not enough of them to keep up with our growing numbers. And no matter how often or how close they get to catching us, the Underground has remained so far untouched. That doesn't mean we let our own guard down. Even so, I decide I need to make an actual appearance at Mother's assembly.

"Absolutely not!" Father slams his fist on the table, causing everything on it to bounce. We're in the artifact-turned-War Room, where I've called another meeting. "It's ludicrous, completely irrational, and an unnecessary risk to show up there."

"I've been going out every day," I say calmly. "It's no more of a risk than that, and we have everything to gain by going."

"Name one thing."

"For most of these people, Mother is still the boogeyman who hides under their beds and in their closets. But if I can visibly rattle her before everyone in Elysium, it will show she's just a human like the rest of us."

"You showing up isn't going to rattle her. She'll just clap and an Enforcer will capture you." He shakes his head.

"Not kill?" Asher asks.

Father shakes his head. "The meeting she held this morning with the Enforcers explicitly stated that if the person behind the mask was you, you were to be taken alive. Anyone else would be quietly eliminated."

Evangeline tugs on her ear. "Why quietly eliminate anyone else? Wouldn't you want to make an example of them?"

"No," Asher says. "If you publicly eliminate them, you make a martyr of them. That's the last thing she wants."

"Then why not quietly capture Evie and kill her, too?"

"Mother made me a martyr already. There was a reason for

it." I glance to Father, who shrugs. "But we haven't figured that out yet."

"And not to mention, you know where you've been hiding and who's keeping you. If she captures you, Conditioning you and getting answers from you will be easy."

"Another reason not to go," Father says.

"I don't have to actually be there," I explain. "Just virtually."

"I don't think I understand."

"We got into the camera system before, we can do it again. I just have to transmit instead of receive."

"It's going to be harder to push a signal than to just piggyback off one to see it," Asher says thoughtfully.

"But it's doable, right?"

"Technically, yes, but I don't think we have a long enough time frame to figure out how to get in. After Joseph, Mother probably has a million firewalls in her system to prevent anyone from doing what he did. And I don't think we have another person willing to open them for us." Asher looks to Father, who shakes his head.

"Well, I don't need *every* Slate in Elysium to see me. Just the holoscreens in the Square so Mother can. What if we just managed to splice into the lines supplying video to the Square? Couldn't we push a signal from there?"

Father steeples his fingers and presses them to his lips. "With your training, I suppose you could. But I don't think you'd be able to keep it open for long. The people in the Palace

Wing would cut you off as soon as they realized what was going on."

"I only need a few seconds."

"I can help," Asher says.

He was a huge help before, it probably couldn't hurt to have him with me again. I nod to tell him I agree.

"I suppose that's it then," Father says. "There's no changing your mind." I shake my head and he sighs. "I have to get back to Mother. With everything going on, she's naturally twitching if I'm out of her sight for too long. Right now she thinks I'm just taking more samples from the anthropomorphic substrate in Three."

I shudder to think of the somehow living creatures made of green muck oozing around Three. "How's that going?"

"Well, we've found that Dr. Friar's device makes them bubble."

I blink and then shake my head. Nope. Don't want to know more. "Are they a danger to us here?"

"No. They respond more like jellyfish. No actual intelligence and they seem to be quite happy staying mostly where they are."

"Good to know." And . . . that's enough of that. If they're not a danger to me, I've got other things to worry about.

I dismiss the meeting and Father and Nadia leave, Father toward Elysium, Nadia in the general direction of the main part of the Caverns.

Asher and I wait, slowly counting down the thirty minutes after Father leaves to make the same journey. Asher squeezes my hand before we go. A subtle *I support you, but be careful,* that I return before I lead the way to the tunnels above the Square. It's not an easy feat today. Twice I have to stop and hide because Mother has her Enforcers in the tunnels. I have to admit, I'm second-guessing this plan with every second that passes.

But we finally make it to the designated location and with our knowledge of connecting our holo-projector to it from before, we easily do the same again. Hopefully, we're not setting off any alarms in the central monitoring center, but there's no way to tell unless they show up here looking for us. Connecting our own camera is a bit more tricky, and sweat trickles into my eyes as before, but finally I think I've managed to get everything set up.

So we hunker down in our spot, keeping an ear out for anyone coming our way. We kill time glancing around the Square with the cams, until Mother decides to grace us with her presence. I'm pleasantly surprised to see six people in the Square wearing masks. The masks they're wearing are obviously not as advanced as the ones we've made. They're extremely crude, like the one Asher first made, but it's the thought that counts. Considering we've only been at this a little over a week, the fact that six people *not* in our original group have decided to put their lives on the line to stand with me of their own accord warms my heart. So I decide to try and figure out a way to make more and get them to the people that need/want them. Solidarity is the key to this particular lock.

However, it does make me extremely worried for them. They're not as observant as I am, and Enforcers are quick. I wish I had some way to communicate with Kara and Tate to try and help the Citizens, but it's too late now. It's just another thing to add to my to-do list. For now, I sit on pins and needles while the masked Citizens move around and manage to steer clear of the Enforcers with the help of their fellow Citizens.

I'm impressed with the way they're working together. Considering everything that's at stake. The fact that those not wearing masks are helping those who are is, in a word, amazing.

Finally a hush falls over the crowd and Mother steps onto the stage. She's clearly wearing one of her "power suits." But this one is subtler. It's blue, probably in the hopes of seeming calming, and its cut and shape are more feminine. It highlights just how gorgeous she is. But even a rose has thorns.

She surveys the people around her. I notice every time she sees someone in a mask, because her whole body tenses and her eyes take on this wild look, but then it fades and she moves on. As if their presence means nothing to her.

Finally she clears her throat, an unnecessary move considering everyone is already quiet, and folds her hands over the top of her podium.

"People of Elysium. Last week, as you all know, I had to make the necessary but regrettable decision to liberate Elysium from the negative impacts of one of our own. It was necessary that I do so publicly so that my children see that although his decisions to betray his brothers and sisters led to the death of my daughter, I am, as always, merciful."

"Merciful?" Asher's voice is filled with derision. "How is murdering someone merciful?"

"Mother has a warped way of seeing things," I respond, then focus back in on what she's saying.

"My decision has upset a few of you, but I assure you that was not my intent. I only meant to cleanse Elysium of the affliction that the Surface Dweller has brought upon us. I was fearful of his influence becoming a cancerous malignancy among our proud and virtuous people.

"While I understand that my resolution of this matter has troubled you, I must insist that this situation with the masks and the lies that are being spread about our great city, including Dr. Friar and myself, stop immediately."

She gestures toward the left side of the stage, where Dr. Friar stands in a relaxed but regal manner. He puffs up his chest a little when Mother continues.

"Dr. Friar has done nothing to deserve this mistreatment. His development of the nanite technology—the technology our city uses to prevent pressure sickness and other ailments that once decimated our population—deserves acclaim and respect. Not intolerance and fabrications."

Father stiffens and his face reddens at her words, but he says nothing. Mother's right. The person who developed the nanite technology does deserve acclaim and respect. It's a shame that hasn't happened and that the man who's helped Mother turn it against her people is the one getting all the credit.

"As far as my Enforcers, they are merely vessels that I employ to keep my children safe. They are not, as the fabricators would have you believe, something to fear. Unless, of course, you are members of the terrorist cell that is using an effigy of my fallen daughter to spread their fallacies. In the name of peace, and to preserve all that she stood for, I will no longer tolerate these injustices."

Her voice hardens and she glares into the crowd of people at her feet.

"If you are a member of this extremist group, if you dare to defile the memory of my daughter by wearing the mask, if you are responsible for misleading my children with their lies, I will have no choice but to have you brought to me, where you will be prosecuted to the fullest extent of the law."

Enough! I think, pulling on my mask. I can't stand to hear any more of her nonsense. I want to stand and scream, "Stop using me to justify your agenda!" But I only nod once to Asher, and suddenly the image of me with my mask on pops onto the screen behind Mother. I don't say anything. I wait for the buzz in the audience to catch her attention. She trails off midsentence, frowning, but doesn't turn around, so I say, "Mother."

Mother spins around, but before she can see me on the screen behind her, my image is gone.

The chaos that ensues is alarming. The crowd is in an uproar, Mother is screeching something to her Enforcers, who have dived into the crowds, and people are running, trampling those in their way as they try to escape the Enforcers.

That's when a familiar sound tears through the bedlam. A gunshot. It's followed by the kind of silence that you can feel. I can only stare at the Enforcer whose arm is still extended, her fingers still wrapped around the grip of a gun. Her eyes are barely visible, but in them I can see the same thing that I'm sure is in mine. Disbelief warring with self-condemnation as she stares down at the boy who can't be any older than ten, bleeding out at her feet. And centimeters from his fingers, splattered with his blood, is one of our masks.

Chapter Seventeen

*The death of the child at the assembly today was an unfortunate
but necessary show of force. My daughter must be taught a lesson
for her insolence.*

—Mother's journal

Evie

We run—Asher and I—as soon as I disconnect all the wires
and shove them in my bag. We crawl as fast as we can on our
hands and knees, practically sliding down the ladder, pounding on the wall until Nadia opens it. We race down the
corridor—Nadia calling after us, asking us what happened—
until we reach the War Room. I lower myself so I'm sitting
on a chair. My legs are jelly and I just don't think I can stand
anymore.

I killed him. Not with my own hand, but I might as well
have.

Asher leans against the wall. His hands are balled into fists,
which are clenched so tightly they're bloodless. He keeps
swallowing as if there's something in his throat. I know the

feeling. I have it, too. The need to cry. To scream. To rage at the unfairness of this all. But I can't.

Tears solve nothing. Emotions are worthless. They only show weakness.

The mask is still on my face. I can feel it tugging at my skin. I rip it off and glare at it, before throwing it at the door and turning away. Nadia and Evangeline step into the room I don't know how long later. Nadia looks a little shell-shocked, so I'm assuming Evangeline told her what happened.

Evangeline immediately takes the seat next to me and grasps my hands in hers. "Evie—"

Right away tears burn the backs of my eyes. I pull away, twisting in the chair to shove onto my feet, but my legs still don't want to support my weight and I have to grab the table for support.

"Don't. Just . . . don't." I can't handle this with her. Not right now.

"It wasn't your fault," she says quietly.

Slowly, I lower myself back down into the chair, trying unsuccessfully to blink the tears away. But they just keep dripping, falling one by one onto the back of my hand. I know she's right, deep down, but I still can't help but feel like it is. My mask. My rebellion. My decision to try and push Mother.

"I stayed behind to see what happened until Mother forced everyone back to their apartments," Evangeline says. I peer up at her through blurry eyes. "It was an accident, Evie. A misunderstanding, actually. Someone dropped the mask when that Enforcer got too close. The boy saw it and, no one knows why, but he was reaching to pick it up. I assume the Enforcer shot because that's what her orders were. That's what most are assuming."

"That doesn't make me feel better." My voice wavers when I speak. In fact I think it's worse. The boy wasn't even part of the Underground and he was killed because of me.

"Well it should!" Nadia says in her typical, no-nonsense tone. "It proves everything you've been trying to show everyone. It is horrible. No doubt about it. But that Enforcer revealed more about Mother in that second than you could have in six months."

"But was it worth an innocent dying for it?"

"No," Asher says. "It absolutely wasn't worth it. Nothing is worth taking another life. But *this* life is on Mother's hands, and that Enforcer's, not yours. And it's been done. There's nothing we can do to change it. We can only make sure he didn't die in vain."

I stare at him. How am I supposed to do that?

I guess the only thing I can think of is to keep doing what I'm doing. But I don't think that's enough now. The random acts of kindness are still needed, especially now, because my people need to know someone cares, but they aren't going to be enough, either. I need for Mother to realize her ivory tower isn't as safe and impenetrable as she thinks it is.

"I have an idea," I say slowly, finally putting into words the plan that's been formulating in my head for weeks. "We've spliced into the cameras twice now, but we can't keep doing that. With the increased security measures Mother's put into practice, and more she's sure to put in now, we're going to have to access the central monitoring completely."

"How?" Asher asks.

"I can install a program that will run in the background of the mainframe—so Mother won't even know it's there no matter how hard she looks—that will allow me complete control of the computer from here using a power line communication system." At least I *should* be able to. If all my time with the Enforcer manuals Father managed to pilfer for me after the almost-mishap the last time has paid off. "That way we can use our terminals *here* to access everything *there*. And at the same time, the computer will appear to be completely operational, except Mother won't be able to access the visuals or audios from the cameras."

"Wouldn't Mother be able to fix that?" Nadia asks.

"That's the best part," I say with a grim smile. "I can"— should be able to—"program it in such a way that there is absolutely no way to even access that part of the code without a data cube that will supply the rest of the 'key.'" I hold up one of the cubes. "But I think we need to take it a step further. We need to cut her off from being able to use it as well. I'm not going to lose another Citizen because they got caught helping me. This way we can control the only way she has to communicate citywide, leaving her blind, deaf, and mostly mute. It should be easy enough, especially if we cause a little bit of a problem first."

"What kind of problem?" Asher asks.

"We set off the alarms. All of them. Fire, water breach,

Surface Dweller, everything. The Guards and Enforcers will be going insane trying to figure out what to do. So will Mother. I can slip in as an Enforcer, run to the CMR, and get the access codes we need. Plus, it has the added benefit of scaring Mother when she examines the very last bit of camera footage we leave her and she sees her little masked friend has infiltrated her sanctuary."

Asher nods. "I like it, but I think we need to go even bigger . . ." He taps a finger to his lips. ". . . like deleting the Citizen registry?"

Both Evangeline and I shake our heads quickly. "No. If we do that, the turrets go off," Evangeline says.

"With nothing to compare samples to, the turrets will just assume *everyone* is a Surface Dweller and will probably kill everyone," I explain when Asher looks confused.

Asher purses his lips. "Can it be done, though?"

Evangeline and I exchange a glance. "Yes, but, like we said . . ."

Asher interrupts me. "If it *can* be done, so can controlling what the turrets respond to. Right? Why don't you just take over the entire system? If you're going to take Mother's eyes and ears, take her arms, too."

Nadia shrugs. "That's . . . actually a really good idea."

I nod. "I agree."

Evangeline still looks slightly unhappy, but says, "You better have as good of a plan for getting out of there alive as you do for getting yourself in unnoticed."

"Of course. The maintenance tunnels."

"When do you want to do this?" Asher asks.

"Today. She'll never think we're planning something of this caliber so soon."

A few hours later, I stand at a hidden door leading to Elysium's maintenance tunnels. I've spent the last two hours memorizing the way through them to the Palace Wing. I close my eyes and take a deep relaxing breath, then another, counting to ten before opening them again.

I turn to leave, but Evangeline touches my shoulder. "You remember the way?"

"Yes."

"Remember to keep your hood up and your face blank. That way even if there's someone in the tunnels they won't think anything of it. And remember, the less emotion the Citizens see, the better."

"Evangeline! I know. I've been going out there as an Enforcer for almost two weeks," I say, trying not to laugh. I'm not sure if it's nerves that make me want to laugh or the fact that she's obviously nervous and doing exactly what I would do.

"When you get to the Palace, keep as close to the shadows as you can. Enforcers never stray too far away from them."

I smile. "I know."

"Don't stop and talk to anyone, even if you recognize them. Enforcers don't have friends."

I fight the urge to roll my eyes again. For real this time. We've been over this hundreds of times in the last few hours. "I know."

"And if another Enforcer stops to talk—"

"I'll tell them I'm on a mission for Mother," I finish with a smile.

She pulls the hood over my face. My mask is tucked safely in the shirt of my dress. I'll need it for when I trigger the alarm.

Nerves threaten to attack me again, but I clear my mind of everything except what I need to do, both hoping for, and worrying about, that click that makes all my worries go away.

I turn and step into the tunnel without saying a word. The door shuts behind me and I take a moment to get my nerves in line. I can't shake the feeling that I won't be returning here.

But then I take a deep breath and move forward, taking what could be the last steps I ever take.

I focus completely on the path I've only ever seen on screen. It's supposed to be straight for twenty meters, then down four flights, then straight again for six junctions, then a left at the seventh—

A scraping sound breaks into my thoughts, and I stop walking, trying to focus my hearing to where I heard the sound. I don't hear it again, so I slowly start forward, pausing only momentarily at one of the junctions.

I glance around and continue forward, but a young man, a few years older than myself, runs around the corner. Not looking where he's going, he barrels right into me, knocking us both to the ground.

Immediately I push myself back up and tug at the cloak,

making sure that none of my skin shows, and turn my head so my face isn't visible.

The young man jumps up and immediately starts apologizing. His heart is racing, visible in the bulging vein in his neck.

I want to tell him it's okay, that I won't hurt him, but that would blow my cover, so I only shove past him. "I will not be so lenient next time, Citizen."

"Yes, ma'am. Of course." He takes off in a fast walk in the opposite direction.

I don't start to breathe again until the echoes of his shoes disappear several moments later. I push away from the wall and hurry on, wondering if I should wear the mask now or keep it off.

I decide to keep it off because I'm so nervous even my lungs hurt as I breathe. I don't want to impede them further by slapping that thing on my face.

When the architecture of the tunnel changes, I take a moment to straighten my clothes again and brush off all the dirt before attaching the mask and readjusting the hood. I find the door that leads to the marble hallways of the Palace Wing without any trouble. According to the missive Father sent a few minutes ago, Mother should be out of the Palace Wing right now, along with most, if not all, of her Guards and Enforcers to determine how my earlier breach of the Square's vid system happened.

But I have to hurry; I doubt she's going to leave the safety of her nest for long.

I push out the door and glance around, looking for people that aren't supposed to be there. Namely other Enforcers. Father's intel is usually spot-on, but after today? Who knows?

I take a moment to orient myself. I know the Palace Wing by heart, but it's been a few months, not to mention I've been through a complete memory wipe. I dart down the path I've outlined in my head to where the CMR is, sticking as close to the walls as possible, and moving quietly in order to hear other people before they hear me. I run until I get to the Citizen's entrance to the Palace Wing. I hit the emergency lock on the tube, shutting off the Palace Wing from the rest of the complex. A necessary safety precaution should there be a leak in this Sector or on the other side, so that as few lives are lost as possible.

Of course, it also allows me to use it as a time delay.

When I reach the door to the CMR, I'm uneasy. I thought this would be harder. Not to mention that déjà vu feeling is back, and that's *never* a good sign. It's usually the harbinger of bad things to come.

Mother is far from stupid. She wouldn't just let me saunter right in here. Then again, she *is* arrogant, and the arrogance is what's going to get her in the end. She may not think we're brave enough—or stupid enough if I really want to admit the truth to myself—to do what we're doing.

The Guard stationed inside is completely fixated on the monitors in front of him, and for the first time in a long time, I feel that little click in my head and all of my senses become heightened. Even though part of me is scared of what I can do in Enforcer mode, I don't feel out of control. In fact, I feel the most in command of myself I've felt in a long time. And I'm going to need as much restraint as I have because with him in that room, I'm going to have to go in hard and fast.

So I do.

I yank open the door. I'm behind him before he even has a chance to turn his head to see who's come in. I hit him with just enough power on the back of the neck that I knock him unconscious and he falls to the floor. After a quick double check to make sure he's only knocked out, I drag him out of the room and into another, locking him in before returning to the CMR.

Following the information I remember, and the advice from Asher, I open the wall where the computers for the cameras are stored and insert the data cube into the computer. Then—after taking a deep breath, wiping my sweaty hands on my pants, and saying a silent prayer—I slowly start tearing down the security walls in the computer until I'm looking at nothing but code. With a few keystrokes, in my program goes. It'll block Mother from using the cameras in any way and run a loop of the past two hours, giving me a much longer time frame before it's discovered the camera system has been tampered with.

I shut down the turret system, remove and redirect their power sources, and then delete the program that controlled them so all the turrets are permanently powered off. Then, with fingers crossed, I delete the entire Citizen register, watching the cameras carefully to make sure the turrets don't do anything.

I think this is the only time I've been grateful for Mother's curfew.

I wait five frustrating minutes for a reaction, and only then, when nothing happens, do I risk breathing a sigh of relief. I've done it. I've essentially made Mother blind and deaf and removed her claws.

I'm sweating, despite the chill in the air, and my heart is racing, but I feel great. Now, I move on to the fun part.

I add in another program that will run—hopefully unnoticed—in the background, automatically setting off the alarms throughout the city and Palace Wing at random times and places. All I have to do is pull one and the rest will follow in a randomized pattern.

When I'm certain I'm completely finished and every trace of me even being here has been erased, I drag the still unconscious Guard back to his rightful spot. If I'm lucky, no one will even know I was in this room.

When I pass the closed doors of the tunnel entrance, I see the Guards frantically trying to open them, but I keep going. I've been here entirely too long. They've probably alerted Mother, and I have no wish for a confrontation. Yet.

When I see the little red lever on the wall, I pull it, but I don't stop even though the bells of the alarm echo in my head. I just keep going before hiding back in the maintenance tunnels, ripping off my mask, and hurrying back to the Caverns, trying not to laugh as a giddy feeling overtakes me.

Chapter Eighteen

Collect the body of the Guard. Hang him from the Square with a noose. His idiocy annoys me.

—Enforcer orders from Mother

Evie

Words fail me as I stare at the image on the screen in front of me. If I didn't know better, I would have thought someone was playing a nasty trick on me. Or that I was having a nightmare after sleep dragged me down following the all-nighter Asher and I pulled getting our new command center set up in the artifact room. It took some time to figure out how to connect Elysium's mainframe into the antiquated machines we have in the Caverns. We don't need to access *everything* Elysium's computer network can do, just the cameras and Father's Slate. So as long as we don't try to view the whole of Elysium at the same time, our devices work well enough. Not fantastic. Not even great. But they'll do.

So when we pull up a camera in the Square and see the

body hanging from the beams of the grandstand, I can't even figure out how I feel, let alone know what to say.

My fault is the only thing that comes to mind. She killed again and it's my fault. Because I didn't think it through. I reacted instead of being proactive. I didn't take her claws away. I just pissed her off.

I should have anticipated this. I should have known she wouldn't go after me personally. She'd use innocent people to draw me out. I've backed her into a corner. What choice did I give her?

I turn and walk from the room. Away from Asher, and Nadia, and Evangeline. They're all waiting for me to do something, because I'm supposed to be in control and know what to do, but I can't. Every decision I make leads to someone's death.

Hell, I've essentially killed *two* people in less than twenty-four hours alone.

I don't know where I'm intending to go. I head toward the bathing area, but part of me wants to march straight up to Mother and just take her out. Like Father wanted. Like maybe I should have done in the first place. Another part says that by doing that, I'm playing right into her game. And yet another part of me reminds me that sometimes the only way to win a game is not to play it at all.

I have to be honest, that part of me is looking more and more right. Yeah, people would still be locked in their gilded cage and the people that have died over the past week or so would still be dead, but if I gave up, Mother would regain control and eventually people would forget what she's done and move on. But most importantly, they'd live.

I can almost hear what Gavin would tell me if he were here right now. That it's too late. Even without me, the people have seen Mother's true colors. The rebellion would continue without me.

"Good," I mumble. "Let them continue it. I can't take making any more deadly mistakes."

"But that would be your worst one yet," the shadow of Gavin's memory says. *"Without you, they'd lose. They're counting on you. You've become more than just a leader to them. You're their symbol."*

"Yeah. A symbol of death," I say and listen as my voice echoes back at me. *Of death. Of death. Of death.*

I sigh. I'm talking to myself. That's fantastic. Keep that up and soon I'll be as crazy as Mother.

I stop then and pause as I realize how dark it's gotten. The lighting that's usually in this section stopped a little ways back. I can see it a few meters behind me. Where am I?

I was heading to the bathing area, but obviously wasn't paying attention, so where have I ended up?

For a moment, panic tingles in my veins as scenarios of me lost and running around endless tunnels here swirl in my mind. But then I notice a big sign nailed to the wall.

WARNING. DO NOT PASS THIS POINT. ELECTROMAGNETIC FIELD ENDS IN FIFTY METERS. Below it is a small yellow triangle with a picture of a magnet inside it.

I stare at it. I know what it means. If I keep going, my

nanos will hardlock again and my memories will disappear. But what's past that point? Why is this even here? A memory hits me almost between the eyes. How Gavin got down to Elysium in the first place.

An emergency exit.

It had been what we were looking for when we'd tried escaping Mother the first time. Even Father's journal mentioned that there were other ways to escape besides the submarines, he just didn't know where they were. We'd assumed they were all in Elysium because we obviously hadn't even known the Caverns existed, but is it possible this is what he meant?

Obviously the workers would need a way into the Caverns as they were working. I'd thought everything had been brought down by submarine, but how much cheaper would it have been if they'd just been able to bring their machines down through tunnels? Tunnels that could then be used as ventilation and an emergency exit during the construction phases, and then again after it was built. You wouldn't want only one way out. You'd want several, so people weren't trapped.

A buzz tingles through me and I turn around, a smile splitting my lips. If I'm right, then I may have just found how I'm going to remove the thousand-plus people from Elysium right under Mother's nose.

I retrace my steps until I'm standing back in the yawning Caverns where our dugouts are. Nadia is speaking with one of her people: a man with skin darker than the color of Dr. Gillian's on the Surface and hair the color of steel. I've seen him around. He's at least thirty centimeters taller than me and his arms are twice as large, but he's soft-spoken and one of the only people here who hasn't completely shunned me.

I don't know his name, but that should change. I need to know the people here. Maybe if I made more of an effort to get to know *them,* they'd be willing to get to know *me.*

As I approach, Nadia holds her hand up to me and I wait impatiently for her to finish speaking with him. I catch something about the crops he's been tending in the very small section by the bathing area. I don't know how they've been feeding everyone here with that small amount of food, but I determine that that will be another thing I will learn before the day is out.

When they finally finish speaking, Nadia turns to me with raised eyebrows. "You were not gone as long as I expected. Have you remembered you are not responsible for Mother's actions?"

I smile at her and bow my head in a nod. "Who is that?"

Her eyes widen and she turns her head toward where the man walks to the small agriculture area. "Jayden? He's in charge of food rations."

"And that small section is enough to feed everyone here?"

"We've kept our population small on purpose, but yes. Mostly. Although sometimes we have to pilfer from the Agriculture Sector."

Now it's my time to be surprised. "And Mother's never caught on?"

"Not that I'm aware. There are no cameras there and we

go only after the workers are gone for the evening. We're careful not to take too much." She sighs. "We've gotten quite adept at 'borrowing' things we need. As I mentioned when you first arrived, the life support system was meant only as a temporary measure. We've kept it alive by stealing parts and tools from Sector Three, but eventually it will fail. I'm not sure what we'll do when that happens."

"I think I can help with that," I say, smiling, and start to walk toward the War Room. "Where do the tunnels by the bathing area lead? I saw a warning sign."

"We believe they once led to the Surface," she confirms. "The old maps say that they're ventilation. Of course, we have no way of knowing for sure. The only thing we know is that anyone who gets too close to the edge of the field—"

"—loses their memories," I finish for her.

She nods. "I have five people that Eli has repaired from that. All were sent to see if we could escape. One even tried twice. He never came back. We hope he made it out, but . . ." She splays her hands out and shrugs. "We tried giving them printed instructions after that, when we realized what was happening. But they just got lost and eventually found their way back. So unless Lenore returns and can make that a nonissue, we're stuck."

I furrow my brow. She speaks about Lenore with such familiarity. "You knew her?"

"Of course. Who else would have given me nanos?"

I nod and glance around the Caverns. "How much room

do you have here? If food weren't an issue, how many do you think you could accommodate?"

She shrugs. "We never came up with a capacity limit. We dug out enough cutouts for fifty people. I suppose there's probably about twenty or so more rooms in the empty buildings."

I purse my lips. "What about this space here?" I gesture to the space between the empty buildings and the end of the Cavern where the bathing areas are.

"Depends on how much room you want to give them, I suppose. If I had to put a number to it, I'd say between the rooms and this space here, two hundred would really be pushing the limits. I wouldn't personally want to go over a hundred."

"Less than a tenth of the population of Elysium, then." I press my lips into a thin line. It's not ideal, but Gavin should be coming with Lenore any day now. With any luck, we could have the people out of here and on the Surface before we ran into capacity issues.

Nadia tilts her head. "What are you planning?"

I don't say anything, I just continue leading the way to where I left the others. Everyone is still there. Asher is talking with Father through the vid screen. A huge weight lifts off my shoulders. At least that part works. No more having to pass around notes that could possibly never make it to their intended recipients.

Asher glances up when I step in. He closes his eyes in relief. "Are you all right?" he asks when he opens them again.

"Yes. And I have an idea I want to run past all of you."

Evangeline gestures to my seat. "We're all here. Even Father."

"It's not safe in Elysium anymore," I start.

"It never was," Asher says.

I ignore him and continue as if he didn't say anything. "Mother's already proven she doesn't care who gets caught in the cross fire. She isn't even bothering to hide it's her anymore."

"She's unstable."

"She was *never* stable," Asher says. I scowl at him and he shrugs. "It's true."

"She's more now than ever. The Guard that was killed was the one in the control room," Father says. "She killed him 'for the breach of safety in the Palace Wing.'"

"You heard that from her?" I ask.

"Everyone here did. She tore into the Enforcer that killed the boy. I was in this office with my door closed. She was at the other end of the hall in the control room with *that* door closed. I heard her clear as a bell. I wasn't surprised to hear the gunshot. I thought for sure she'd had the Enforcer killed. But I risked a peek out of my door and saw her at the end. She told the Enforcer to collect the body of the Guard and hang him from the Square with a noose. He was the one in charge and he's the one who had to pay the price for the breach of safety in the Palace Wing." He rubs his hands over his face. "I've only seen her lose her cool like that once before. That was when she realized Lenore and I were together."

I remember how Lenore described it, but still. "She didn't

kill the Enforcer though. She hasn't gone off the deep end completely, but it's probably only a matter of time. Which means that my plan is even more important. We *have* to start removing people from Elysium and bringing them here."

"I must object," Nadia says. "It is an unnecessary risk to my people. Not to mention yours. If you're caught . . ."

"It's a risk we have to take. I can't have any more innocent people on my conscience. All I'm doing is provoking Mother with these raids. I'm at a crossroads. I either do nothing or I keep going. If I keep going, she's going to find us here eventually anyway."

Nadia doesn't look happy about it, but nods.

"Why here, though?" Asher asks.

I tell them about my discovery of the possible escape tunnels and that when Gavin gets here with Lenore, we'll be able to just escort them out.

"Will they go?" Evangeline asks.

"Mother has done a good job of terrifying them about the Surface, but that commercial we aired from when this was a resort was ingenious. It has a few questioning what the Surface is really like. If we start handing out information about the reality of it, it shouldn't be that hard to persuade a lot of them."

That could of course cause Mother to kill more in the meantime, but I don't see another way. "So we continue to do our normal maskings, but with pamphlets about the Surface . . ."

"Since we have control over the network now, we might as well use it. We could show them some of these pictures and stuff." Asher gestures to the artifacts still spread around the room.

"It could be a good distraction, too," Evangeline pipes in. "When you finally get a few people to leave, just make sure the Enforcers are occupied with a masking."

"I'll keep my ear to the ground and see who's ready to go," Father says.

"Kara and Tate could help find out who's ready to leave, too."

"Slow down. There's nothing in place here to make sure people aren't working with Mother," Nadia says.

"Blindfold them so they can't see the way. Once they're here, they can't leave," Asher says. "And maybe we do a security screening. Check them and their belongings. I'd also suggest that we confine them to an area constantly watched by one of us so they can't escape."

"No!" I slam my hand down on the table. "These people aren't the enemy. If we do that, they're just trading one cell for another. The point is to give them freedom."

"It only takes one person to screw everyone else," Asher says quietly. "Are you willing to risk everyone? It's only for a short time."

I glare at him. "No imprisonment." But I do see the point he's trying to make. "But fine on the not going back. We can set up a guard at the entrance to the tunnel."

"And the search," Nadia says. "Just to make sure."

I don't like it, but I'm sure she's not going to budge on it, so I nod. "A search. Once. When they get here."

"Then it's set," Father says. "I need to make my breakfast appearance with Mother."

He disconnects and Nadia excuses herself to explain the new situation to her people. Evangeline, Asher, and I put together our first advertisement for the Surface.

We start that day, using the Guard's death as a reason for leaving. Still, it takes four days before we get our first couple to join us. Kara's the one who tells me about it. They're friends of hers. They're already members of the Underground, but the woman is pregnant. She and her husband are willing to risk the Surface if it means her daughter living in freedom.

So I escort them personally, while Tate and Asher distract the Enforcers by leading a masking. They meet me in the maintenance tunnel by their apartment. Kara's standing with them.

She smiles when I take off my mask and they both gasp. The woman says, her voice slightly breathless, "It *is* you. We'd been hearing rumors . . ." She glances to her husband, who's staring at me in awe.

"And the masks," he continues for her.

"But we didn't think they were true," they say together.

"Evelyn, this is Beca and Adam. Beca and Adam? Evelyn."

An uncomfortable smile tugs on the corners of my lips when the woman curtsies. "It's a pleasure to meet you," I say.

"No," Adam says. "It's our pleasure."

"We're just so excited to meet you! It means so much that you're willing to let us into the Underground." Beca pats her belly. "Considering."

Guilt tugs at me. They're risking so much for me. I hope I don't let them down. Or worse, get them killed. But . . . I have to admit it's probably safer for them to be there than here if they're going to insist on helping me. Which I have no doubts that they will.

Apologizing, I blindfold them. Shame and regret pull at my heart as I tie the black cloth around Beca's eyes, but she assures me she understands.

When they're both blind, I take Beca's hand and she takes her husband's. I lead them through the tunnels. When we get to the Caverns, it's Nadia who does the security check. I think Kara must have told them how different the people are here, because they don't do more than hesitate for a second when Nadia starts talking to them.

Evangeline takes them from there. Her naturally bubbly and welcoming nature is a huge help and I take a moment to watch the woman who birthed me talking to Beca about the baby and when it's due until their voices fade.

Over the next two weeks, we do six more transfers, using the chaos of the 'malfunctioning' alarm systems and the random masking to help divert attention and keep them away from the maintenance tunnels. People are a lot more willing to leave than I expected. The groups grow exponentially. Mostly families. It shouldn't surprise me, but it does. I thought for sure the bravest would be the ones with nothing to lose if things go wrong, but that apparently isn't the case.

The group I'm escorting now is the biggest yet at ten people. At this rate, we're going to reach our maximum way before I thought. But it keeps me so busy between maskings and these transfers that I can't think about how Gavin should be here by now.

I'm just about to turn down the corridor leading to the door to the Caverns when I hear the telltale sound of an Enforcer's shoes against the concrete.

My heart jumps into my throat. I glance around, looking for anything, and see a small maintenance closet. I don't think it'll hold all of us, but I don't have a choice. I slide as quietly as I can to the door and pull it open and gently push them into it. As the Enforcer gets closer, my heart slams harder against my chest. I squeeze in last and pull the door shut. My thumb searches frantically for a lock to turn to no avail.

"What's going on?" someone asks too loudly.

"Shh," I hiss. "Enforcer."

Instantly the word has the effect of everyone holding their collective breaths.

The Enforcer pauses at the door and I grip the doorknob like it's my lifeline. I bite my lip to keep from crying out in shock when the knob tries to twist in my hand. But I hold it as tightly as I can, hoping she'll just think it's locked.

The pressure on the doorknob fades, but I don't hear the Enforcer walk away. I listen carefully, as my training taught me, and barely hear the swish of her clothes as she, I assume, kneels to the ground. The swatch of light leaking underneath the door becomes dark in the middle and I have the worst feeling she's trying to peer under the door.

Please don't move, I think to the group with me. Stay as

still as statues. I keep my death grip on the door handle. My muscles are so tense they're screaming at me. Sweat drips down the middle of my back and I take the shallowest breath I can manage. Finally, the light returns, but I still don't budge. Even when she walks away and I'm sure she's gone, I wait for a long time. My hands cramp around the doorknob and my leg muscles are as taut as violin strings.

Eventually, when I know I can't stay any longer, I slowly twist the knob and peer into the corridor. "Stay here," I tell the group and venture a few more meters away to double- and triple-check the Enforcer's gone before I risk letting my group out of the closet.

I hurry them faster than I should to the door to the Caverns and then to the security checkpoint. I don't take a deep breath or relax until every single one of them is settled and Asher makes it back from the masking.

But the horrible feeling in my gut continues the rest of the day and into the next morning. I find out the reason why when Asher and I, on our way to do another masking, pass the broom closet I hid in . . . and see the Enforcer. She's propped up against the door as if sitting and waiting for us. Blood seeps from the hole in the dead center of her forehead.

CHAPTER NINETEEN

I dreamed of him again last night. Gavin. He came back to see me, but twenty years had passed for me, while none had passed for him. He didn't recognize me when he saw me. He passed right by without saying a word.

—EVIE'S JOURNAL

Evie

Six weeks. It's been six weeks of maskings and infiltrations into Elysium to move Citizens from there to the Caverns. Six weeks of sneaking around like thieves, worrying about the almost two hundred and fifty people now under my authority and protection in the Caverns, and six weeks of learning from Nadia and her people and trying to get the Citizens from Elysium to work *with* the people from the Caverns instead of being afraid of them. Not to mention six weeks without even a word of what happened to Gavin.

I stare at the Slate I snatched from Elysium. There is no extra space here. We can take on no more people. I've already pushed Nadia's limits by fifty people, but there's still so many people left on the other side. So many more that need to be free of Mother's tyranny.

But the food supply is not enough to sustain the people already here. The top priority on my to-do list is to secure more rations from the Agricultural Sector and the Fishery. And to figure out how much of a problem Sector Three really is. Or, more precisely, the anthropomorphic substrate affectionately known as the green goo. It's now causing structural integrity issues with the building. I can't spare any of my people to fix it and Mother doesn't seem to care one way or the other about it. The only thing she cares about in that section is the ooze.

And that's what Father has been working on to no avail. He's only managed to come up with a theory that the seawater seems to damage/kill them. Because in all the areas that have flooded, the green goo has lost all of it's viscosity and no longer consumes anything. He even touched it and nothing happened. I'm not sure how that'll help our situation with Three, but I've filed it away for later.

But my mind isn't on any of that. It's crept over, unbidden, as it has so many times in the last six weeks, to the image seared into my brain of the fallen Enforcer.

My mind slides over the details of the hours before we found her. Of the one wound. Of the way she was placed. An obvious assassination. One by another Enforcer. One more than likely ordered by Mother, because of her failure to find us. It didn't escape my notice then, or now, that that was an extreme move. One that makes me question how far I've pushed her, if she was willing to kill one of her most important weapons. Especially since Enforcers are an endangered species.

But, so far my plan is working. More and more people are carrying the masks. Each time something new pops up on a vid screen or a wall, or people wear the masks, Mother loses it more. And I'm not just talking about losing her place in Elysium. I'm talking everything.

She gets a little more unpredictable. A little more unstable. Unfortunately that means innocents suffering and dying. Two people died last week when a Guard came out at a masking and started firing into the crowd. But it's also showing the people who she really is, and every time one of them defects and turns to our side, that makes her even less sure of her position. Or at least that's what Father reports. But she's been keeping Father at arm's length, so his intel is increasingly unreliable.

It's been slow going since we took over the control of the main computer system and the cameras and turrets. Mother's had to resort to using her version of a town crier to try and mediate some of the damage we've done. It isn't working.

Gavin was right about the masks. It's taken off so much more than I think even he expected. I think even Father, whose only wish for the longest time *was* just to kill Mother, is quite pleased with our current progress and sees that staging deliberate and purposeful, yet veiled acts of protest against Mother will make her regime fall.

Gavin was definitely right. I wish there was a way I could tell him that his plan is working. And that, because of him, we're closer than ever to getting our people freedom.

"I miss you," I whisper into the air, wishing he could somehow hear, but knowing he can't.

A knock sounds and the door opens behind me. I turn and look to see Asher step in quietly. He's been nothing but a blessing during all of this. He's helped keep my feet under me with his unwavering support and willingness to share his political knowledge.

He smiles at me and takes a giant flourishing bow, before offering me a bouquet of flowers. The colors of every single one of my favorite flowers shine like a kaleidoscope.

"Happy birthday!"

My lips curve into a wobbly smile and tears spring into my eyes. Hopefully he'll see just the surface and not the fear—and most recently, hurt—that's filled me, thinking of Gavin. But I know better. No one's better at seeing the fake than Asher.

I take the proffered flowers and bury my face in the blooms, breathing in their sweet scents, and using these few moments to collect myself. I gather the memories of Gavin and lock them away.

When I pull my face from the flowers, I'm not forcing my smile any longer and the tears are safely tucked away.

"Thank you. These are lovely. I didn't even know it was my birthday."

But even as I say it, bits and pieces of old memories burst into my mind's eye. Most of the time there was no celebration. Pretty presents wrapped in even prettier paper sat on my vanity and Mother and I would have cake with our tea, but that was the extent of it.

Asher clears his throat, and smiles back. "Evangeline was talking about it with Eli a few weeks ago. I didn't think you remembered, so I was hoping to surprise you."

I crinkle my nose in another smile. "I'm very surprised."

"Liar," he says softly and taps my nose. "But I'll forgive you." He turns to my dresser and fiddles with my perfume bottles. Father snuck them out of the Palace Wing to try to fill in any remaining holes in my memory. So far it hasn't worked.

"So, what's on the agenda for today? More meetings? Vandalism? Random alarms and a carefully planned trip into the Palace Wing for more psychological warfare against Mother?" His voice sounds purposely bored, like he's checking things off my schedule and it's all old hat to him.

Suppressing a laugh, I press my face into the flowers again, looking over the blooms at him. He's trying to appear nonchalant, but his eyes are a storm of emotion. He's so much easier to read than Gavin was. He's scared I'll say yes to any of those things. But mostly he's worried because of my worry about Gavin.

Because of that last thought, because I don't want my best friend/maybe brother sad because I am, I force an even brighter smile. I walk over to him, putting a bounce in my step before threading my arm through his. I lay my head on his shoulder and look up at him.

"Did you know it's apparently my birthday?"

He meets my eyes in the mirror. "I'd heard something like that."

"I think we've worked hard up until now. One day off won't hurt things. Maybe the break will lull Mother into a false sense of security. I think we should make this a day of celebration. What do you think?"

A smile slowly spreads across his face as he watches me. "That sounds like an awesome idea."

He kisses the top of my head. Then we leave my room as I mentally cancel my plans for the day.

Slowly and carefully I cross the Cavern toward the cutout in the rock wall and the stone passageway that leads to the bathing area. I flip the OCCUPIED sign nailed to the rock outside of the bathing cavern, then remove my clothes and carelessly toss them aside. I slide into the pool of hot water with a hiss.

Sometime during the course of the day, the fact that Gavin isn't here hit me square in the chest. Something's wrong. It's been too long. He wouldn't have left me here this long by myself. I actually hope it's that he decided not to come back; that I, and my foolhardy decision to save my city from Mother, was just too much. But a worry is lodged deep in my heart that that's not what happened at all, and the reason he's not here is because something stopped him from returning. Endless possibilities of his horrible demise flash through my mind in a flood of unwanted thoughts. A sob escapes me and I press a hand to my mouth to push it and the blasted tears back in.

I slip farther into the pool, letting the water close over my head.

Asher has hinted that maybe something happened to Gavin, but I refuse to believe that. I'd feel it if he died. The string I've always felt tethering us together would have been snipped in half and I'd no longer feel him . . . but I do. I refuse to believe that he's dead. I want to go back up there, to find him, to see if anyone knows what's happened to him.

But if something did happen . . .

No! Don't think like that. I shove myself out of the water and stand on the earthen shelf, water dripping and pooling at my feet. I scoop my clothes from the ground, snatch two towels from the shelf, and wrap one around my body and the other around my hair. I stride in long, purposeful steps down the little walkway to the dressing area.

I force myself not to think about Gavin; I force myself not to worry about him. I'm not going to be *that* girl. The one who pines for her lover, moping around like a living corpse.

But when I glance up into the cracked and dirty mirror, water still dripping down my face, in my mind's eye I see the two of us as if it's a window to my past. We're walking hand-in-hand along the beach, and even though I feel awful and scared of almost everything, I'm happy. Because I'm with him. He makes me feel like I can do anything as long as he's with me.

Without warning, he spins me around and tugs so I tumble into his chest.

Laughing, I tilt my head up, but before I can say anything, his lips are on mine. I melt in his arms. Into his kiss.

His fingers flit at the waistband of my skirt, teasing the skin underneath. My head spins. I feel like I'm falling. But I don't want to stop. I want to just keep falling.

"I love you," he says. "I'll *always* love you."

It's then the bubble breaks and I find myself staring at my own reflection in the mirror. "You can't," I whisper, my voice hoarse and cracking with raw emotion. Anger, resentment, and sorrow fill me, crashing into me like a tidal wave and drowning every other feeling. "Because of you!" I glare at my reflection. At the girl who's me, yet not me. "Because of you!" I slam my fists into the mirror.

It explodes. The glass shatters, sending shards all over the cavern floor, slicing my hands in several places.

Pain blooms across my hands like the blood pouring from them.

Chapter Twenty

Dispose of the Tippet family. Inflict as much damage as you can before death. Make sure they know it is their leader *that kills them so unmercifully.*

—Enforcer orders from Mother

Evie

Damn it." I race across the room to press a washcloth into my palms.

The glass on the floor slices into my feet. I curse with each painful step. Just as I sit on the bench to check my wounds, one of the girls in the Underground bursts through the door. She glances around the room in an obvious panic. She frowns when she sees I'm the only one there, standing in my towel. Her eyes widen when she takes in the broken mirror and the bloody glass spread across the floor.

"Evie?"

For a minute I'm speechless.

How do I answer?

I lost control, but not in the Enforcer I'm-going-to-kill-anyone-who-moves kind of way. In a completely emotional and irrational kind of way that both embarrasses and pleases me. Surface girls—normal girls—throw temper tantrums all the time. They're not soulless automatons. They have real emotions.

However, all of this makes me look insane, and I can't help but remember a similar tantrum Mother had not so long ago. Just then Asher dashes into the room.

He stops short to stare at the blood soaking the cloths in my hand, then at the floor and the blood on the rock. His gaze rises to the mirror, before moving to my hands. His eyes close briefly. When he opens them, he gives me a look that has my stomach burning with guilt and dismay.

He pushes past the girl and, with a grunt, lifts me up. "Please clean up this mess for Evie." Then he carries me over the remaining glass, which crunches under his feet, and through the courtyard to the cutout in the rock that's my room, and places me on my cot.

My skin is on fire. I've never been so embarrassed. The courtyard was filled with people who saw Asher carrying me. It won't take long before the whole camp knows of my temper tantrum.

"What happened?"

"Nothing. Lost my temper. No big deal."

"Let me see." He kneels in front of me.

I hiss as he gently unfolds my hands and pulls the washcloth from them. He sighs and my stomach turns when I see the slices across my palms. It's not a pretty sight by any means. I look away.

"Come on. Let me bandage these."

His hands are gentle as he cleans, then wraps gauze around my hands and feet. The way the light plays up the gold hue in his hair makes me gasp at the suddenness of the déjà vu that hits me square between the eyes.

"I'm sorry," he murmurs. His touch turns even lighter. He reminds me so much of Timothy in this moment, I can only stare. Mother was right. He's practically a double of the boy I once loved. I want to cry as the last lock smashes open and every single forgotten memory bursts into life.

But I choke them back.

Still, my eyes sting and I sniff.

Asher looks up from where he's kneeling and he sighs, then leans forward. "I'm sorry, Evie. But you can't keep doing this to yourself. He'll come back when he can." What he leaves unsaid is clear as a bell. *If* he can.

I don't say anything; I just look away. He's right, of course.

"I can't pretend to know what you're going through," he continues. "But I know all this waiting you're doing. All the sleepless nights. All the food you *aren't* eating. All the time you spend just sitting, staring into space isn't helping you do what you wanted to do before he left. What he left to help you do. Save your people." He takes my chin in his fingers and forces me to look at him. "You can't help them if you can't help yourself."

Asher's right. I have to let go of the past and make the best of the present, to make a better future for everyone.

There's a knock on my makeshift door. Asher hesitates a second before he answers it, slipping out of the door to talk to whomever it is and leaving me to get dressed.

I pick my favorite dress: one with a loose, flowy fit. A frilly neckline, exposed shoulders, and an eyelet cutout pattern on the hemline and frilled sleeves. A gift Evangeline managed to smuggle in for my birthday. It's my "power" dress. A trick I picked up from Mother. Except it's not red like hers usually are, but white.

The color of innocence instead of the color of blood.

I pull the dress over my head, listening to Asher outside the door.

"What?" His voice is cold and hard.

A man says something, but it's too muffled for me to understand.

"She's busy."

The man keeps talking, but Asher interrupts. "My orders stand. Now leave." The door shuts quietly and I slip out, wincing at the pain erupting from the soles of my feet.

"Everything all right?" I ask.

He nods, but then there's another knock. He yanks open the door, but stops short when he sees Evangeline standing there.

"I apologize," she says, obviously sensing the tension in the room as Asher steps aside to let her in, "but it's of the utmost import that you come with me. There is . . . an issue."

"What's going on?" I ask.

"There's been an . . . incident."

Asher narrows his eyes. "What kind of incident?"

Evangeline refuses to meet either of our eyes. "A family's gone missing. One of the ones that didn't want to leave just yet."

Asher's whole face darkens. "When?"

"A little while ago."

"Who?" I demand, even though I have a sinking feeling I know who it is already.

"Kara and Tate . . . and their little girl, Myra."

I pull my shoulders back and straighten, even as everything in me is telling me it's already too late. "We need to find them."

Evangeline swallows. "We've already found them."

Asher and I both stare at her. Even though I already know the answer, I ask, "Are they alive?"

Her lower lip quivers for a fraction of a second before she bites down on it. She shakes her head.

Despite the fact that I'd been expecting the answer, my head spins. I lose my balance and stumble when my legs wobble. Asher touches a hand to my shoulder. I can't tell if it's to steady him or me.

"Even little Myra?" I whisper. This time I really don't want to know. Myra's only three. Evangeline merely shakes her head and even though I know she's having as much trouble as I am with this, a little bubble of anger and resentment floats through my grief.

"Why are you shaking your head?" I demand. "What kind of answer is that?"

Asher squeezes my shoulder. "Easy," he says under his breath, reminding me to keep my temper in check.

"She's alive. She was found a little while ago wandering around the maintenance tunnels."

I let out the breath I was holding and close my eyes in relief.

"Well, that's something," Asher says quietly.

"She won't talk," Evangeline says.

My eyes fly open. "What?"

"She won't talk, but she led us to her parents."

"Show me."

Four eyes jerk up to mine.

"What?" they both say.

"Take me to them. I want to see this for myself."

Asher shakes his head, but I cut him off. "No. I need to see them."

"Very well. Follow me." Evangeline turns to Asher. "You should come, too."

I may have only known them for a little over two months, but they were my friends. Actual, *real* friends who trusted me to keep them and their daughter safe. They would have done anything for me, and I couldn't even keep them safe.

Without a word, we follow Evangeline out of the camp and sneak quietly into the Residential Sector on the farthest side of the Sector. We take the six flights of stairs two at a time because the elevators are death traps. At the top, I'm not winded, but Evangeline and Asher are, so I wait impatiently until they can catch their breaths, before continuing forward all the way to the last door in the hallway.

Evangeline knocks. I reach for Asher's hand. He grips mine and squeezes back just as tightly. I honestly don't know who's supporting whom.

The door is slowly opened by one of the Underground. The man glances at Evangeline before his gaze settles on me. He straightens as if he'd been pulled into place by a rubber band. "Ma'am. I don't think you'll want to see this."

I straighten my own shoulders, but keep my hand in Asher's. "Yes. I do."

He opens the door wider, letting us in before shutting it behind us with a snap. I stop almost immediately. The scent of copper chokes me.

This was no murder.

It was a slaughter.

It's also a message. To me. To the rest of the Underground. To every single person who wears the masks.

Blood is splashed against the walls in numerous places. One of the bodies—I can't tell for sure whose, the face is too badly mutilated, but I assume Tate since it's definitely a male body—lays stomach down in the living room, blood pooling around it. Bile crawls up my throat and snakes wriggle in my stomach, but I swallow repeatedly, trying not to vomit.

Asher, however, can't do it and runs straight to the bathroom. The sound of his retching reaches my ears as I continue to gaze down at the body.

I squat down to try to see closer and Evangeline pulls at me. "Oh, Evie." Her tone is that of a mother talking to her three-year-old who's playing in the mud. "Don't. You're going to get your dress all bloody."

I barely spare her a glance. "My dress is hardly a consideration compared to what's happened here."

I roll him over and see the same mutilation on the front of his body as on the back. Again, I have to force myself not to vomit, or cry, scream, rage. Everything I want to do. I force myself not to feel anything as I try to study the body, but it's futile; there's nothing here I don't know already.

Mother had her Enforcers do this. The cuts are too precise. Made in exactly the right spots to cause as much damage and blood as they could.

The only thing that surprises me is it appears he was attacked from behind. The way the slash wound on his neck is angled suggests that, and explains the blood splatter on the walls. But that wasn't what killed him. It may have been the first move, but the killing blow was obviously when she rammed his head into the concrete wall.

His skull is completely caved in on the left side. Blood and things I don't even *want* to think about spill out of it.

However, it's that long cut across his neck that's caught my attention. It starts just to the right of the top of his spinal column. Then slides down across his neck, and over his jugular. The slice is smallish. Possibly from some sort of thin blade. I touch it gently, studying it and what it means, only glancing over when Asher kneels next to me. He still looks a little pale, but he seems in control of himself.

"What is this?" He points to where I'm touching.

"A mistake. I think." I sigh. "See this part here? There's a hole in the skull right there. If she would have stabbed him here, it would have killed him instantly. I think that's what she was trying to do." I push myself up, still frowning. "I don't understand why, though. If she was ordered to kill and make it as messy as possible, that wouldn't make any sense. Unless whoever did this didn't want him to suffer."

"Why do you say that?"

"She came at him from behind; probably from the maintenance door, then grabbed him in a strangle hold so he couldn't call out for help." I can imagine the whole scene in my head as if I was the one who did it. "She probably was going to plunge the knife in here, but he must've moved. So all she ended up doing was slicing his throat. It was still very fatal, but she chose to bash his head in, too. But just once, which suggests she wasn't angry." I point to the splatter. "Since it appears she was trying to go for a quick kill, I think she smashed his head in so he wouldn't suffer as he bled out."

"So it was a humane killing?" I can't tell if the disbelief in Asher's voice is directed at me or the possibility.

"I think so. Yes." As ludicrous as it sounds.

I need time to think on this latest development. Enforcers are trained—Conditioned—to follow orders. Explicitly. Any deviation from the orders could be deadly and would be met with harsh punishment. So . . .

"Why?" Asher asks.

"Maybe she didn't agree with her orders and wanted them to suffer as little as possible." But how did she fight her Conditioning? And is she the only one?

The other Undergrounds in the room mumble to themselves, but I interrupt. "Where's Kara?"

"Kitchen," the man who let us in says. "You can't miss her." His tone is curt, but I know it's not directed at me. The fury boiling just barely under the surface in him is the same one burning my skin.

My Enforcer self tries to fight her way out of me and take over, but I take what I need from her and force the rest away. Going Enforcer isn't going to help.

When I first push through the swinging door, I can't really see Kara, but there's a hand clutching a large knife sticking out from behind the kitchen's island. A whole fat lot of good it did her, I think. More splatter streaks mark the kitchen counters and refrigerator.

She's slightly less mutilated, but it appears she suffered more than Tate. She must have seen her attacker, because she struggled; that much is obvious from the blood smeared and flicked everywhere. Almost every surface has something on it. This is probably more like what Mother wanted to happen.

Kara is lying on her back; her lifeless eyes stare at the ceiling. The fact that her own knife is covered in blood says she may have gotten a piece of the Enforcer that killed her.

Good for you, I think, feeling oddly proud of her.

Avoiding the knife, I kneel next to her and study her as well. The slash marks are almost exactly the same as they were on her husband, but there are a few more, probably gotten during the attack. But when I carefully roll her over, there's a small hole in the back of the neck, just where I described to Asher.

The Enforcer didn't want her to suffer. She even took a few hits in the act of trying to get to the right spot at the base of the neck to make the killing blow and get it right this time. Interesting. Still absolutely horrible, but interesting.

I stand again, brushing my hands on the skirt of my dress. "I don't know how you're going to do it, but I want to know which Enforcer did this. And I want the entire room gone through for anything that might tell us why them. And to make sure there's no damaging evidence against us." The man nods and the two other men go to work.

Suddenly Asher gasps, "Oh my God!"

I glance up and follow his gaze, expecting to see the Enforcer . . . but it's worse. Myra. She's covered in blood, as if she was caught in a rainstorm of it. There are tear trails in the gore on her face. Her dress is pretty much nothing but a blood-soaked rag.

When she sees me, she starts to cry again and I kneel down, almost oblivious to the blood soaking the hem of my dress. I hold my arms out to her and she runs to me and hugs me tightly around my neck. Her little body is shaking and I hold her firmly as I push back up.

"Shh!" I say, rubbing her hair. "It's okay." It's not, of course. She lost her parents and nothing I say will bring them back, but I don't know what else to do.

"What is she doing here?" I glare at the man who's been giving us the tour of the apartment. "Isn't it bad enough that she obviously had to witness this?" I gesture to her dress.

"We thought it better to keep her here in case you wanted to question her yourself."

"She's a *child*!" My voice breaks. "Show some compassion! She needs to get out of those bloody clothes and to be cleaned up and most certainly does *not* need to be *here*." I hug her more tightly. "I've got you now. I'll take care of you now. Is that okay?"

She pulls back slightly and her big round blue eyes stare into mine. Then she nods and places her cheek on my shoulder.

That's when I feel something sharp poking me in the chest. I push her up a little and see a piece of paper pinned to Myra's dress. It's soaked through with blood, which I guess is why I didn't notice it before now.

It's a note, and it's addressed to me.

I unpin it and let her lay her head on me again, while I read aloud to everyone in the room. " 'Abdicate your place as revolutionary leader and leave Elysium. You've been tainted by the Surface and this is no longer your home. If you do not leave, those loyal to you will continue to be slain and you will swim in their blood before we come for you.' "

Chapter Twenty-one

The storm is coming.

—Lenore's journal

Gavin

The water is so blue. Just like her eyes.

Evie's eyes.

I can't get them out of my head. The way they'd crinkle around the edges when she smiled. The way they'd brighten the second before she understood something you were saying. The way they blurred when I kissed her.

They haunt me even in my sleep.

She haunts me in my sleep.

I'm so far gone on this girl, some nights I feel her next to me. The warmth of her body pressed to mine, the pressure of her arm lying across my stomach, her soft breaths against the back of my neck. Of course, that's when I wake and roll over to an empty bed and cold sheets.

Reality's a bitch.

I kick a rock into the water, then turn around so I don't have to see it, but I still hear the waves whisper to me.

"Go back. Go back," they say incessantly. Morning, noon, and night.

A guy can't get any peace with those whispers. I can almost imagine it's her saying it, pleading with me to go back.

My imagination's a bitch, too.

I want to go back. More than anything. But I'm terrified of what will happen to my family when I leave. Lenore says the mayor has no interest in them anymore. But Lenore's living with us now. I'm not sure how much intel she can have when she's over here all the time and not there.

But the reason she's here is because she says we can go back anytime. She even made sure to replace my destroyed raft with a small boat she'd procured from Rushlake in ways she told me I didn't want to know. According to her, the mayor has moved on to other sources that have said they've seen Evie and Asher somewhere to the north of us. Witnesses paid for by the mistress herself, most likely, in order to lead away from the true answer that Asher and Evie are at the bottom of the sea, fighting a battle I'm not sure they can win. That maybe they've already lost.

That thought has kept me awake more than once.

I wonder if I'm delaying going back, because if I do go back, I'll see that she's gone. Either dead, or dead to me. Because she was caught and Mother erased her memories and replaced them with others. Making her forget me. Forget us. Everything we had together.

But I've found Lenore *and* I was able to save my mom and brother. And, at least for now, they're taken care of.

Unless Mayor St. James reneges on the promise to take care of them once he notices I'm gone.

He's far from dumb. He'll know I went back to her. Or at least suspect it. There's no telling what he'll do. He's almost as insane as Mother is. But my only other choice to assure myself they're safe is to bring them with me, and that means sentencing them to another type of punishment—possibly something worse than what the mayor can do, especially if Evie's not there or doesn't remember me.

I can't do that.

I could try to make a sneak trip down. Take a look around at things. Verify that everything is mostly safe down there and that Evie's even still alive, *then* bring my family down. Of course, I don't know what I'll do if I find out she isn't.

And . . . I'm overthinking things again.

I *want* to be with Evie. I *need* to be with her.

And now she's down in that vipers' nest, trying to fix a problem that's no one's fault but Mother's and Father's in the first place.

I wander around the cove soaked from the rain and the waves that crash onto the shore. I find myself remembering all the sadness and frustrations of my time there. Remembering running terrified and sick down the hall that led me to

Evie. Remembering how she stood up for me when she didn't even know me. Remembering how she nursed me back to health when she didn't know if I was as dangerous as Mother warned or not. And how she risked—and lost—everything for me; just some stupid Surface Dweller kid with a bad attitude.

My mind whirls like the storm brewing around me just off the coast; then, suddenly, it's all clear. I break out into a run before my thoughts can catch up with my actions. I have to get to my house and do what I should have done a long time ago. Evie trusted me when she had absolutely no reason to and I trusted her then, too. Now it's time to trust her again.

My mother is kneading bread on the counter in the kitchen and she and Lenore are talking when I burst in through the back door. They both glance behind them with a half-confused, half-fearful look until they realize it's just me.

Mom smiles. "I haven't seen you burst through a door like that since you were younger than Tristan." She laughs and goes back to kneading the dough.

I go up behind her and kiss her cheek and hug her, as hard as I can without hurting her. Who knows when I'll be back? I want to say soon, but the answer might be never.

"I love you," I tell her.

She turns slowly from the dough, her hands and the entire front of her apron covered in flour. "You're going back."

I glance toward Lenore, before returning to my mom. "The storm's here. It's going to be big and mean and the perfect cover to head back down."

"So when will you be leaving?"

"As soon as the storm reaches its peak. So no one sees anything."

"And if the mayor comes looking for you?"

"Tell him Gavin couldn't bear to stay here with all the memories of Evie slapping him in the face," Lenore answers for me. I don't argue, it's the truth after all. "Make sure to say he was heading as far in the opposite direction Evie took as he could."

Mom gazes between Lenore and me as if she thinks I have something to say. Then her lower lip quivers.

She touches a floury hand to my cheek. "I'm proud of you. So very proud. We'll be fine. It *is* time for you to go. It's *been* time for you to go."

Screams wake me. I hadn't even realized I'd fallen asleep. It takes me a minute to realize that this time, it's not an echo from my dreams. It's the scream of the wind from the storm raging outside my window.

This isn't any normal summer storm like I'd thought earlier. The whole house shakes from the winds, making my blood run cold. This is a hurricane. Or at least it will be. It's just starting. We're probably in the last of the rain bands before the actual full-blown hurricane. But still . . .

We haven't had one in so long. I should have known it was just a matter of time. I should have seen the warnings earlier. But I was too distracted with thoughts of Evie and going back. Then packing and making sure Lenore was all set.

Thunder booms, causing the whole house to shake, and catapults me out of bed. I have to get Mom and Tristan to the shelter before Lenore and I leave. Our house barely withstood the last hurricane and that was five years ago.

I rush out of my room, but stop in my tracks at the door, spin around, and run back to my dresser to grab the most important thing I own. A branch flies through the window by my head and I duck, tucking the picture frame in my waistband. Maybe not the most appropriate place for it, but at least it won't get damaged.

Mom's already rushing down the hall toward me. When she sees me, she lets out a breath. "Get your brother. Make sure he brings *just* the essentials. Don't let him dawdle. If he doesn't get up, pick him up and carry him. There's nothing he absolutely needs anyway. I'll get some things to take with us to the shelter." She doesn't give me a chance to respond. She's already hurrying away with Lenore at her heels.

I rush into Tristan's room. He's lying facedown in the bed, one arm flung over his pillow, the other hanging off the edge of his mattress, his fingertips brushing the floor. I shake him.

"Tristan!" He doesn't even move. "Tristan!" I say again, louder, shaking his shoulder. Still nothing. "Okay. Fine." I pick him up, sheet and all, and sling him up over my shoulder. Tristan doesn't even bother waking up. Which is probably a good thing. He'd just get frightened.

I race back out into the hallway, where Mom and Lenore

come rushing back in from the kitchen. They both have bulging bags and Lenore is struggling to carry hers. I sigh and take it from her, and then the one from my mom, too.

"Let me take Tristan," Mom says.

"No. It's faster if I take him," I say.

She looks like she's going to argue, but another crack of thunder shakes the house.

She just nods and leads the way to the back door. The hurricane shutters—I almost want to laugh at the term—bang against the house as another huge wind gust swings them back and forth. If I wasn't afraid the house was going to collapse around us, I would insist on waiting until the eye of the hurricane passes. But with every gust, the whole building leans in the direction it's blowing and groans.

Mom grabs the handle of the door. "Ready?"

I don't know why she's asking, it's not like we have a choice, but I nod and she pushes through the door. As soon as she opens it, the wind catches it and sends it crashing against the house.

She gives me a look that says, "Yikes," then rushes out into the rain, which immediately plasters her hair and clothes to her head and body. The wind pushes her back a few steps before she plods forward and I lose her in the curtain of rain falling from the eaves. Lenore follows and is quickly swallowed up by the storm.

Bracing myself, I take one last quick breath and push into the rain. Instantly water sluices over me. The wet mud-sand sucks me in, but I trudge forward, trying to find my mom and my way.

Of course, the rain does what I'd failed to do and wakes Tristan.

He starts thrashing around like a maniac, until I shout, "Relax! I've got you. We're going to the shelter."

"I can walk," he yells into my ear so I can hear him.

"No," I yell back. "*I* can barely walk. You're so small the wind will blow you away. It'll be faster if I only have to watch out for Mom and Lenore."

"Fine."

The rain comes down so hard it's almost impossible to see where I'm going, but I know the general direction of where the shelter is and I just keep going in that direction, my feet plunging and pulling from the muddy sand. I feel almost like I'm going backward. My hair is in my eyes and face and, of course, I don't have any hands to brush it away. I don't see Lenore has stopped until I run directly into her.

She stumbles forward onto her hands and knees. I put Tristan down to help her up.

"What's wrong?"

"The shelter. It's blocked."

I take the extra hand I now have free and push the hair from my eyes, squinting through the rain. She's right. It is blocked. By a branch I'm sure is the size of a tree. Mom's tugging at it, but she can't get any traction on the slippery ground and isn't even budging it. I push my mom aside and tug on the branches, but my feet just slip in the wet sand as my mom's had and I fall onto my ass. I try a few more times, and finally manage to budge it enough to push the doors open.

I usher Tristan and my mom into the little concrete building. Mom lights a small lantern so we can see long enough to say good-bye. I hug her and she holds me so tightly and for so long that I wonder if I'll have to find a crowbar to pry us apart, but then she lets go. I can't tell if the water on her face is tears or just the rain, but still.

I kneel down in front of Tristan. "Take care of Mom until I'm back. Okay?"

He nods, and for a second just stares at me. Then he wraps his arms around my neck and hugs me, too.

"We need to go before the storm gets worse!" Lenore yells from where she's huddled by the door.

"Go! Be careful," my mom says.

I give her a grin. "I always am." Then, before I can second-guess my decision, I step into the pelting rain again. Lenore follows, gripping my hand this time. In a lightning flash, I can see there's fear in her eyes, so I give her hand a squeeze. "We'll be fine," I yell.

I hope it's true.

We rush as fast as we can to the trees on the other side of the cove. It still takes longer than I want, and I'm out of breath within just a few minutes, but when we hit the trees, most of the rain is caught by the branches and only a bit hits us. We race toward where the inconspicuous little rowboat is hiding.

When we reach it, I push the boat into the water. There's an immediate tug that almost rips it from my hands, but I manage to hang on and yell to Lenore, "Come on! Get in!"

She scrambles into the water and carefully crawls into the boat. It rocks precariously, but I ignore it as I scoot into it, too. My only worry is that with this rain, the boat's going to take on too much water. With the surges and waves this big in the cove, when we get into the open water, I'm going to have a hell of a time keeping it from being submerged.

It takes only a few minutes with how fast the current is dragging us to the island, but it's the most terrifying ride of my life. And that includes running for my life in Sector Three with Evie, unsure if she wanted to kill me or save me.

Waves almost capsize us countless times. They swamp the boat. Saltwater splashes into my eyes, blinding me with searing pain and sending us off course until I can see again.

Lightning flashes across the sky, followed almost immediately by the crash of thunder. I worry that one of those lightning strikes will hit us, but they don't and finally we crash onto the beach. Even though we brace for the impact, it still throws Lenore and me off. I roll across the rocky ground, scraping my already raw skin.

Lenore fares no better, and even though she stands, she limps as we race as quickly as we dare to where I moored the submarine. I hope and pray the entire way that it's still there. And worry as we slip down the cliff that nearly killed me the last time. But when I get there and see the submarine, exactly where I left it, I almost whoop in happiness.

I slide open the top hatch, and carefully help Lenore in, before I push the thing into the water and grab onto the side, hitching myself up and over into the passenger compartment. I hit the button for the hatch, waiting for it to close over our heads.

Immediately the sounds of the storm cut off. The silence is deafening in contrast to the cracks of thunder and the shrieking of wind. And even though we're soaked and gasping for breath, it's almost heaven not getting pelted by the freezing rain. It was like being sliced by tiny little knives.

Eli said something to me about there being a button that would take me back. After searching for a few minutes, I find it in the instrument cluster. I hit it and the submarine moves around in a hundred and eighty degree turn until we're faced away from the island, then it speeds us away.

Hopefully it's taking me back to a place that still exists.

Chapter Twenty-two

Myra is mine now. I am responsible for the death of her parents and so I will take on all the duties as her caregiver. It is the least I can do, for those that gave the ultimate sacrifice for the new Elysium.

—Evie's journal

Evie

I sit in the darkened War Room. It's the middle of the night, but I don't care. It's the only time that I can be alone. With my thoughts. My memories. My mistakes.

I thought I'd had everything figured out. I thought we'd been *winning*. I was wrong. I'm as lost as I was in the beginning. I *don't* know what I'm doing. How could everything be so wrong even after so much time?

How could something as horrible as that *still* happen? And for what? Why? To send a message to me?

If that was the case, why not just send me the message? Why pin a note to a little girl's pajamas and hope she found me?

My mind flashes over that note.

I'm not a fool. I know what they want.

I *don't* know what I need to do. What I *should* do. If I do abdicate, I'd be giving in to a terrorist and that's not something I'm willing to do. If I don't, more innocent people will lose their lives. Am I willing to pay that cost?

I think of Myra, asleep in my bed because she's terrified the monsters will come for her.

Tears slide over my cheeks and I pull my knees up to my chin and sob into my thighs.

After who knows how long, I feel a hand on my back, and look up to see Asher frowning down at me.

"Evie," he says. The sadness in his eyes melts in his voice.

I quickly wipe my face with the backs of my hands. They're still bandaged, but they're bloody. I don't know if it's my blood or Tate's and Kara's. I blink as if I haven't just been bawling my eyes out.

Tears are a weakness.

He grabs my hands. "Stop that," he says. "You can't keep your tears from me. Even if I hadn't seen it, I'd have known." He pulls me up and into his arms, but I pull away.

"I don't need you to do this. I'm fine." I hiccup. "I'll be fine." It comes out as barely a whisper.

"You're not fine, Evie. You've been here for half an hour. And I'm sure you've been crying the whole time." He lifts my chin with his finger. "It's not your fault."

Even more tears slide down my cheek. "I know," I finally choke out. "But it's so hard to know that when I'm the one who's putting this whole thing together. I'm the one who's supposed to be leading these people to their freedom. Supposed to be keeping them *safe*! But I'm also the one who pushed Mother over the edge. I knew she was close. I wanted her to fall off that ledge, but they wouldn't have died if I hadn't done what I've been doing. Undermining Mother all the time."

"Mother went over the edge a long time ago. Way before you were born. You're just showing the people who she really is." He hugs me. "What you're doing *is* the right thing."

I lean my cheek on his stomach, soaking up his never-ending support. My tears come again, and this time, I let them. Drowning me and soaking Asher's shirt. But he doesn't say anything. He just sits and pulls me tightly into him, letting me cry without saying a word. A strong rock in the storm of my emotions.

And as I'm sitting there, letting him comfort me, I realize something. I can't lose him. He's all I have of a real family. My brother. Whether that's true in the genetic sense or not. He is mine. And I can't lose him.

I have to take the next step. This stupid cat-and-mouse game of Mother's needs to stop. Mother needs to go and I need to be the one to make it happen. I've been afraid to; my instincts were telling me not to. To wait until Gavin came back with Lenore. But Asher's right. It's time to really show Elysium what Mother is. It's time to take back the city. Mother isn't going to change. It's time to stop chipping at her base and just take her down.

"I think you're right," I finally say. "Gavin isn't coming.

And I can't continue to keep the people here. It's not safe, here or there. It's time to finish this." I know he'll know exactly what I'm talking about. That's the great thing about Asher. He always seems like he's one step ahead of me. Watching out for me. The best big brother a girl could have.

He pushes me away, but grips my shoulders, staring me directly in the eyes. "Are you sure? Maybe you should wait until you're not so . . ."

"Emotional?" I say with a laugh.

He nods, but sighs. "You know I'll stand with you no matter what you choose."

I smile. A real one this time. "You've always stood with me. There's no one I trust here more than you. You're my best friend. My brother." I kiss his nose. "I don't know what I'd do without you."

He pulls me back into his chest for another tight hug. "I don't know what I'd do without you either."

A throat clears behind me and I turn to see Nadia standing in the doorway. I palm my tears away and stand, straightening my dress. Asher stands slowly as well.

"Yes, Nadia. How may we help you?"

"I'm sorry to bother you after . . . everything." She looks as lost for words as I feel.

I wave my hand. "Nonsense. You're not bothering me." But the catch in my voice gives me away.

She steps farther into the room. "We have another issue."

My legs wobble as my knees weaken. "Not another . . ." I can't finish the sentence. I have the horrible thought that if

I say it, it'll make it true. Asher's arm snakes around my waist, taking on my extra weight.

Nadia shakes her head. "No, ma'am."

"Then what?"

In answer, Nadia steps aside, and my breath catches in my throat. Asher's whole body tenses beside me. Behind her is Gavin.

He looks awful. His hair is a rats' nest of snarls and sopping wet. Water drips over his entire face and onto his clothes. Those are soaked as well, and his arms and face are covered in mud and scratches.

He reminds me of the first time I saw him.

My first instinct is to run to him. To hug him. To pull him to me and tell him I'm so glad he came back, but just seeing him has me in a chaotic mess of emotions. I'm so completely relieved he's here I'm light-headed, but I'm also filled with pure irrational anger that he's okay and it took him so long to come back. I don't care that he probably has a good reason. He scared the hell out of me.

I do walk to him, but when I reach him, it isn't to hug him or kiss him or any of my initial instincts. I glare at him. Then I punch him in the face.

"Oh my God! That was awesome!" Asher says, laughing, from behind me.

"Oh!" Lenore says next to him.

Immediately, shock and embarrassment replace the anger. I can't believe I just did that! What in the world is wrong with me? But I can't control the whirlpool of emotions in me.

"You were just supposed to be gone a little while," I yell at Gavin, who holds a hand to his nose. His eyes are wide with surprise. "Like going into the next room. It's easy. Here, I'll show you."

I storm past him and a shocked Nadia to walk through the door they came in. Am I being completely irrational? Absolutely, but I don't care. I slam the door behind me, wait to the count of three, then swing the door open again and walk through again, completely focused on his amused eyes. "See! That's how you do that."

Then I burst into tears and barrel toward him. His cold arms immediately wrap around me and pull me closer. I don't even care that he's soaking wet. Or dirty. Or freezing. I only care that he's here.

"Good-bye," I whisper into his chest.

He chuckles and presses his lips to the top of my head. "I think you have that backward."

"No. I have that in just the right order."

I knew I missed him, but I had no idea how much until just this moment, and I can't bear to let him go. So I don't. I stand there, holding him, letting him hold me—the only good news this day has given me.

Asher is greeting his grandmother in a much less dramatic way than I greeted Gavin, so I back away from Gavin slightly, but I refuse to let go of his hand. Not just yet. Asher gives me a questioning look and I nod. I'm fine. In fact, I'm more than fine. I'm great. I'm perfect. And—as a fire lights in my blood—I realize I'm ready. Finally.

I turn to Nadia. "Please get Evangeline and send for Father. Thank you."

It's time to finish this poker game, as Asher calls it. I've learned so much from him and the best advice he gave me was to keep my cards close to my chest until just the right moment. It appears that moment's now.

It takes a few minutes, but finally Evangeline and Nadia arrive and we all take seats around the table. Asher sets up the vid screen so Father can be a part of the communication using the only computer from the Palace Wing we've let access the mainframe. When his face pops onto the screen, Lenore stares at him. "Eli?"

Asher glances to his grandmother, and pats her hand. "It's too risky for him to try and come here, so we do this."

"Hello, Lenore. It's been a long time."

"Too long," she whispers in a wavery voice, but doesn't say anything else. She gestures for me to start.

I glance around the table, taking in everyone around me, gathering my thoughts and figuring out exactly what I'm trying to accomplish.

I squeeze Gavin's hand. "A lot has happened today and while I'm so very glad you're back safe, I'm afraid there's no time for a welcome back party." I move my gaze to encompass everyone when I speak next. "Mother has finally shown her true colors tonight. She will, of course, try to blame the Underground. This time, there is no hiding that she was behind this. But I believe we have the upper hand."

Father speaks up. "She'll wait until the morning to make

her announcement. She thinks we have time since what happened should be devastating to Evie."

"She's right," I say, glad my voice isn't showing any of the inner turmoil I feel. "But we can't wait until tomorrow. We have to expose her, before she exposes us."

Nadia nods. "I agree. There are still too many of her Citizens stranded in Elysium, but we cannot let her have them."

"How do we do it?" Evangeline asks.

"Through the vid screens. And we'll tell everyone—including those in the Caverns—what she's done." I turn to Nadia. "I need everyone in the common area. I want it on the big screen. There's been some dissent. Some questions about what we're waiting for. This is a horrible way to answer them, but it's what I feel needs to be done."

"Of course."

"Try to make sure the children are not able to see this. I'm not going to sugarcoat what happened. In fact, I'm not going to hide anything. I'm going to literally show the Citizens what she's done. The *people* will be shown what she's done." I focus on Father. "Are the bodies still there?"

Gavin stares at me. I ignore him for now. He'll know everything soon enough.

"We're still conducting our investigation and documenting the scene." He glances at his watch. "They're probably finishing up now though."

"Good. We need to act now. Mother's waiting to make her move. We're not. We'll take her thunder from her *and* use her own ammunition against her. I won't let my friends' deaths be in vain."

"But you're covered in their blood," Evangeline says. "If you show them what she's done, she'll use that to blame you anyway."

"She can try," I say. "But she left too much behind this time. Too much that points to her. I think the Enforcer that did it made sure of it." I pull the slip of paper from my dress pocket and flash it out. "She'll also have to explain why this note exists."

"She'll blame you," Evangeline says again.

"But how many will believe her?" Father asks. "Her followers are few. Some have *joined* our ranks. Half the city wears the masks. A quarter of her population is in the Caverns. We walk freely among the rest. This might be the final crack in her wall."

"I think we're underestimating Mother and the power she has over the city. Over us. This is a trap," Evangeline whispers. "She's using this to prove you are a monster and anyone who follows you will die by your hand."

I smile. "Of course it's a trap. But we have nothing to hide. I just have to show the people what we've seen and know. I will prove who the real monster is."

I grab my mask, while Asher gathers his equipment. Evangeline and Lenore decide to stay back with Nadia to help the Citizens shelter the children. Gavin, however, wants to go with me.

I've noticed his attention on my bloody dress a few times. It doesn't take much of a logic leap to figure out he wants to know what happened and where we're going. My first thought is to protect him from the sight. I can't imagine how hard it'll be for me to step back in there, let alone him. But, in the end, I decide to let him go. He needs to know everything that's happened since he left and we don't have time to ease him into it.

Carefully, we dart through the passageways that lead to the Residential Sector until we get to the apartment again. It should be mostly empty now, except for the bodies and the crew who'll take them to give them a proper good-bye. Father waits for us outside the door. The coppery scent of the blood is unmistakable even before we open the door.

"This is going to be bad," I say to Gavin. "Very bad. There's no shame in deciding you can't handle it. But, please, if you can't, don't go into the hallway alone. The bedrooms and bathroom are safe. Wait in one of those for me."

"I understand." His hand brushes mine, but I don't take it. Even though I really want to.

I push open the door and step in, trying not to gag on the much stronger stench of coppery blood. Father and Asher rush in, keeping their attention away from the bodies. Gavin follows at a much slower pace, his eagle-eyed gaze taking in everything in the room.

When he shuts the door, he leans against it. "Jesus!" He looks at Asher. "Mother did this?"

Asher gives him a sympathetic look. "An Enforcer carried it out, but Mother ordered it."

"Why?"

"Because they were part of the Underground," I say quietly. "They were two of our first members and our most avid supporters. We were close. Mother found out somehow." I have a sick feeling starting to claw at my stomach, but I force it down. We've got a message to get out.

I turn to Asher. "What do you think? Should I be here first?" I stand by the wall covered with Tate's blood and brain matter. "I'll say what I have to, then Father can pan down to the body, before we move to the kitchen."

"That should work. It'll get the point across nicely. We'll show how only an Enforcer could have done this. And since Mother doesn't want to publicly announce you're alive, she can't say you did it."

I nod. "Tell me when you're ready."

I wait while he sets things up and turn to look at Gavin. He's slightly pale, but holding on quite well, considering. I guess all the hunting he's done over the years has made him slightly numb to, or at least able to tolerate, the sight of this much blood. I am definitely not numb; I'm incensed by it.

"Ready," Asher says.

"Don't say a word while we're recording, okay?" I tell Gavin. "Unless it's an emergency. I don't want Mother to have any more information than she already has."

"Okay."

I take a shaky breath, then pull the mask over my face. The mask instantly aligns itself with my head, making me want to shudder. I hate that feeling. When it settles, I signal Asher

Enforcer could inflict this much damage to a human skull." I gesture for Asher to pan along the body. "You can see from several of the slash marks, these are no ordinary marks. There's no hesitation. They're all clean, straight lines made in exactly the right spots to make this appear as bloody and messy as possible. There's only one 'mistake.' It's obvious that she tried to stab him in the back of the neck, but missed or slipped and sliced the jugular instead." I gesture to the red stained walls. "Take note of the spray of blood on the wall across from the body." I stand, and walk backward through the kitchen door.

Father shows Kara now, including the bloody knife. "The woman, a mother herself, tried fighting back, but still had her life stolen from her. These people were Citizens. People from the Metalworking and Agricultural Sectors. People just like you. But they were also so much more than that. They were parents, friends, and now . . . martyrs. Symbols. Mother killed them simply because they believed differently than she. The Underground has never taken a life. We've gone to extreme measures to not only avoid it, but to stop several assassination attempts. We've never done anything but show people the truth about Mother. To prove you don't have to live in the constant fear of Mother and her shadows. But now because these people disagreed with her and sided with me, Mother decided to take their lives. Their blood is on my hands. Literally and figuratively." I lift my arms, showing my blood-covered, cloth-wrapped hands. "We all know these Citizens weren't the first, and I know they won't be the last. The next death could be you or someone you love. Do you really want a woman who kills people because they believe differently than her to be in charge of absolutely everything in your life? Do you really want to live in this gilded cage, believing everything this woman says because you're afraid to find out what's outside of it? Do you really want to live in fear for the rest of your life, which could end tomorrow or the next day or the next? Most importantly, do you want your children to grow up in a world filled with fear and death? She calls Surface Dwellers monsters, but looking at this massacre, I know who the real monster is. Do you?"

Chapter Twenty-three

Mother's laws have dictated and ensured the Citizens' predictability for so long that Mother has become quite cavalier in her assumption they will remain so. Therefore, in order to get something we've never had, it's important to do something we've never done.

—Evie's journal

Gavin

Seeing those poor people was probably the worst and most heart-wrenching experience of my life. Now I know why Evie looked so broken. I have more questions, but they can wait until later. Eli rushed back to the Palace Wing after Evie finished with a promise to vid chat. So now I follow Evie and Asher back to the Caverns, keeping as quiet as I can while I let things percolate in my brain.

Back in the Caverns, Asher puts the equipment away and Evie just keeps walking past all the people gossiping. A few try to talk to her, but I don't even think she notices them. She just continues past them as if they aren't even there. At first I think I should follow her, but I veer off when I get to her—our?—cutout. At a loss as to what I should do, and after a few minutes of trying to decide whether I should try and sleep on the floor, or wait to try and talk to Evie, I go back to the War Room and wait.

Asher sits at the table, staring at a box filled with equipment, cords dangling from his fingers. He seems as unsure of what to do as I am. Evangeline sits next to him, tears spilling silently down her pretty cheeks. Her back is ramrod straight and her hands are folded on the table as she stares straight ahead at the wall. Nadia looks defeated. I think that's the scariest of all of this. I don't think I've ever seen her show an emotion. Defeat shouldn't be the first one. I take the seat next to Asher, leaving a space for Evie in the middle, should she join us.

Uncomfortable with the silence, I finally bite the bullet and ask, "So . . . who wants to share what I missed?"

Asher turns his head up, only to return to staring at his cords without saying anything. Nadia stares into space for a minute, but then she sighs and spends the next several minutes catching me up.

"So . . . now what?" I ask.

Asher lifts an eyebrow. "We do the only thing we can. Wait for the backlash."

"And what's the backlash?"

"Who knows?" Asher yawns and sits up as the screen next to him lights up with a picture of Eli. The vid screen.

I look at Eli. He was with Mother. He should know.

Eli seems to guess what I'm thinking. "She's extremely careful not to tell me anything anymore. She's paranoid, and Dr. Friar is the only one she shares anything with lately. When I returned, I could hear her screaming and breaking things from the Maintenance tunnel. I followed her voice to her room where she was dressing down every single Enforcer we have left. She saw me and immediately demanded answers, but I played dumb. I don't think she believed me, but she kicked me out after that, so I have no clue what's going on in her head or what her next move is."

"So how do we prepare?"

"We're already as prepared as we're going to get," Eli says.

"So we're just going to sit around doing nothing?"

"No," Evie says behind me, startling me.

I twist around and see her wearing a new dress. Her hair is wrapped in a towel. She looks absolutely exhausted, but despite that, there's something shining through her. Something I've only seen peek through when she's gone into Enforcer mode. Except she's *not* in Enforcer mode. She's quite obviously in control of herself. I've never seen her look so beautiful.

"You're going to do another masking," Evie says. "Tomorrow. This will give the Underground enough time to spread the word on it and let Mother tell her lies about Kara and Tate."

"You said *we'll* be doing it," Asher says. "What are *you* going to do?"

"I'm going to talk to the Enforcers." She straightens her shoulders.

Suddenly the room is in an uproar and my heart has jammed itself into my throat, while my stomach seems to have taken up residence on the floor. I can't make out one voice from the next. After a minute, she holds her hand in the air. "One of Mother's Enforcers did this. I know which one." She holds her Slate up. "The one that hurt you originally, Asher." The two of them share a look full of meaning that I don't understand, but clearly they do. Asher purses his lips as she continues. "Her actions suggest she might not be as okay with what Mother is doing as Mother wants to believe. If that's so, she's probably not the only one."

"You can't just walk in there. They'll kill you on sight," Lenore says, popping up from behind Evie. She must have followed her in, but I didn't see her.

"Possibly. Maybe even probably. But," she fans out her hands in front of her, "it's a chance we have to take. Unless and until you can figure out how to deactivate the nanites, it may be our only choice. If we can get them on our side, we'll have the final blow to Mother's support system."

"They're monsters, Evie. You can't reason with them," Asher says.

"*I* used to be one of them."

No one seems to know what to say to that. But I do. It's something I should have said a long time ago. "You were never a monster, Evie. From the first time they Conditioned you, you fought back. That's why they kept brainwashing you over and over again. To get you to go along with their plans, while thinking they were your own. It's possible these girls could be fighting their own battles like you did. But it's just as possible they never have and never will. Honestly, it wouldn't surprise me in the least if this was all some part of Mother's plot to get you back."

She frowns, and I can see she's thinking it over. "Yes . . . I suppose that you're right." She nods and looks directly at me. "Actually, that makes a lot of sense."

"If that's the case," Eli says, "which I'm inclined to agree it is, then it is even more imperative that you *not* do this. We've said our piece. Let's just give Mother time to make her own statement, then hold a masking in the Square the following morning. It'll tell us how many people we still have supporting us and how many are still too afraid. You're forgetting that while this *could* go in our favor, it can just as easily go against us. Fear is the most powerful weapon and Mother wields it well."

Evie rubs her fingers in circles around her temple. Little tiny cuts dribble blood, and I wonder what *that's* about but I don't ask.

"We'll see what Mother has to say. We've waited this long. One more day isn't going to hurt." They all breathe a sigh of relief, but I know better. I'm not surprised when she says, "Besides, that'll give me time to prepare a plan for going to meet with the Enforcers." She looks at everyone in turn. "I *know* this is what needs to be done and no one is going to stop me."

I can't sleep. I can't stop pacing. I can't stop thinking about Evie and her idea. It's solid. It scares the hell out of me, but it's smart and resourceful and *if* she can get the Enforcers on our side, that will leave Mother open to an attack that would otherwise be impossible to execute. While I understand why the others don't want her to do it, after what I had to do with Mayor St. James, I completely understand why she does.

When I'm in the corner of the cutout I hear footsteps at the door and stop pacing long enough to see Evie standing in the doorway, the light from the common area turning her to mostly a shadow. But I'd know her anywhere.

She turns her head and moves her eyes until they meet mine. She jerks back, slapping her hand to her mouth to muffle her scream.

She moves a hand to her chest and lets out a little laugh. "Oh, you scared me. I thought you'd be asleep."

"Couldn't." The main reason why is staring right into my eyes.

She nods. "Same here. Couldn't even if I wanted to." She steps farther into the room, then hikes herself up onto the cot. I can't help but notice how her dress goes up and shows her knee and a lot of her thigh. I have to admit: she has awesome legs.

She clears her throat and I realize she's caught me staring. I look up guiltily, but I don't see a frown, I see amusement. She's actually laughing at me!

I sit next to her. "Are you sure you don't want to try and sleep?"

She shakes her head. "Mother is probably planning her next step right now. I want to be awake when it happens. There'll be plenty of time to sleep once we finish this."

"I agree with them," I say, cautiously. "I don't like the idea of you just walking up to the Enforcers like a lamb to slaughter."

She purses her lips. "I guess it's a good thing the decision isn't up to you then." Her tone is considerably cooler than it was a few seconds ago.

I sigh. I wasn't planning on telling her, but this is the first time we've really talked and I don't want to fight before we've even said more than a few words. "I don't like it, but I think it's a good plan."

She blinks as if she can't believe her ears. "You do?"

I shrug. "I don't like it, but . . . I believe in you. I love you. And I trust your decisions. If you think talking with the Enforcers is what needs to be done, I'll be standing right there beside you. No matter what."

"I'm sorry for punching you," she says.

An obvious ploy to stop talking about her idea, but I take the bait anyway and laugh. "No, you're not. But I kind of knew it was coming. I've seen that look on my sister's face a few times before she slapped my brother-in-law. Of course, it wasn't a sucker punch in his *nose*, but . . ." I break off when she giggles. An actual giggle, and I'm in heaven even if this place is hell. "I missed you," I blurt out.

The silence after my admission is almost deafening.

"Was it horrible up there?" Her voice is so quiet I almost miss the hidden worry and hurt hidden in her words. Her eyes meet mine, and in the dark they look huge.

I pull her into my arms and hold her as tightly as I can

manage. Her whole body shivers, as does mine. Six weeks was much too long to be away from her. I kiss the side of her head as she snuggles into me.

"Was it hard to come back? To this?" She tosses her arm out, obviously meaning not just the Caverns, but Elysium as a whole. She peers at me out of the corner of her eye. "To me?"

"No. It was hard to stay away."

"What happened?" There's no censure in her voice. No accusations. Merely concern and curiosity.

I tell her the entire story from beginning to end without leaving out a single detail. By the time I'm finished, she's the one pacing the floor. I swear if the mayor was here with us, she'd beat the hell out of him. I'd almost like to see it.

"I can't understand how Asher came from such a . . . a . . ."

"Asshole?" I suggest.

She bobs her head once. "Yes. Such an *asshole*!" She grits her teeth when she says it and I can't help laughing. I don't mean to, but hearing her say the word is hilarious.

She whirls around and stomps over to me, glaring up at me. "What?"

I swallow back another laugh. "Nothing. It's nothing." I pull her to me and kiss the top of her head.

She leans into me and wraps her arms around my waist, her head resting against my chest. "The city wanted me," she says. "That's probably why he was looking so hard for me. I hurt a bunch of people at the medical center after a hallucination. I thought I was back here. After that they wouldn't let me go and wanted to run a bunch of tests on me. That's why Asher snuck me out and brought me back here. They're probably still looking for me."

"Seems like it might be time to bury the hatchet completely and talk to Asher. It seems that I've been angry with the wrong people the entire time."

"Will you tell me what happened? You were obviously close at one time."

"Thick as thieves, as my mom would say." I look down and turn my hand over to stare at the little scar in the center of my palm. "Blood brothers."

"You're brothers?" Her eyebrows pinch together. "How can that be?"

"Not *real* brothers. But we were so close we might as well have been. So we did this thing where we both cut our palms, then pressed them together. Blood brothers."

I can tell she doesn't understand, but she nods anyway. "Oh. Okay."

"From the time we were babies until . . . well, until we weren't friends anymore, we spent all of our time together. Told each other everything. He told me his worst secret and I told him something I should have kept to myself. Ultimately it was our bond that made us enemies."

"How?" She touches the back of my neck when I lean over. Her fingers play with my hair.

"One winter we didn't have enough food. Hunting had been slim all year and Tristan had just been born, so my mom needed every scrap we could find. But we were completely out. My dad had continued to hunt, but the winter was especially cold that year, so there wasn't anything. Not even a squirrel. We'd been without food for a week, so my dad stole meat from the butcher. I caught him. He was trying to hide it and present it like a kill, but I knew better. I'd been hunting with him earlier and knew. He admitted it to me, but promised that as soon as spring came around he'd repay the butcher with twice as much meat as he took. He made me promise not to say anything, because the others wouldn't understand. I tried to keep it a secret, but I had to tell someone, because it was just eating me up inside. So I told the one person I trusted most. Asher.

"About a week after I told him, the mayor came by with a few of his 'special' hunters. The ones that supplied the city with fresh meat. He wanted my dad to be an official hunter for the village. He'd pay him for his services and allow him entry into Rushlake so we'd never go hungry again. My father didn't know how the mayor had known we needed food, but I knew it was because I'd told Asher and Asher must have talked to his dad. It made me glad I'd told them. I'd helped my family. Without even meaning to.

"After a bit of negotiating, my dad and the mayor came to terms and my dad headed out the next day. He never came back. He just . . . disappeared. The hunters he was with came back, but Dad was just gone. The official story was he was probably taken in his sleep by a coyote, but I know my dad. And the hunters he usually hunted with never believed it either. Not surprisingly, the 'special' hunters were sent back to the city within a few days of their return. It was a commonly held belief that the mayor had my dad killed, but no one knew why. But I did. Because I told Asher my father had stolen the meat and he told his dad. My dad died because I couldn't keep a secret and neither could Asher."

"Oh . . . Gavin."

She steps toward me. Her blue eyes are a melting pot of emotions as they sparkle with unshed tears. Her arms come around me again and she just holds me. Her quiet support is more than I expected.

I expected her to tell me I was wrong to feel the way I did, or that I should forgive Asher. But she does none of that. Again there's no judgment. No criticism. She just hugs me.

I don't know what to do, but finally I solve the matter by kissing her. It feels like it's been forever, until I lift her chin up and lower my lips to hers. Then it feels like it's been no time at all.

She kisses me back, but it's not enough, this small taste of something I've been craving for weeks. The air changes between us, becoming charged with a familiar, primal kind of energy.

Her eyes flutter closed when I slowly slide her dress off her shoulder to bare the skin there and trace a path with my lips from her shoulder to the curve at the base of her throat.

My lips slide along the edge of her jaw, suckling softly at the tender spot where I feel her racing pulse against my tongue. She sighs, making my stomach twirl like the girl on my sister's jewelry box. Torturing myself, I let my hands drift excruciatingly slowly down her body, stopping at the hem of the dress. She trembles when I pause to let my fingers brush the sides of her thighs.

She digs her own fingers into my hair, tangling them through the strands and pulling me closer to nip at my bottom lip. My pulse jumps, but I force myself to take this slowly. I move my hands unhurriedly back up—under the dress— savoring the feel of her skin against mine.

It's the most delicious sensation I've ever felt.

My hands grip her hips and pull her closer, so my pants and her thin dress are the only things separating us.

I push her back against the wall and she makes this little sound that makes my blood pressure skyrocket.

She moves her hands under my shirt and I shiver when her cold hands press against my flesh, but I love it. Almost more than I like the feel of her silky hair between my fingers or her taste that's unlike anything else.

All of the past emotions disappear. Evie is what matters now. Anything else is inconsequential.

She moves her hands from my stomach to my back and up to my shoulders, and I move mine to her thighs and hitch her up, so she wraps her legs around my waist.

My hands return to their previous position on the naked skin of her waist and continue their upward track, sweeping over her rib cage, as our breaths turn to ragged gasps. My whole body is on fire, each movement scorching my already smoldering flesh.

I love every moment of it.

I pause again, just below the curve of her breasts. My whole body is shaking with want and need.

She kisses right under my ear and I shiver. "I love you, Gavin."

"Say it again," I whisper.

Her eyes are confused, but she says, "I love you and—"

I kiss her again. "That's it. That's all I need to hear," I say against her lips. "I love you."

She pulls me closer, then whispers in my ear. "I need you."

I push back, my brows furrowed to look at her, confused as to what she really wants.

"Don't you want me?" Hurt swirls in her eyes.

"More than I want my next breath," I say.

She smiles. "Then what's the problem?"

"Are you sure?"

"As sure as I'm here right now." She drags me back down to her, and says in my ear, "I want you to be my first, last, and only. I want to be *your* first and only." Then she presses her lips against mine in a way that leaves no room for questions or doubts or nerves.

Chapter Twenty-four

Today I wear the dress of the Enforcer and the mask of the revolution. I wear them not to hide, but to reveal my true self.

—Evie's journal

Evie

I wake feeling lighter than I have in a while. And not just because Gavin's in my bed either. Although that's not exactly a hardship. It's because, with him, there's no pretense. I don't have to be someone I'm not. I don't have to pretend I know the answer to every question. Or the solution to every problem. I don't have to be Evelyn, Daughter of the People. Or Miss Evelyn, leader of the revolutionary Underground. I can just be Evie.

It's wonderful having him back, I think, looking over at Gavin.

"If you're going to stare, can you do it more quietly? I'm trying to sleep over here."

I laugh and shove him slightly. "I'm so sorry I woke his royal highness with my loud thoughts."

Gavin opens his eyes. Before I can do more than laugh-scream, he's got me tackled on the bed, his hands on mine. And then he's kissing me and I stop thinking altogether.

When he kisses me until my mind is completely empty and the breath stolen from my lungs, I gently try to push him away, but he won't let me up.

"Come on, Neanderthal, let me up. I've got to get clothes on."

"What's wrong with what you're wearing?"

"I'm not wearing anything!" I say with a laugh.

"I'm still not seeing the problem. You look gorgeous. You're absolutely perfect."

I push slightly away from him. "Asher told me something about perfect once. When we were on the Surface."

"Asher isn't exactly someone I want to be talking about at this moment." He lifts an eyebrow. "But . . . what was it?"

"That there really is no such thing as perfect, because every-one's version of perfect is different. And that no matter how perfect you think something is, there's cracks and flaws."

Gavin shrugs. "I can't argue with any of that."

"So . . . my question is, am I perfect to you because I'm perfect? Because that's what Mother made me to be? Or do you see *me*?"

He laughs. "Oh, you're far from perfect, Evie. Just like me. You're stubborn—"

"What's wrong with being stubborn?" I interject.

He kisses me, to shut me up, I'm sure. "You're *annoyingly* stubborn. About *everything*. You always think you're right. And you usually are. You have no sense of what your true worth really is, even though everyone around you sees it. And the most annoying of all: You have this habit of tying a guy up in knots and making him want to do absolutely anything for you—no matter how difficult or impossible the task—just to see you smile."

For more than a second I'm speechless. Finally I manage a question. "And that's a bad thing?"

He laughs and presses another kiss to my mouth. "Yes, but also absolutely, beyond a doubt, the reason I love you. So, yeah, I see you."

The muffled sound of a throat clearing comes from the doorway. Gavin groans and pulls away, making sure we're both covered with the blanket.

"I don't mean to interrupt your reunion," Asher's voice calls through the wood, "but Mother's made her move. You're probably going to want to see this."

Gavin and I toss on our clothes and hurry out the door, catching up to Asher just as he turns into the War Room. Everyone is already there, including Lenore. I thought she looked bad when she came back, but now she looks even worse. She appears to have aged more than a few years in the last few hours.

In her hands is a data screen, but she's not looking at it. She's gawking at the picture on the monitor Asher set up for us to keep an eye on activities in Elysium. The one where two

Enforcers lay crumpled and piled on top of each other on the floor just outside the Palace Wing, as if they'd just been tossed out like trash.

A fresh wound slices across my heart.

"She's completely unhinged," I whisper. I turn away from the image. I can't take any more death. "I have to talk to them. This has to end."

No one argues with me this time.

I turn to Lenore. "I know you've just gotten here, but I need to know if you can deactivate our nanites."

She stares at her data screen. "I've been trying to answer that same question since you left. I don't know." She meets my eyes. "The changes that have been made since I left have made them almost a completely different machine than the ones I designed. I need more time and samples. I need to see the new machines in person."

"Fine. We'll make sure you get them."

"Also," she says. "The files here are just a bunch of technical specs on the device Evangeline told me Mother gave the Enforcers. Is there anything else?"

"We have access to all of Mother's records she kept on the mainframe. I'm sure Dr. Friar's notes are there as well. You're welcome to pull anything you need from them. Asher." He looks over at me. "Help her access them."

He nods and signals for his grandmother to join him.

I pull Gavin off to the side. "While she's working on the nanite issue, I have another problem only you can help me with."

He nods solemnly. "How can I help?"

"There are tunnels that we believe lead to the Surface. We thought we could funnel people from Elysium through here to them and up to the Surface, but we still have the nanite problem. As soon as anyone comes close to the end of the field, their nanites do what mine did. But we have Lenore now, so I need you to make sure that the tunnels are even viable."

He groans. "The last time I followed tunnels I didn't know, I almost died."

I pat his arm. "And you also met me."

"I got it. I'll take care of it."

"Good, because I have to give these people some kind of good news."

I walk him to where the tunnels start and hand him a few flashlights. He isn't gone long before he returns. "I need rope. Or string. A lot of it. That way I can use it to make sure I find my way back."

"There's some where the life support system is," Nadia says behind me. "The excavation crews left huge spools of it. Hopefully it'll be enough. I'll have people bring them here."

Ten minutes later, he's got the metal rope tied to his waist and he's starting back into the pitch-black tunnel. I sit on the ground next to a spool that's twice as tall as I am with instructions that when the first spool runs out—if it does—I tie the second spool to the first line and do the same for the second and the third. Until he returns.

Somewhere near three hours later and getting close to spool three, I begin to get worried. The rope hasn't moved for almost an hour. I've been pacing around the spool for the last thirty minutes. People have filtered in and out, so I know word's gotten out that I'm doing something about a way out, but no one says anything to me. They just peer into the dark. Some sit, but most leave after a few minutes.

Suddenly, I see something coming at me through the dark. I can just barely make out the light beam. I sincerely hope it's Gavin, but I prepare myself for the possibility that it's not. It doesn't take long before Gavin, dirty but unharmed, steps back into the light.

I lift my eyebrows in question and he grins, nodding. I whoop and jump the distance between us as he hugs me one-handed. Today's the day everything changes. I can feel it.

Even though he never actually states it's an exit, word spreads like wildfire around the Caverns that the tunnels are a way out. I get stopped I don't know how many times so people can ask me if it's true as I make my way toward the War Room to find out if Lenore's made any headway.

I only happily smile and nod to their questions. The relief on everyone's faces as I pass them bandages a small part of my heavy heart. We still have a ways to go, but we're closer than we've ever been before.

When I step into the War Room, Lenore and Asher are still poring over files and I stop myself from demanding an update. It's obvious that they haven't come up with a solution yet, or they'd have told me. Besides, it's only been three hours. Lenore said she needed time. I just have to be patient.

"Evie!" Father's voice booms from the vid screen, startling

everyone in the room. Lenore slams a hand to her chest and for a minute I worry something's wrong with her heart, but then she glares at Father.

"You scared me."

"Sorry." He barely spares her a glance before returning his attention to me. "Mother is planning something. She has all of her Guards going door-to-door with this." He holds the paper and reads from it. " 'Citizens of Elysium, there will be an assembly at four p.m. in the Square. Attendance is mandatory.' "

Conversations burst to life again. Part of me is completely gratified that Mother has had to resort to this to make sure the word is passed along about the first assembly she's held since we cut her communications, but part of me is worried, too. *Why* is she holding an assembly? Surely she got her point across with the Enforcers' bodies in the Square. Technically, it's my move. Not hers.

I guess I was right. Today *is* the day that changes everything.

In four hours there will be the moment of truth. Will there be anyone who stands with me? Or will I stand there alone?

"Well, I guess it's time to recruit some Enforcers," I say.

Gavin takes my hand and squeezes it. I squeeze back, letting him know I appreciate him standing beside me when I need him the most.

Asher readies the vid system to link into the com channel as I walk to my room and grab my garb. The dress of the Enforcer. The mask of the revolution. And today I wear them not to hide myself, but to reveal my true self.

I slip into the clothing, but leave the mask off and the hood down. For now. With all the children now here, it's best I not scare them. I step from my room and back into the War Room. Asher glances over before quickly returning to his work, but Gavin stops and stares at me.

"Promise me you'll follow your instincts. If they're telling you to get the hell out of there, do it. We can always have a go at it another way."

"I will. I have no wish to die by Mother's hand today," I say.

"It's not Mother's hand I'm worried about."

I kiss his cheek. "I'll be fine. Mother's killing *them* now. I'm sure they'll hear me out."

"Just . . . don't take any unnecessary chances."

My heart beats frantically in my chest, but I smile. "Shouldn't I be saying that to you? You're the Surface Dweller."

He doesn't smile. "Promise me."

I roll my eyes in the hopes of teasing out that smile. "All right. All right. I promise."

He leans down and whispers in my ear. "You have my heart, Evie. Make sure you keep it safe."

"I love you," I whisper.

He presses his lips to mine and I can feel him fighting to stop himself from demanding more before he gently pushes me away.

The worry in his eyes is doing nothing to help my nerves, but as I take those steps away from him, I go with a light heart. Because I know today is the day that, for better or worse, everything changes.

Chapter Twenty-five

It is the cause, not the death, that make the martyr.
—Napoleon Bonaparte

Gavin

My heart really does feel like Evie took it with her when she left. Despite my confidence and trust in her that she's making the smart move, I'm terrified for her. I don't know how many times in the past hour I've walked to where I watched Evie disappear only to stand there for a few minutes, then pace back to the center area of the Caverns again.

It's on one of these trips back from the entrance that Asher rushes out from the direction of the War Room and barrels into me. "Gavin!" He grasps my shoulder.

His expression makes hope flutter in my chest. "Lenore figured it out?"

He beams. "We think so. Yes. Come on!" He drags me by the arm back into the War Room.

Lenore is slouched over the table, staring at something on the table with a giant table top magnifying glass. Asher and I cross to the other side and Asher gestures toward her when I frown at him. Her fingers are deftly fiddling with the silver device Evie recovered from Dr. Moreau.

"What's going on?" I ask. "Asher says you might have found a way to neutralize the nanites?"

"Yes," she mumbles barely loud enough for me to hear, her fingers still tinkering. "This device is used to control everything the nanites do. It would stand to reason that if they can control them, they can also power them off."

"Is that smart?" I peer down at the remote. "Won't turning them off do what happened to Evie?"

"No. According to Dr. Friar's notes, the nanites are programmed to destroy the neuro-pathways of the subject only if the proper shutdown sequence isn't activated. So, if I can *properly* shut them down, I should be able to negate that consequence."

I blink as I stare at her. Then turn my attention to Asher, who's grinning from ear to ear. Apparently what she just said was supposed to make sense to me. Unfortunately, speaking geek isn't one of my many talents.

"Would you mind saying that in a way I can understand?" I ask.

She frowns as she peers up at me over the top of the glasses that have slipped down her nose. "Pardon?"

"I didn't understand what you said," I repeat. She still looks puzzled, so I tap the machine.

The light bulb goes off above her head and she nods quickly. "Ah! Sorry. Basically the nanites are programmed to 'erase' someone's memory if they're not shut down properly. Like what happened with Evie."

"But you can turn them off properly?"

She puts the remote back together as she talks. "I think so. Yes. Dr. Friar has lots and lots of notes on his experimentations and a few of those experiments were testing the efficacy of the field on the nanites. He had to know how to properly turn them off to test it, so it's all here in his notes."

A spark of excitement singes my nerve endings, but I squash it down with logic. "We're going to have to test this to make sure it works before we send a whole city of people away."

"Yes. I know." Her voice is quiet again, but it's not because she's focused on her task. She's staring at her hands as if questioning how to work them. "We already have a volunteer."

"Who are you—" I start to ask, but when she looks at me with so much pain in her eyes, *I* almost crush under the weight of it, I realize exactly who would do such a thing.

I turn my attention to Asher, who returns my gaze without wavering.

"Me," he says, confirming my suspicion. He splays his hands out in front of him on the table. "I'm willing and able to do it."

I shake my head, even though I know the fruitlessness of my protest. "Let's wait until Evie gets back. She'll know how to best proceed from here."

He shakes his head. "We don't have time to wait. Mother's

assembly is happening in four hours. We don't know what she's planning, but it's not going to be good."

"We don't know that—"

"Evie thought so. That's why she went to get the Enforcers now instead of waiting."

I can't argue with that so I don't. "But Evie—" I start to say again.

"Evie's not here. I am. She trusted me enough while you were gone to put me in charge whenever she was out. You need to trust me, too."

I open my mouth to protest again, but the look he gives me tells me that he's not going to listen to any of my arguments and I'll be wasting time we already don't have. "I don't like this, but—" I say finally.

He purses his lips. "You don't have to."

"*But*," I continue as if he hadn't interrupted. "I trust you. So . . . how can I help?"

His mouth is open as if to argue with me, but apparently shock has robbed him of his voice. Lenore is the one who says, "The only thing you can do, is once I've turned them off and we're sure he's all right, you'll need to help him get to the Surface and back again. If it doesn't work, he'll need your help to get back."

I swallow and nod my understanding. "I can do that."

She pushes her glasses back up her nose and reaches for one of the Slates. "I'm ready whenever you are." She holds the machine in one hand and her Slate in the other.

Asher opens his mouth to tell her to go ahead, but I interrupt him. "Wait. Before you do this, I need to say something. Something I should have said a long time ago."

He frowns up at me, but gestures for me to continue.

I shove a hand through my hair, but keep my eyes steady on his. "Look. I . . . I just want to say I'm sorry. About everything. When my dad died, I thought I knew what was going on. But, obviously, I didn't have a clue. You had my back this whole time and I was so stuck in the pain of losing my dad I couldn't see it. I should have known you wouldn't have betrayed me like that. I should've asked what your side was. *You* should have forced me to see your side of it." I glare at him.

The shock on his face gives way to amusement. "You always find a way to turn this back around to me, don't you?" He laughs. "But when you're right, you're right. I should have told you my side. But would you have listened?" He lifts an eyebrow.

I shake my head with my own chuckle. "Probably not." I let out a sigh. "Man, your dad's a *dick*!"

Lenore snorts. "Now *that* I agree with."

"Grandma!"

"What?" she demands with a shrug. "Sometimes the truth is vulgar."

Asher and I exchange a look and start laughing for a few stress-relieving minutes, before he stops and holds out his hand. "Friends?"

I grip his hand and return the shake with a nod and a bro hug.

"Well, that was lovely," Lenore says, her tone as dry as the dirt under my feet. "But we have work to do. Are we ready?"

Asher swallows, but nods and sits back next to Lenore. I move to his other side just as Lenore presses a button on the remote. I quickly look up at Asher, who has his eyes closed, but nothing happened.

"Did you do it?" I ask.

"Yes." Her voice cracks and she clears it quickly. "I turned them off. See?" She gestures to the Slate where a bunch of random letters and words are scrolling over the screen.

"What's that?"

"The shutdown sequence." The screen goes blank and her eyes jerk up to Asher, who's still sitting completely still in his chair. I can hear his slightly faster than normal breathing, but that's it.

I touch his shoulder. "You okay, man?"

His eyes open and he blinks a few times before he nods. "I don't feel any different." He glances at Lenore. "Is that what's supposed to happen?"

"Yes." She lifts a shoulder, but she's paler than she was a few minutes ago and I have the feeling she expected something different as well.

Asher pushes to his feet with a shrug. "Well, then, let's see if it worked." He saunters out of the room, leaving Lenore and me to follow in his wake.

When we get to the area where the start of the EM field ends, we all pause and stare into the dark abyss. After a few seconds, Lenore clears her throat and hands me a flashlight, which I promptly turn on. I didn't much like the tunnels the first time I went through them and I don't care for them now. But it's a way to the Surface and if what Lenore did to Asher worked, it's the best chance we've got of saving the people in Elysium.

Lenore hugs Asher tightly before she pushes him away. "Godspeed," she says quietly and then steps back and gestures for us to go ahead.

I clap Asher on the shoulder. "Good luck," I say, then lead the way.

For the next hour, we follow the wire I'd left to the Surface. Neither of us say anything, but I'm constantly turning back to make sure he's okay. I don't know what to expect. Evie passed out when her nanos stopped working, but I don't know if that was from blood loss or from the nanos.

We wander in the dark, the path in front of us only illuminated as far as the light from the flashlight beam goes. But finally I see the light at the end of the tunnel. Literally. Fresh air blows in our faces and when we exit the mouth of the cave, I take a huge breath of the sweet air.

Asher and I just stand there, watching and waiting for something to happen to him. But after a few minutes, I wander to the edge of the cliff beyond the cave opening and sit, looking out over the whole area. I can just barely see my town and the cove from up here.

Asher joins me and for a while we just sit there without talking.

Finally Asher says, "I guess it worked."

I nod, as the pressure that had been squeezing my heart lets up a little. "Yep."

"Now what?"

"Now we figure out how to get over two hundred people who've never seen the sun before out of the Caverns and into a safe place here."

He shoves to his feet, then holds out his hand for me. "Let's get the party started."

Evie

Mother has the maintenance tunnels so full of Guards that I don't even risk using them. Not today when no one knows what Mother has up her sleeve. Instead I decide to slip in by way of Sector Three. It'll give me the added benefit of checking on the damage to Three and seeing what the green blobs are up to.

I slide the airlock door up just enough to allow me to peek under it and make sure everything is safe, before wedging it open with a large piece of rock from the cave-in, I crawl through the gap, then remove the rock and let the door drop into place.

Lights buzz and flicker, casting eerie shadows on the wall next to me. The building creaks and groans, causing the hairs all over my body to stand on end. I shudder. I thought this place was creepy the first time I came through, but that's nothing compared to how it is now.

The stench here is so bad I have to bring my shirt up to

cover my nose, but that doesn't help much and I'm constantly swallowing at the lump of bile in my throat. Maybe it wasn't such a good idea to come this way. But I had to see if Three was as bad as Father said. I have to admit I think it's worse.

The exit to Sector Two is on the complete opposite side of the building from where I am. Memories from the first time I was here echo in my head. I *really* don't want to cut through the building, but unless I feel like taking on all the Guards in the maintenance tunnels single-handedly, I have no choice. So I straighten my shoulders and walk as quickly as I dare without running down the corridors.

Every so often I hear what sounds like feet sliding across the floor, and I stop immediately to do a quick visual to make sure I'm alone. When I'm sure there's no one there, I continue, my heart hammering away at my rib cage.

Finally, I see the dark glass of the corridor and staging area for the Tube leading to Sector Two. I let out a large breath I hadn't been aware I'd been holding until just now. I have to force myself to slow down as even my body tries to rush me toward the airlock door of the Tube.

But it's the goo that stops me in my tracks. It's definitely moved since the last time I was here. It's now in a big puddle by the glass wall. Part of it is reaching up the metal beams toward the ceiling, stretching out across it in a pattern not too different from that of a spider web.

Despite myself, I give in to my curiosity and shove down my misgivings to cross to where it is. Carefully, I steer clear of the massive puddle and narrow my eyes at the stuff strung across the girders. It's unusual to say the least. The parts not touched by the green stuff are completely intact. The areas that have been touched are rusting. And not just a little—some places are so pockmarked and filled with holes they look like Swiss cheese.

That can't be good for the building. That must be what Father was talking about when he said the structural integrity of the building was compromised. I make a mental note to make sure no one goes this way anymore. This Sector has to be officially off limits to everyone. Including Father. I'll have to figure out a way to keep him from here. I don't care about the green junk anymore. It's not worth dying over. I'm just about to step away from it, and the window beyond, when a dark shadow passes by on the other side of the glass.

The water's so murky here, I'm not exactly sure what it is I saw, until a shark rams the glass with its jaws fully open, showing off all the rows of its super sharp teeth. I jump back with a yelp. My feet slip out from underneath me, and I fall mere centimeters from the puddle.

"What in the . . ." I mutter. Why did it do that? That's not normal, is it?

I shove myself away from the puddle, but don't stand just yet. With my heart going a kilometer a minute and my legs shaking, there's no way I'd be able to even if I wanted to. So I press my forehead to my knees and count to twenty.

I've just reached nineteen when I hear someone running down the corridor to my right. Not caring if my legs will hold me or not, I jump up to my feet and press myself as tightly as

I can to the wall. Whoever it is, it probably isn't someone who's on my side.

As they approach, my mind goes through all the possibilities. If it's an Enforcer, I'm going to have to be smart how I approach this. I am trying to get them on my side, after all. If it's anyone else, whether it's a Guard, or some other random Citizen, then I'll just knock them out and drag them out of here so they don't get hurt.

Either way, I tell myself, the worst case is it's an Enforcer, and I'll have to hope they're as willing to listen to me as I think they might be. The footsteps slow down as they draw closer, but it isn't until they stop just on the other side of the green stuff that I can make out who it is. My heart stops. It's worse than my worst case. It's Dr. Friar.

I push myself even flatter against the wall behind me. If I can just wait him out, he'll probably leave and I'll get on my way and leave him to whatever horrible thing he's doing here.

He's muttering to himself. ". . . know I heard someone . . . just the building giving me the creeps . . . should just flood the whole thing like I said months ago."

But instead of leaving and returning to what he was doing before like I'd hoped, he kneels next to the green ick and pulls his Slate out. For the next several minutes, he continues tapping away at the screen. Then he pulls out one of those silver remotes and touches a button on it. The blob bubbles and makes a horrendous sound, almost like it's screaming.

I slam my hands to my ears and the movement must give me away, because Dr. Friar's head jerks up and his eyes meet mine. I stop breathing and don't even dare to blink. I'm in a shadow. It's possible he can't see me. I hope.

Until that sickening smile of his slices across his face and he pushes up to his feet. "Well, well. What do we have here?" He slowly walks toward me, while I measure my choices.

It seems I only have two. Run deeper into the building and hope to outrun him—if I remember correctly, there's a stairwell around here—or stay and fight.

When the building lets out another loud groan, I realize I have to fight. There's no way I'm running around a building that even he thinks should be abandoned completely.

His grin grows even more wicked when I step into the light of the hallway. "Evelyn! How wonderful to see you alive! Mother will be so pleased to know that."

I just stare at him. Really? Does he really think I'm that stupid?

When he laughs, I realize that no, he doesn't think I'm stupid. He's just as mad as Mother is.

Suddenly, my whole body feels aflame. Screaming, I collapse to my knees, and even though they hit the concrete with all of my body weight, the pain of that doesn't even compare to the agony ripping through my body.

As quickly as it started, it stops, and I peer up through tear-coated lashes to see Dr. Friar standing over me. "Mother doesn't want me to kill you, but she's not happy with you."

I try to force myself to my feet, but before I can even get one foot under me, I'm back on the ground writhing as more volcanoes erupt through my skin to scorch my flesh.

"No. Don't get up. I need some answers from you." He leans over me as I curl into myself, trying to escape the pain, but I see the silver remote between his fingers. Not that I'm surprised. "Where have you been hiding?" he demands.

The pain stops long enough for me to spit out, "Not. Telling."

He presses the button again, and this time the pain feels like I'm being electrocuted. I bite down so hard on my tongue, I taste blood in my mouth, but I can't let up as what seems like every muscle in my body contracts at once.

"Want to try that again?"

He releases the button and, with it, my muscles.

I glare at him, but don't answer him. I don't care how much it hurts or if he *does* kill me. I'm not telling him anything.

"Aw! Catfish got your tongue?" He laughs at his own joke as more red-hot agony tears through me.

I struggle against it. If I can just manage to tap into the Enforcer part of me, I'll be able to ignore it. Or at least I think I can. I did when I got shot, back when I first met Gavin. Every time the Enforcer part of me kicked on, the pain dulled. This has to work the same, too, right?

He leans down, presumably to whisper something in my ear, but I force myself to focus all my energy on him and I shove up, slamming my head against his. He howls in pain, dropping the device to grab for his nose.

While he's busy with that, I belly-crawl toward the silver object. I hope he's too busy dealing with his own pain to worry about me, but just as my fingertips touch the cold metal, he stomps on my hand, breaking fingers I'm sure, before he swipes the device from the ground with clawed fingers.

Suddenly, I feel like he crushed my trachea instead of my fingers. I can't breathe. I scratch at my throat, trying anything to get oxygen flowing again. But all I'm doing is tearing my flesh from my body.

"Can't . . . kill . . . me," I gasp out, hoping a reminder of Mother's wrath will stop him, but it doesn't.

"She'll never know," he hisses at me. "And with you gone, your mutiny dies with you." He glares at me.

Spots form in front of my eyes and I realize, I'm going to die. He's going to kill me and he doesn't care what Mother wants. I have to stop him, no matter what it takes. I survey my surroundings for anything that could help me. That's when my eyes land back on the goo again.

Somehow, during the fight, I forced him closer to the spider web of ooze along the window and beam. One shove and he'd end up right in it. It's my only choice, if I want to live.

Gathering all my strength, my lungs burning, and red and black spots flashing in my eyes, I lunge toward him again and push with all my strength. He lets out a surprised gasp and drops the remote, pinwheeling his arms as he falls backward into the goo.

I don't waste even a second. My fingers just barely find the remote as darkness leaks in from the sides of my vision. I mash down on what I hope is the right button as I collapse face first onto the concrete.

Almost immediately the pressure in my chest leaves and I'm

able to drag in enough air to push back at the darkness. But as the pounding in my ears dissipates, I hear another sound. High-pitched screaming. Dr. Friar. Panting, I push onto my hands and knees and watch in horror as the slime sucks him into it as fast as it had done Asher's shoe when we first ran into the stuff.

Guilt now eats at me instead of my own nanos, but I don't have a chance to even remind myself it was either him or me, when the sludge suddenly lurches toward me. I push myself up and hobble toward the Tube. Last time, we were faster than it. I have to be faster than it now.

But it's different than it was before, and I'm slower, so by the time I force open the door to the Tube, it's practically at my heels. I rush through and immediately shove the door back down, but it slides through after me before I can get the airlock closed and grabs ahold of my ankle.

The fire I thought I'd felt when Dr. Friar turned the device on me is nothing compared to acid devouring my leg. I rip my leg from it, but it clings to me and I can't shake it off. Stupidly, I try brushing it off, but it sticks to my hands, burning them as well.

Then, as if someone is screaming it at me, I remember what Father said about seawater and its effect on the goo. Without thinking of the consequences, I run to the control panel near the door, and shove up the lever that fills the Tube with seawater.

The water rushes in so cold and so fast it takes my breath away, but it's relief I feel most as the goo just falls away from me like it had never been. My flesh underneath is bloody and raw, but at least it'll heal.

Relief making me giddy, I try to yank on the lever to stop the flow of water, but it doesn't budge. Frowning, I tug again only to be met with the same resistance. I laugh and roll my eyes when I remember I can't shut it off because I have to unlock it. Only Citizens can unlock it. A safety measure in case of Surface Dwellers. I press my hand against the plate and wait for it to flash green, but it doesn't. It flashes red.

I press my hand against it again. And again. The water starts closing in over my head. Panic kicks back in as I remember.

I deleted the Citizen's registry.

I can't open the door, because the registry that the computer needs to unlock the door is gone.

Chapter Twenty-six

The beginning cannot start without there first being an end.
—Unknown

Gavin

It's been four hours since Evie left. I thought being away from her for two months was bad, but I was wrong. These have been the longest four hours of my life. Each tick of the second hand on my watch is like a countdown. I'm in the Square, standing in a sea of sameness. All the people here are dressed the same as me, with exactly the same face. The mask, of course. I can honestly say I'm proud to be here, with all these people showing their solidarity against someone they've feared since they came to be living in the city.

Some people at first glance would say that nothing has changed. But I can see that everything has. Even in the short time since I came back, since Mother's irrational and wildly publicized atrocities have taken place, I can see it. This time they *choose* to be the same. They're not forced to be that way by selective breeding, or whatever Mother calls her brand of hate.

The stage lights shine brightly on a banner that states LONG LIVE ELYSIUM. But a smile pulls at my lips when I see the small, hand-painted message under it. LONG LIVE EVIE. It's painted in the same stark white color as the printed words on the sign. And even though it's smaller and messier than the original words, somehow it stands out more, its message as loud and clear as the masks the people around me wear: "We're here. We're alive and we're not disposable."

I look around and see hundreds, if not thousands of replications of those words. Written in different colors. Different hands. Some still wet and gleaming. Others faded because Mother tried to wash them away. But they all are still there, and just the thought that they couldn't be washed away sends a happy thrill through my veins. Mother can't get rid of them, any more than she can get rid of the things Evie stands for. She could kill Evie today. Take the very breath from her lungs. But she'll never take what Evie's done.

I glance around again, this time looking for Evie. I know even in her mask I'd be able to see her. It worries me that I can't. She should have found me already. In fact, she should have met us back in the Caverns, but she never showed. We had to make the decision to continue without her. The snakes writhing in my stomach tie themselves into knots as I think about what that could mean.

"Does anyone see her?" I mutter into the mouthpiece attached to my mask.

"No," comes the answer from the three other people in the crowd with earpieces.

"Asher?"

It's quiet, except a soft buzzing, and my heart beats a little quicker. What if Mother got to her? Maybe the reason Mother is ten minutes late for her own assembly is because she's got Evie and she's planning on executing her publicly.

Finally the earpiece buzzes again. "No," Asher says, and I let out the breath I didn't know I was holding. "I just did another quick scan, but I can't see her. If she's here, she's well hidden."

Damn! I want to leave my post to find her, but if she's around here and I do find her, she'll be upset I'm not in my position. Besides, I'm closest to the stage. If Mother is planning something on the stage with Evie, I'll be able to get to her faster than anyone else.

"She's here," I finally say. "She has to be."

No one answers me.

Finally, the Square dims, and the spotlights highlighting the sign focus instead on the podium. A group of ten Enforcers step onto the stage. They line up next to the podium, five on each side. My eyes scan them quickly, trying to see any differences in their stature or stance. Anything. But there's nothing.

Shit! I scream in my head as my heart shatters and the hole it leaves in my chest threatens to suck me in.

"She didn't do it. She couldn't pull it off," Eli says, and along with the pain I hear in his voice there's also something like disappointment.

"We don't know that," I say. "Enforcers are trained not to show anything. We must continue with the plan as if nothing is wrong. Even if Evie is . . ." I can't force myself to say dead. ". . . gone. We have to finish what she started. For her. So that her sacrifice isn't in vain. That's what she'd want."

I shove my own pain down. I'll deal with it later. I have to finish this for her. I do another skim of the crowd around me to see if I can see any other Enforcers.

"I can't see any more Enforcers than those on the stage," Asher says just as I'm thinking it. "The infrared doesn't show anyone in the shadows and unless she's got more hidden somewhere with her . . . Eli?"

"No, Mother's placed everyone she has left on the stage with her," Eli says.

"She's scared," Evangeline says and I can hear the smile in her voice. "She's never had more than two on stage with her. The rest circulate through the crowd."

She says it like it's a good thing, but I know better. "She may be scared, but she's still being careful. A scared animal can be even more dangerous than a confident one."

The mumbles in the crowd quiet slightly as Mother takes the stage. She's wearing a red suit. The color of power. Of blood. Of death. It's not a good sign. But I try not to let it get to me. It's probably just a show. Like how an animal tries to make itself look bigger to scare things away.

As soon as Mother takes her place behind the podium, the

crowd starts shouting at her. Every once in a while I can make out the chant of "Evie lives," but mostly it's just a mess of voices tangling in and around each other.

She glares out over the crowd, but no one stops. She holds her hand up, calling for quiet, but again no one listens. They just keep up with their chant.

The microphone turns on with a click and her voice fills the Square. "Attention, Citizens. I call for your immediate silence and attention." Her voice is stern and not just a little unnerving and scary. It's laced with the insanity that we guessed at earlier, but there's something else there. Determination? Conviction? For the first time since I got down here, terror freezes my bones. Not for me or Evie, but for the people around me. Those rallying against Mother. Who knows what Mother really has planned? She's already proven she has no fear of death. Or murder of innocents. Even of her precious Enforcers. As long as it suits her needs, she'll do whatever it takes.

The crowd doesn't quiet. In fact they only get louder. Even from my spot I can see the anger spinning in her eyes. She's edging closer and closer inside the door of lunacy.

I sneak a little closer to the stage. If Evie's compromised, I make a promise to myself for everyone standing here, I won't let Mother get away with it. Not this time. Not after everything Evie's done to make sure they get a chance at freedom.

She raises her voice louder. "Citizens of Elysium! Control yourselves, before I'm forced to restrain you myself."

"Like you did with that family?" someone yells from the back of the crowd.

Mother glares into the crowd, her eyes rolling with madness as she tries to find the person. She leans to the Guard standing next to her in front of the stage. "Find whoever said that and take care of them." Her voice echoes across the room since she didn't cover the microphone.

Apparently she realizes that her people aren't going to quiet so she can spout her lies, and she speaks even louder into her microphone, almost screaming. "I apologize for the lateness of my reply to the traitor who feels it necessary to use my late daughter's effigy to make her futile point. But I wish to reassure all those who may believe her, that her accusations that one of my Enforcers killed that poor family under my orders are completely untrue and unfounded."

The buzz blares into my ear again. "There's no one left in the Palace Wing and the Enforcers' quarters are empty," Eli says.

". . . I am not sure why this traitor is targeting our city, but I assure all of you that Elysium is still the completely safe and wondrous place it's always been. I want also to remind the renegade that all traitorous actions from anyone will be dealt with swiftly and as harshly as the law allows. Renegade, that family's blood, and anyone else's who sides with you, is on *your* hands, and the only one to put it there is yourself . . ."

"There's still no Enforcers or even Guards in the crowd that I can see," Asher says a few seconds later.

God damn it, Evie! Where are you?

Just then there's a movement to my right, and I quickly turn to see what it is. My entire world rights itself again as I watch someone that can only be Evie slither onto the knee-high wall around the fountain and push herself up onto it, pulling herself to her full height. She stands there, staring at Mother, and I have to force myself not to run to her. To grab her off that wall and hold her to me, to kiss her until I'm sure that she's not just a figment of my imagination.

Instead, I say, "Evie at my six."

"She's there?" Eli says so loudly I wince.

"Yes," Asher confirms and the joy in his voice is nothing compared to what I feel.

My smile is glued to my face, and I don't think I could rip it off even if I wanted to.

Mother must finally notice Evie, because she stops in the middle of a word. I turn and see her staring at Evie in shock, her eyes following Evie's hand with the mask in it as she lowers it to her side.

The crowd slowly turns in the direction Mother's staring, but I keep my body angled so I can see both her and Evie. I don't want to leave anyone from my sight. When the crowd sees Evie, they stop shouting, and the entire Square is filled with the kind of noise that can only be heard in complete silence. Silence can sometimes be even louder than shouts.

Evie stares at Mother, who swallows, then smiles wickedly at her. The look isn't even directed at me, but it still makes me shudder.

Then Mother turns to her Enforcers. "Get her."

They don't move. They just keep their ramrod-straight stature, staring over the heads of the crowd as if the people don't exist at all.

Did she do it? Did Evie actually convince them to join us? Shock makes me numb.

The screen behind Mother now shows Evie. Asher's got all the monitors in the entire facility focused on her.

Evie turns her attention to the people standing around her.

"I *am* Evie. And I live." A cheer goes through the crowd. She waits until they quiet before going on. "People of Elysium, I want to first thank you for all the support you've given me these past few months. Just you being here with these," she lifts the mask, "shows what a group of people can do when they stand together."

A cheer goes up in the crowd, and my own smile grows larger, pride flowing through me. She's absolutely the most beautiful thing I've ever seen. The power and confidence I knew was there is bursting out of her, brighter than the sun.

She puts her hand up like Mother did earlier, but unlike with Mother, the people instantly quiet. "But it wasn't me who did this. It was you." She smiles. "It was all of you. Pulling together and coming to the realization that you weren't really living in paradise. Not when everyone has to be the same. When you can't make your own choices on anything. Not who you're friends with, where you work, what you say, or even who you can mate with."

A murmur grows through the crowd and Mother calls for her Enforcers to do something again, but while they're focused on Evie now, they seem to be listening as intently to what Evie's saying as the Citizens are.

"Look at what you've done. No one told you to do this. This

was all of you. Working separately, yet coming together for a single cause. You knew that life didn't need to be the way it was. That being afraid to breathe the wrong way, or look at someone wrong, isn't really living. And that 'living' every day in fear isn't and won't ever be acceptable."

I want to stand up and cheer, but I don't. I just keep staring at her and marveling at how far we've come.

As if thinking the same thing, she glances in my direction. I don't think she sees me, but it feels like she might when the smile on her face softens. She moves her gaze to encompass the crowd around her again. "But *you* didn't choose to live like that. *You* chose to realize that a leader who has no more respect for her Citizens than she does for the floor she walks on doesn't deserve her place, and you've rallied together to oust her. Look at all that you've accomplished." She spreads her arms out and spins in a circle as if encompassing all they've done. "All because you believed in something. Someone. It didn't even matter if I existed or not because I only gave you the ability to see that things were not as they seemed. *You* decided that things here weren't what you wanted. *You* decided *you* wanted to change it. And *you* accomplished it."

She focuses her attention completely on Mother, who seems to have lost her ability to speak. "The people have spoken, Mother. *Your* people. *Your* Citizens. *They* don't want you in power anymore. They don't want someone in your position who could massacre a toddler's entire family in front of her and then leave her to wander around covered in their blood." She narrows her eyes as the crowd turns, refocusing their attention on Mother. "As the rightful heir to your throne—the Daughter of the *People*—I am the people's voice. *They've* demanded *your* abdication." She places the mask back over her face, and while the next sentence is slightly muffled, I'm sure it carries directly to Mother. "I am Evie. I live and I *am* part of the people."

This time there's no cheer. Only people, their own masks still on, facing Mother. The monitor behind her blinks and shows Mother now, as it was originally intended to do. I feel a small bit of satisfaction as she remains quiet. She glares out over the people, and I can see her rage in the whiteness of her knuckles as she clutches the podium, but her blue eyes swirl with something close to madness—not anger. Insanity.

My heart thumps in my throat, competing with the ever-growing lump as I wait for her to say something. She turns toward her Enforcers again. "What are you waiting for?" Her voice squeaks. "I don't care what she or they say. *I* am in charge. *I* am Mother and *I'm* Governess. Retrieve her. *Now!*" Her voice steadily rises with each word and she shouts the last bit so loudly I'm tempted to cover my ears.

Again the Enforcers stay motionless. She did it. Evie did it. Enforcers are programmed to follow orders implicitly; if they're not following them, something big has changed.

Then a movement toward the stairs leading from the left of the stage catches my eye. I immediately tense, focusing on the Enforcer standing there.

Without moving her gaze from Evie, the Enforcer slowly removes her hands from behind her back and moves them to the front of her body. I nervously lick my lips, but stand my ground. Evie isn't moving. She doesn't even seem surprised. Since I trust her, I wait and see what the Enforcer does. But I'm completely astonished it isn't a gun in her hand, but one of the masks. She slowly pulls it over her head and adjusts it on her face, so she looks just like everyone else here.

The next Enforcer does the same, then the next and the next until the entire line of them from stage right to stage left has masks on. Then, in one movement, as if they've practiced this move for hours, they all turn toward Mother, their boots making a thumping sound on the stage.

"Long live Evie!" They say it together in their emotionless voices.

"Whoa!" I can't help but say aloud. Not at all what I expected to happen.

Then something else I didn't expect to happen, happens. The people chant for Mother to step down.

You can tell she has no idea what to do. She stares at her Enforcers, then at the people, then at Evie, then back at the Enforcers. Then she bolts. Straight past the Enforcers and me, jumping down the stairs.

Evie

After everything that had gone wrong this morning . . . the fight to the death with Dr. Friar. The murderous goo. Nearly drowning, only to be rescued by the very people I'd been trying to find in the first place—the Enforcers. I was sure the entire plan was doomed to failure. But my heart is singing in triumph. We did it. I can't believe it, but we did it.

But I don't even have time to let that sink in. Mother races away from the Square, toward the Palace Wing and the Tube Station. The Enforcers immediately give chase, along with one of the Citizens—one I'm almost positive is Gavin. I rip off my mask to push through the crowd.

By the time I catch up to her, she's already at the Guard station in front of the tube leading to the Palace Wing. The Guard tries to stop her, but she only shoves him down and runs down the tube. An Enforcer takes aim and shoots at her, but the bullet misses by mere centimeters. I hear it hit something metal.

"Stop shooting. We're not like her," I shout.

She suddenly makes an abrupt turn and disappears into a stairwell. I put on an extra burst of speed. Adrenaline pumps through my veins, pushing me to go faster and faster, and I bypass the first Enforcer and plunge into the stairwell directly after the only person between Mother and me: Gavin.

I keep them just in sight as we run down the stairs and watch them vanish through a door at the bottom. I follow after them, the Enforcers immediately behind me. I'm sure we've got her trapped. This should be a storage room with only one door. The other walls are exteriors. The Enforcers will apprehend her and we'll continue our plan to exile her without any further surprises until Lenore can free the rest of the Citizens and myself from our invisible bonds.

But when I rush in, I stop in my tracks. It isn't a storage

area. It's another submarine dock. Similar to the one in Sector Three, only smaller. And Mother is in the lone submersible—also much smaller. The circular door that leads to the spherical vessel slams shut just as Gavin reaches it.

She waves her fingers at him with a smile so bright it's manic. She presses a button and with a burst of bubbles the sub rushes away from the glass into the open ocean.

Gavin slams his hand against the glass door hard enough to shake the whole thing.

"Stop that," an Enforcer hisses. "You'll break it and the pressure will kill us all."

Gavin ignores her. "What is that?" he demands, though the answer is obvious.

"It's obviously an emergency escape pod." My voice is devoid of emotion. How could this happen? Father had to know of this. Why didn't he tell us this was here?

"She's going to get away?" Gavin demands. "That's it?"

But I'm studying the little round vessel. Why isn't she trying to get away faster? She's not that far from the building. A meter at most. And the submersible is just slowly floating upward, as if the vessel doesn't have its own power and is reliant on the air inside it to make it buoyant.

"Come on." I turn away toward the door. "As slowly as that thing is moving, there's plenty of time for us to get to the other subs and tow her back." The Enforcers immediately follow my command, vacating the space in just a few seconds. I hear their footsteps moving up the stairs, but then a speaker crackles and Gavin and I jump and look around for the sound.

In the corner is a tiny square speaker. Mother's voice emits from it. "Foolish child. Did you really think I would just 'go quietly into that good night'? You should have let the Enforcers kill me when you had the chance, Evelyn. I will not allow you to take my city from me."

I shake my head and gesture for Gavin to turn around to leave. "Let's get the other subs."

I jump when I hear a long, low beeping sound.

"What was that?" Mother demands and both Gavin and I turn around to try and find the source.

But then it cuts off and there's a *thump*, which sounds like it came from the speaker.

Gavin echoes, "What was that?"

But I don't answer, because while I don't know exactly what it was, I can see what it did. There, on Mother's pod, the glass dome is cracking. Spiderwebs of cracks grow larger every time I blink. I can hear it through the speaker.

She runs to the hatch, and her face presses against it. "Help me," she says. "Please. Help me."

Both Gavin and I are frozen. I can't do anything. I'm rooted to the spot. My feet refuse to budge even a centimeter.

Mother is staring at me. "Evelyn! Help me!" she says again. "You have to help me! I saved your life. Made you my own. Don't just *stand* there. Help me!" she yells, her voice screeching.

In horror, I watch as the cracks grow larger and longer. Even from here I can see water pouring in from a few of the larger ones.

Mother starts screaming louder. Shrieking about the

pressure. Yelling at us to help her. But we can't. There isn't anything we can do. We're too deep and the cracks are too big. It'll all be over before we even reach the top of the stairs.

She's only meters from us and there's nothing we can do to help her.

Her screams turn to gurgles and red foam froths from her mouth. The sound is horrifying. Someone places their hands over my ears.

"Don't look, Evie," Gavin says. "Just close your eyes."

But I can't. Even with Gavin's hands over my ears, I can still hear her screaming. See her clawing at her throat as if she can't breathe. Then, just when I don't think I can take it anymore, the glass splinters one last time and the entire vessel implodes.

"Mother!" I yell, pushing past Gavin to run to the glass, even though I know it's too late. Had been too late from almost the beginning.

Just as I reach the glass, the shockwave hits it with a boom and rocks the entire room. I'm thrown into Gavin, who is directly behind me. My head smashes onto the concrete floor and stars explode in front of my head before darkness yanks me down.

Chapter Twenty-seven

"She's planning a rebellion."

"Yes."

"Should I terminate?"

"No. It's just getting fun."

—TRANSCRIPT, SIM 6, SUBJECT 121

Subject 121 failed . . ." The somehow familiar yet unfamiliar voice, along with the sound of beeping, greets me as I slowly come to.

The air around me feels heavier than I remember; the smell of it staler. I think I might even smell a hint of chemicals. I must be in the Medical Sector. Father must have brought me and Gavin here after the explosion.

Gavin! The thought gives me a quick electrical zap in my nerves, but my limbs are still so heavy that the thought of moving my fingers—or even just my toes—is exhausting. My body wants me to succumb to blissful sleep, but I struggle through the fog in my head to tug myself into full consciousness. Even then I can't open my eyes. There's something keeping them shut.

Slowly—excruciatingly slowly—I force my fingers to move. But when I try moving my forearm, I make it only mere centimeters before I realize my arms are strapped to whatever I'm lying on. My legs are shackled with the same soft restraints at the ankle.

Tingles of panic slice through the fog in my brain, and I struggle against my restraints. The beeping next to me turns into screaming alarms.

I sense more than hear the movement at the bottom of my bed. I force myself to stop my fruitless floundering and to slow my rapid breathing. Of course, that doesn't stop the pounding of my heart, but there's nothing I can do about that.

The warmth of someone standing near me heats my left side and then suddenly, as if I've been hit with a hammer, pain pools like a wet heat at the nape of my neck. The tape is ripped from my eyes leaving me blinded not by darkness, but by a searing white light. I blink rapidly, trying to get my vision to focus, and stop the pain shooting from my eyes to my brain, but no matter how much I blink, everything remains a blur.

Finally, after several long moments, I'm able to make out a nurse standing beside me, making notes on a Slate and mumbling numbers to herself.

"Wh—what?" I start, but my voice is rusty. My throat is sore and my tongue is thick and dry, sticking to the roof of my mouth.

The woman barely spares me a glance. "Don't talk. You've been under awhile." Her tone is gruff. Almost mean.

Once again, I try to move, only to have the nurse glance at me and roll her eyes, before returning her attention to the Slate.

The sound of a door opening and the familiar click of heels against tile has me freezing and the nurse turning away from me. Confusion and terror war in my mind.

Is that . . . No. It can't be.

I struggle against my bindings again, trying to peer around the nurse, but she's a perfect door when all I want is a window.

"I'm just finishing taking my vitals for her report, ma'am," the nurse says.

"I saw what happened. I don't need a report. Or her vitals," Mother's voice says clearly, making my veins run cold and leaving no room for doubt that it's her.

How could that be? I just saw her die!

The nurse rushes out the door and Mother strolls to stand beside me. "Relax, Evelyn." She presses a button on the beeping machine and cold replaces the heat on my neck.

My eyes clear and I scour the room for a clue as to what's happening. I'm not in the Medical Sector. I have no idea where I am. And I'm alone aside from Mother. Where's Gavin? I glance up at the ceiling and my mouth falls open. A naked girl stares back at me from a mirror angled above the bed. She has my same blue eyes, even if they're a bit sunken. The same blond hair, even if it's lost some of its luster. And the same star-shaped scar I've come to accept as mine on her left shoulder.

But the rest of what is obviously a much grimmer version of the me I remember is covered in wires and electrodes. There are four electrodes on my upper chest, four on my abdomen. Two on my thighs and biceps and another two on my lower legs and forearms. And my head has so many of them, that I might as well be wearing a hat made of wire. There's a tube going into my nose and one resting just under it with two prongs blowing oxygen into my nostrils. There's what appears to be IV lines in my neck and another one in each arm.

"Where am I? What's going on?"

Mother peers down at me with pursed lips. "How do you feel, Evelyn?"

"Where am I? How are you alive? Where's Gavin?" I know I'm in no place to make demands, but I have to know.

The door behind her opens again with a swoosh and she glances over her shoulder. Without a word, she leaves me to join the new visitor in the corner of the room. My heart lurches when I see it's Dr. Friar. Did no one I killed actually die?

They're whispering, and my head is swimming with confusion. Reality and fantasy war in my memories. Memories, or echoes of memories, flood into my brain in a tidal wave of jumbled thoughts and pictures, filling in the gaps, and pushing away the memories I'd had just moments ago to make room for others, duplicate and triplicates of things that couldn't possibly have happened. I don't know what's real and what's not.

"She remembers," Mother hisses. "She's not supposed to remember anything that happens in the sims."

Sims!

More half-memories flood in. Mother captured me. Knocked me out with . . . something, and I woke up in here. She'd been planning this all along. It had all been just one giant test and this was to be my final exam. To make sure that when the time came, I would rule Elysium as she did. With an iron fist and an empty heart. And I'd walked right into the trap. But . . . someone—who? A friend? Yes! Someone in the Underground—came to my rescue. They had a plan. I could use the Sim to find Mother's weaknesses.

But I've been doing this for too long. None of this is going to plan.

"It was traumatizing. Her brain recorded it like it would a nightmare." Dr. Friar shrugs. "It's nothing. In time it will fade."

"If we ran it again, would she remember?"

Again? That's right. I failed again. Both the Underground and Mother. They had to run the sim again so I can try . . . wait . . . no. I *didn't* fail this time. I bite back a grin as more memories slide in. I'd done exactly what I was supposed to do this time. Find a way to take Mother down in the sim for the Underground to use in real life. But there's more I'm supposed to do.

"Doubtful. But, she's much too weak . . ."

Mother waves her hand. "She's the strongest subject we've had. I handpicked her myself. Despite her unfortunate decision this last time to start a rebellion against me, she showed true leadership potential. I'm not wasting all the time I've spent grooming her over such a small issue."

How many times have I done this? When was I put here? Too many conflicting memories float around in my mind to snatch the real answers.

"I must insist . . ."

"I can't risk her remembering these . . . revelations. Erase her and run it again."

"Her brain may not be able to take it . . ."

"I can do it," I gasp out, desperate to prove myself one last time. I'm not finished. I've only completed half the task. Dr. Friar *has* to let me go again. And Mother *has* to believe that I'm doing this for her. That I *want* to pass her test so I can be her heir. Because as long as she's focused on me, she *isn't* focused on the Underground.

Mother glances over her shoulder, a smug grin resting on her face before she turns back toward Dr. Friar.

"Dr. Friar. You are my most trusted advisor." Her voice is sugar sweet when she says it, but her voice hardens to cold steel and the smile goes dark when she adds, "Don't make me find a new one."

I can see his Adam's apple bob, but he hesitates again, so I plead, "Please let me try again. I won't disappoint you again, Mother."

"Get the tech. Run it again." She turns and walks to me.

"As you wish, Mother," he finally says.

Dr. Friar rushes from the room, but Mother stays standing over me.

She touches a hand to my head, pushing my hair farther from my eyes. It takes everything in my power not to flinch away from her.

"You'll do this city no good if you're brain damaged, Evelyn," she says as if she were the one questioning my ability instead of Dr. Friar, but she smiles down at me. "You'll have one more chance to choose the *right* side in the sim to become my heir, Evelyn. And just to make it clear, starting a rebellion isn't it. Otherwise, I'll have no choice but to terminate you and choose another."

"Where's Gavin?" I have to ask. I have to know he's okay.

She narrows her eyes, and she nods to herself as if she's just realized something important. "He's dead, Evelyn. You killed him yourself."

Despair pools in my stomach like molten lead. "No. I love him. I would never hurt him." I know I wouldn't. But that doesn't mean that Mother didn't kill him and blame it on me. She's done worse.

She only shrugs, that same horrible smile on her face. I just want to rip it off when she says, "But you did, dear." She pats my shoulder. "But don't worry. In a few moments, you'll never know he lived at all."

I close my eyes, letting Mother think that she's upset me. My eyes sting, but it's more from frustration than pain. Frustration that I can't sort the reality from the fiction even after all this time. *That's why I'm here.* That's why we chose *this* plan. Because I was the only one able to fight my Conditioning. I *have* to remember.

Another familiar female voice vibrates into my ear. "You sent for me, ma'am?"

"Prep her for another run." She leaves the room with a clicking of her heels as her only sound. The door whooshes closed behind her as the tears I've been fighting since Mother appeared leak from the corners of my eyes to slide down into my ears.

I fight for control over my emotions as the newcomer walks closer. She stands next to me for so long I get the sense she's watching me and I open my eyes to glare at her. It's the only emotion other than despair I can muster.

But the minute I see her, I gasp. It's an Enforcer. In fact, it's *the* Enforcer. The one I was sure had killed Myra's family in the last sim. And she's holding none other than Dr. Friar's device. The one that disrupts my nanos and can turn me into nothing but a quivering mess of dead tissue with a push of a button.

But . . . no . . . Mother called her a tech.

More fog clears from my brain as I force myself to remember. The device doesn't disrupt my nanos. It's what starts the program. And the tech *isn't* an Enforcer. She's part of the Underground. My only contact with them. My only way to know for sure if Gavin is dead or not.

I open my mouth, but she shakes her head. Just once, but firmly. Her eyes lock onto mine. "Looks like you have a loose wire here." She bends next to me, her attention and fingers on one of the electrodes behind my ear. "Gavin's not dead," she whispers and the way she says it makes me think that even though I can't remember it, this isn't the first time we've had this conversation.

I just want to weep in relief. Deep down I knew he was fine, but hearing it lifts a huge weight from my shoulders. I sniff, as more tears leak out from my eyes and I jerk my arm, ripping the electrode from my skin, in my haste to wipe the tears away.

"Sorry!" She steps back a little, speaking a lot louder than I expected, but I don't care. She just said the only words that matter to me right now. "I should have warned you it pinches a little." She leans back down and the stinging sensation comes back. "Don't move," she whispers. When I don't, she continues, "Gavin's fine. He's worried about you, but he's still with the Underground. He says, 'We're in this together. Remember?'" She pauses and makes a few more adjustments to the wires on my head, before she goes on. "The Underground already has the results of the last sim. They know the key is the Enforcers. Just one more time. You can do it."

I shake my head, not really sure I can. What if Dr. Friar is right? What if I've done this too many times already and my brain can't do it this time?

"Yes you can. Do it for Gavin." She squeezes my arm.

She moves away before I can do anything else and adjusts a few more things around my body while my mind races.

I can do it. I *have* to do it.

Finally, she returns to my head and peers down at the leads there. In a normal voice she says, "We're going to begin the infusion. This may sting a little." Then, speaking in a voice just above a whisper, she adds, "We have everything we need this time. And so do you. I'm going to restart the program. You know what to do." She presses the button on the silver remote.

My whole body heats as the infusion fills my veins. The same warm cloudy mist fills my head as it's done more times than I can remember, but this time I don't fight it. I only smile.

This time I won't fail.

Acknowledgments

Once again, I have a never-ending list of people to thank for turning my mess of words into a readable book, but since this book is already too long, I'll make it short. *smiles*

A huge thanks to my wonderful agent, Natalie Lakosil, for being in my corner when I needed her the most. And to my editor, Mel, for her awesome insight and patience. And as always, a huge thanks to the cover artist, Eithne, for yet another beautiful cover.

I definitely couldn't have done this without the support of my family, specifically my husband for all the times he saw the simple in the complicated, brought me coffee at three A.M. and ice cream for breakfast. And, of course, there's no way I could have done this without my awesome kids for putting up with all the time my imaginary friends took all my attention.

And to my crit partner Liz Czukas for all the last-minute brainstorming, freak-outs, and encouragement. Thank you so, so much. You have no idea how much that means to me.

And to my other crit partner, Larissa Hardesty, thank you for being my friend and confidant.

A special shout-out and thank-you to Laura Helseth (Little Read Riding Hood). Your insight was absolutely invaluable. Gavin and Evie's story wouldn't have been complete without you. Thanks for everything.

And, of course, thank you to God for giving me the talent and perseverance to make my dream a career.

And last but not least, a huge thank-you to all my fabulous readers who loved *Renegade* and *Revelations* and loved and rooted for Evie, Gavin, and Asher. I hope you enjoy the last chapter of their story. I couldn't do this without you. XOXO